T0272590

Walk the Earth as Brothers

A Novel

Henry J. Rozycki

Walk the Earth as Brothers

A Novel

Addison & Highsmith

Addison & Highsmith Publishers

Las Vegas ◊ Chicago ◊ Palm Beach

Published in the United States of America by
Histria Books
7181 N. Hualapai Way, Ste. 130-86
Las Vegas, NV 89166 USA
HistriaBooks.com

Addison & Highsmith is an imprint of Histria Books. Titles published under the imprints of Histria Books are distributed worldwide.

Library of Congress Control Number: 2023948374

ISBN 978-1-59211-386-6 (hardcover)
ISBN 978-1-59211-408-5 (eBook)

To the men in whose footsteps I tried to walk —
my father, Kazimierz Rozycki, and my uncle, Joseph Ronar

As individuals, men believe they ought to love and serve each other and establish justice between each other. As racial, economic, and national groups, they take for themselves whatever their power can command...

— Reinhold Niebuhr

We've learned to fly the air like birds, we've learned to swim the seas like fish, and yet how to walk the Earth as brothers we don't know...

— Maxim Gorky

Henry — Nancy, France, 25 July 1976

The plaque confirmed that I had found the right place, but because it was Sunday and stiflingly hot, there was no one else in sight, not in the shade of the courtyard or on the street. If anyone were to look out from their window and ask why a backpacked American, dripping sweat, was standing in front of the locked gate to an engineering school, how would I answer?

It was the summer before my last year of college, and after wandering clockwise around Britain and counterclockwise around France, I detoured to Nancy in Lorraine before going directly to Paris. An unease had been growing in my mind as graduation loomed, and I hoped that coming here might make things clearer and calmer.

Had it been as hot that summer day, thirty-seven years before, when my father arrived? Did he also come directly to this same spot? He would have been about my age, leaving his home in Poland for the first time to begin his studies at this school. Alone — like I was at that moment. Except I knew that, come fall, I would be sitting in a classroom. When his September came, Germany invaded Poland, nations declared war, massive armies clashed, and he never attended a class or saw his home again. Had he been scared? Or did his way of becoming so absorbed in the analysis of his situation keep him calm? All I knew is that he somehow managed to make it to England.

The quiet solitude made it easier to imagine myself in his place, and what led me to Nancy coalesced into a question. Two questions, actually. First, how could I reconcile this picture of him here in 1939 with the careful, private, wary, even milquetoast man he was to me then? And second, and more frightening, could I have done what he did? Nothing in my young life came close to what my father had faced as a man of similar inexperience. Could I have acted as decisively, made the same right choices? Would I have survived? I could not begin to answer, in part because I did not yet know myself as well as I thought I did, but more because there was so much missing from his story. And not just his story. His brother's story, my mother's story, the stories of all their friends — fellow survivors who would sometimes stop in the middle of whatever they were saying as a shadow passed over their faces.

Remembering was pain, and a dutiful child learned at an early age never to ask questions.

Ian and Daniel — Warsaw, 17 June 1939

Where was Daniel?

A half hour scanning the face of every man crossing the concourse, and still no sight of his older brother. He'd even sent a telegram this morning confirming that everything was on schedule to follow up the letter in which he'd specified the time his train was due to arrive. He wondered if Daniel was running late, maybe rushing to finish something at his office. He considered the possibility of an accident as the cause, but as the summer heat began to make his new wool suit itch, Ian wondered whether meeting him as promised hadn't qualified as something Daniel could be bothered to remember. Dammit, where was he?

Pigeons cooed and rustled from the scaffolding that rose into the shadows of the unfinished train station. Where the soaring vertical elements, meant to symbolize Poland's progress and promise, met the shed roof, Ian noted a crack of light. That must be how the pigeons were getting in, he decided, where some engineer had badly miscalculated. Below, businessmen strode purposefully, carrying thin portfolios of contracts and accounts under their arms. Young men, navigating their way to join army units massing at the border, stopped to look from the paper in their hands to the display board. A dozen soldiers in new uniforms and shiny boots marched past, their heel strikes on the marble floor sounding like a battalion. The sergeant went eyes right, his unspoken question to Ian: *Why is a nineteen-year-old man not in uniform?*

Where was Daniel?

A violent boom suddenly reverberated off the walls, the floor, all the surfaces. The birds launched themselves in every direction, unable to localize which way was safe. One of the businessmen fell flat to the floor. The soldiers stopped and tensed. Only the sergeant stood unmoved. Turning to where dust now rose over sheets of fallen plywood, he barked at his recruits to double-time out of the station.

Staccato beats now, coming from a young woman in high heels, her summer dress lifting off her legs with each step. The women in Warsaw looked so different from the ones back home, carrying themselves as if, like those soldiers, they were prepared to repel any feint or thrust.

"Hey, little brother, look at you!" Daniel must have come through one of the side doors. He pulled Ian into a back-pounding hug, pushed him away to admire him, then enveloped him again.

"Look at you!" he repeated. "I never pictured my little brother as a gentleman in Warsaw, but here you are! Wow! Come on. My apartment is not far."

Ian reached the handle of his suitcase first, so Daniel went to the other side and put his arm loosely around his brother's shoulder to direct him out the front doors and into the sunshine. A policeman, whose white gloves made his hands appear twice as big as normal, stopped lanes of streetcars, sedans, and carts so the brothers could cross the impressive Jerzolimskie Street. Ian focused on not smashing his bag into the shins of the many passersby and heard barely half of Daniel's commentary on the big city. Only when they turned onto a less-congested Emilia Plater Street could he understand Daniel's question.

"What do you think of that train station?"

"It's hard to tell right now," Ian said. "What do you think?"

"It's a sell-out," Daniel declared. "Anyone who sees that amalgam of clichés will know that Poland keeps at least one foot in the past."

"What would you rather see?" Ian asked.

"Everything! That stone they chose! It invites ornamentation — before you know it, there'll be eagles with their legs splayed open carved all over the place. And the space! Ridiculous! No, what they should do is what we are working on; we call it Functional Humanism, a new theory of architecture. We marry the aesthetic of modernism with the humanity of the Renaissance." All the rest of the way, Daniel outlined how he and his best friend were about to change how people lived. Very soon, their manifesto would be ready to publish — in five languages, no less — after which they would open their own office and select which of the inevitable prestigious commissions to accept.

Daniel finished as they reached his apartment door, which looked as if neither lock nor wood would deter anyone who wanted to enter uninvited. Daniel ushered

Ian into the main room, a kitchen with a small table on one side and two stuffed chairs around a coal fireplace on the other. Beyond was the bedroom, which had the only window, opening onto an airshaft.

"My first morning, I stuck my head in to look up and check the weather, and it was gray, like it was raining. But when I went out, there wasn't even one cloud, and I realized that skylight is probably covered by a hundred years of smoke and dirt and pigeon shit."

Ian changed out of his suit in his brother's room while speculating on what Warsaw specialty Daniel might serve. He'd had nothing since a quiet goodbye breakfast with their father, but when he re-entered the main room, he found Daniel in one of the chairs, smoking a cigarette and reading a newspaper.

"Ian, listen. I know of a small party starting soon, very low-key, but it's an interesting group of people I think you might like. Not just architects," Daniel reassured him.

This was very much like Daniel's last visit. Ian met his brother at their little train station and Daniel filled the walk to their apartment with stories about his exciting life in the capital. But all the things Ian wanted to talk with him about, things their father never discussed like his dreams, choices, and future — there was never the opportunity because as soon Daniel threw his suitcase into their room, he was off to see his friends, followed by the inevitable argument between father and son, after which Daniel was on an early train back to Warsaw.

Ian tried to use travel fatigue as a reason to avoid the party, but Daniel would have none of it.

"Don't be like that. You need to open yourself to the new, the unexpected." They both knew what he was really saying: *Don't be like Father.*

On their way, Daniel cataloged how each of the likely guests was going to be the one to lead their respective fields into the future. By the time they arrived, Ian was at least a little intrigued to meet such noteworthy individuals.

Most of the advertised people were there, in an apartment only slightly bigger than Daniel's. Ian smelled something wonderful. A beautiful woman with long black hair left the pot she was stirring to greet Daniel with air kisses past both cheeks before leaning in to listen to something he whispered only to her. Whatever it was made her tilt her head back and laugh, exposing her delicate white throat. This gesture of freedom surprised Ian. All the girls he'd ever known just tucked their head into their shoulders and giggled.

"Daniel!"

Several young men following the brothers swept Ian to the wall like a dust ball. One held up a bottle, another a loaf of bread. It quickly became a hubbub of people greeting each other as if it had been years since they were last together. A record came on, and Ian heard snatches of French lyrics about love and walking by the Seine.

"Everyone, everyone! Listen!" Daniel now stood next to Ian and raised his voice above the music. "This is my brother, Ian. My younger brother. He is here for a few days to get ready to start school in France."

A few congratulations and telegraphed smiles from around the room were sent his way before the matter was dropped. Ian returned to inspecting unfamiliar album covers and labels. What was playing, he was happy to admit, was not unpleasant.

"Daniel says you are off to France," said a serious-looking young man who appeared next to him. "*Vous parlez francais?*"

It took him a second or two. "*Ah, oui, mais je lis mieux que je le parle.*"

Daniel popped up to hug them both, grinning from one ear to the other. "Perfect! Ian, this is Joseph, a classmate of mine and, what's more, my best friend and future partner. I am sure I mentioned him before. I wanted you to meet him because he lived the bohemian life in France, and I thought he might have some advice for you." With that, Daniel was off again to chat with one of the young women.

Joseph had a shy smile and a bird's nest of black hair, and to Ian's relief, his questions were not in French. Destination? (Nancy, in Lorraine.) Intended course of studies? (Engineering.) Timetable? (Obtain the necessary visas early this week, train to France, maybe language lessons until classes began the last week of August.)

"When were you in France?" Ian asked in return.

"Oh, Daniel makes it sound so adventurous. I thought I was going to be a famous painter, so of course, I had to go to Paris. Stayed about nine months. It was 1933, in a horrible, dark little space. France can be very expensive when you have no money because you cannot sell any paintings." Joseph gave a little shrug.

"And so, you came back to your homeland," said another smiling young man who joined their conversation, blond, with a broad face and small wide-spaced eyes.

"Warsaw is not Paris, Peter," Joseph said.

"I cannot say, of course, since I never had reason to leave," Peter responded. "There are some pretty places and such, I suppose. And I hear that the women are very modern, if perhaps a little louche."

Daniel was back, a diplomatic smile on his face. "Peter is quite proud of Warsaw," he said.

"And why not? You are not, Danik?" Daniel's grip on Ian's elbow tightened at Peter's use of his diminutive name. "They have a Grand Palais, I hear, which is what? A fifty-year-old, decaying exhibition hall. Compare that to our Royal Castle which has stood for five centuries."

"Come on over to the table, Peter, and I'll get you something to eat," Joseph offered.

"I don't want to eat. I want to tell you what I think of your France. It is a pisspot. I have never been, true, yet even here — what, a thousand kilometers away? — it pollutes our air. Can you smell it?" Peter looked directly at Ian.

"I smell nothing," Ian answered.

"Peter, you are drunk. Go home."

Peter ignored the directive. "If you put a Rococo pediment over a modernist doorway, it offends the eye, no? So it is with the odors from the cooking and the bodies and the breath of so many people who gather in places like Paris." The music was gone, the other voices stilled. Ian quickly scanned the faces to measure the score. Two other men might be with Peter.

"No harm in visiting or studying, is there, Peter? Learn and then bring the best back, eh?" Joseph kept trying.

"No need! Look at what we've accomplished since we sent the Russian bastards back to their villages. And in the meantime, France jumps from one government to another, there are strikes and riots, and they even elect people like Blum." Ian tensed. "But that's just it, it's not France anymore, it's a cesspool of all manner of peoples."

"We have been friends for many years…" Daniel started his warning, until Peter interrupted.

"We sat next to each other in a lecture hall." Peter aimed his little eyes directly at Daniel, while his lips began their slow journey towards a smirk. "And every day I had only one question. Why was a Jew in that seat and not a proper Pole?"

The hand that had been on Ian's elbow knifed towards Peter's throat. The momentum slammed the two men into a wall as someone shouted, "Stop it!" Daniel's other hand joined the first, and Peter's face went from white to red to a shade of purple before others pulled Daniel off.

Peter rose to his full height and glared across the room, like a matador planning his *coup de grace*, until Ian's goddess placed herself in front of Peter's face.

"Peter, you are drunk. Go home. If you do, we may be able to consider forgiving you at some point, but you must leave, now."

Hers was the best side to be on, Ian thought.

Peter directed his parting shot at the younger brother. "Good luck in France! The air here will be a little cleaner and sweeter when you are gone."

Only the hands still grasping Daniel's arms prevented him from trying to finish his murderous goal.

After the trio left, the group was unable to revive any feelings that justified a party, and soon afterward, Ian and Daniel thanked their hostess, said their good-byes, and started the walk back.

Daniel still buzzed with energy. "That was something, eh? No parties like that back home!"

Ian had no answer all the way back to Daniel's apartment.

Daniel — Warsaw, 27–30 August 1939

Something carved into the table was so fascinating that Joseph barely touched his beer. The light in the café was too dim for Daniel to see what it was. Instead, he drained his own glass and went to order another. He was at the bar when the door opened, admitting Sylvia, the summer evening sunlight behind her catching her long black hair. She paused to acclimate to the gloom before she was able to see Daniel holding up his glass and shook her head at his offer. Mieszko the bartender gave him his refill, and Daniel went back to where Sylvia now sat close to Joseph.

"You are both such bad actors!" he said, after watching them for a few seconds.

"You haven't told him?" Sylvia asked Joseph.

"I was waiting for you," he replied.

"Told me what?" Daniel loved party games. "What are you two up to?"

Joseph put his hand into Sylvia's. "Well, Danik, we wanted to tell you that… We have decided to be married."

Daniel leapt up and clapped his hands. "What? Wonderful! Oh, but I am not surprised. Congratulations! It's about time," he said in rapid fire and went round to hug them and kiss Sylvia. "Mieszko, do you have champagne?"

"Of course, but it is expensive," the barman called back.

"Never mind that," Daniel said. "These two are getting married! Bring it, and four glasses!"

These three were regulars, after all, and really, when would there be another occasion in the foreseeable future to sell or even drink champagne? Mieszko mumbled something about a reduced price and popped open the bottle. All raised their glasses and waited for Daniel to find the words.

"I always believed that you two would marry, but, no, wait. I knew there was no man and woman who deserve each other as much as you, two people who were always fated for each other and who will be each other's deepest friends and…

muses… I realize this is not why you are doing it, but you must know that you could not have done anything that would make me happier. Ever."

In Daniel's memory, he and Joseph became friends the very moment they sat next to each other on the day of their first architecture lecture, now almost six years ago. They studied together, lived together, argued with each other about the purpose and meaning of architecture, and fought side-by-side when the antisemites of the National Green Camp tried to force Jewish students into segregated 'ghetto benches.' They were as close as brothers, closer than he was with Ian. And when Joseph met Sylvia, she became the third equal partner in their relationship.

Mieszko drained his glass in one quaff. "You will be best man then, no?" he asked Daniel, who looked to Joseph.

"Of course!" said Joseph. "And we want to hold a small reception here for our friends, is that okay?"

The barman was honored as well as pleased and accepted a second large glass of champagne to seal the pact.

Daniel let loose with questions, and the engaged couple tried their best to keep up. There would be a simple ceremony the day after tomorrow, in the late afternoon, at the registrar's office at Plac Bankowy.

"Are you sure you won't just slip into the shul?" teased Daniel, since the Great Synagogue also fronted on the Bank Plaza, but he knew that for all three of them, Judaism was a meaningless part of their past. He sat back and marveled at how congruent this felt, the first wedding amongst their contemporaries and friends. Finally, there was nothing left to plan or say and Mieszko returned to his bar.

"Danik, there is something more." Joseph spoke up with a solemnity not befitting the occasion.

Daniel waited attentively.

"The day after the reception…" Joseph paused; he and Sylvia looked at each other before turning back to Daniel. "We have a boat to Sweden arranged."

Every word now passed, one after the other, clear as broken glass, to slice into Daniel's brain.

"Sylvia's brother-in-law knows a fisherman, a raging antisemite, but now that only means he charges us double, but, you see, there is not more room…" His voice trailed off.

Sylvia took it up. "We tried to get passage — for the three of us — on a ferry to Malmo or Gothenburg, but it is impossible now. They are sending their ships to safety until they see what happens."

Joseph's turn. "Tuesday, we will take the train to Gdynia, and they will put us on a small fishing boat from a village called Hel, to Oland. In Sweden."

From the alpine height he'd ascended to at their marriage announcement, Daniel felt himself plummeting into a black hole that was the imminent loss of these two, people he loved more than anyone, people against and with whom he defined himself. His arms, legs, hands, brain, all felt paralyzed as he fell, faster and faster.

"It is not tenable here, not to work, not even to live, Danik," Joseph said with more urgency. "That treaty, Stalin and von Ribbentrop, that decided it for us. There is nothing to stop Hitler now. First Danzig, and then anything else he wants, and you know the Poles. They will resist to the last drop of blood, so that any who are left will sing sad, heroic songs and write epic, tragic poems." He paused for breath. "Any day now, they will put even you and me into uniforms and send us out to die." He sounded like an advocate in front of a skeptical jury.

Daniel's brain became an amoeba, sending out pseudopodia of random thoughts to grab at anything they might catch along the sides of his abyss. "What about… I heard." He threw out names and thoughts. "Chamberlain. Raczynski… Britain will send her army… France's honor."

Sylvia answered his desperation. "Maybe that is true, maybe it will work, but what if it doesn't?"

Then Joseph. "And if it does, how long until the next crisis? We are builders, you and I, designing a better future. There may be some kind of future here, only I cannot imagine it, and if it doesn't come to pass, who do we design for?"

Daniel felt like he was alone in the ring against two boxers. He tried to counterpunch.

"No matter what, there will be a need to build or to rebuild. I mean, at that point we will be vital. No one will want structures made for the state, for the party. These will be abhorrent; they will represent what led to this hell. It will be the time for Functional Humanism. How can we have it ready if you are in Sweden?"

One late evening, in that very café, after another of their innumerable arguments, a frustrated Daniel had asked, "Why must we only do what has been done, when we know it is wrong? Architecture must be in service to man, not the other way around!" A week later, Joseph presented him with sketches for an auditorium where the audience rose up around three sides of the stage in a series of scalloped shells, each holding no more than twenty patrons. Daniel immediately recognized what he was trying to say — that power belonged as much with the viewers as the speaker, and that the individual was never simply one in a mass; they were, at most, a part of a family or a neighborhood like the one defined by the shells. Joseph already had the name: Functional Humanism. The two immediately began formulating their manifesto, dreaming and sharing, arguing and editing, imagining its publication, the acclaim that would follow, and the commissions that would overwhelm them after the world learned how man should truly live. Thinking about it had been enough to make him forget everything else happening in the world, up until this moment.

"We are sorry, Danik." Joseph looked down at his lap, the apotheosis of resignation. "This is something we must do while we can. We will be together again when it settles down and until then we will work by post. We will put together our manifesto. I promise."

Sylvia reached out. "We considered not going. We searched for another boat with another space, but my brother-in-law said that it was this or none."

He did not want to hear the *groszy*, the pennies they offered to buy off their guilt. He knocked his chair down as he stood and without another word, ran out into the daylight.

Daniel did not leave his apartment the next day. His supervisor sent him home early on Monday after finding too many mistakes in Daniel's plans. "We are all under stress. Get some rest and come back tomorrow when you can concentrate."

He wanted to be angry at Sylvia and Joseph's betrayal, yet all he felt was tired. He lay in bed, curled into a fetal position at the bottom of his hole. The pinpoint of light above was what he was supposed to climb up to, a climb for which he lacked any desire or strength. When his mind grew tired of circling the same thought patterns, he got up and paced his room, like a prisoner measuring and remeasuring the dimensions of his cell. When he got tired of that, he dressed and went out, because by leaving, he proved to himself that he was not in any kind of prison, and walked aimlessly around Warsaw until, just after ten at night, he arrived at their café.

From the number of empty bottles and glasses left round, many had been there earlier, but now it was only Sylvia, in a yellow dress, and Joseph, in his best suit, sitting next to each other at their table like it was just another ordinary night, when whichever two arrived first sat waiting for the third.

"Mieszko, more champagne!" Daniel yelled. The barman looked to Joseph for guidance before bringing a bottle and three clean glasses, which Daniel filled and distributed. He raised his toward the couple. "Well, I assume the deed is done. Congratulations! *Moje gratulacje! Mazel Tov!*"

Sylvia took a quick sip. "We missed you, Danik. It was not what we imagined it should be."

Daniel couldn't help himself. "Your imagination seems to be doing quite well without me." He regretted the words as they were leaving his lips.

"That is unfair of you, Daniel," said Joseph, who hadn't touched his glass. "I thought our friendship meant more than our philosophical discussions, our dreams of the future. It was a… I don't know, a connection beyond words. We wanted to build structures within which individuals can feel like a hero in their own lives. I thought that grew from how we felt about each other."

"These decisions were not easy, Daniel," Sylvia said. "Joseph at first refused to go. We have been struggling with it and suffering from it for weeks now."

All three looked into their glasses or the table or anywhere except at each other.

"There's another thing, if you must know," Sylvia said.

"You are pregnant," Daniel announced.

"Yes! How did you know?"

"I didn't, until just now," Daniel said. He sat up straight as tears came to his eyes. "Can you forgive me? I was only thinking of how you were abandoning me and abandoning our plans. It was so selfish of me."

Sylvia came around to pull Daniel up into a fierce embrace and cried into his shoulder. Joseph brought out his handkerchief to wipe his own eyes.

"Danik, this could all be temporary. I have an invitation from Markelius in Stockholm. First thing, I will get him to send for you. In the meantime, we will be forced to write, and that is good. We will write every week, every day if necessary and we will finish the manifesto."

Joseph put his arms around them for a good minute, and they went back to the arrangement of bodies anyone who'd seen them on countless happier nights would have recognized.

Daniel poured more champagne and raised a proper toast to the new couple, to their baby and to their future.

"Wait, what time is your train tomorrow? I have to see you off!" Daniel exclaimed.

Joseph insisted that Daniel not be there, ostensibly so he wouldn't lose his job. Daniel reluctantly agreed because he too was not certain whether he could handle the emotions.

It was Joseph who realized they had not addressed what Daniel should do. "You need to think about it, Danik. What if they mobilize everyone, even Jews with a bad ear and a heart murmur?"

"All I know is that I have to get to the office tomorrow morning. There's too much happening, too fast to do otherwise."

She wouldn't let him get away with that. "What about your father? He is alone now."

Ian's departure had essentially severed Daniel's last tie to his home. He hadn't spoken with his father in over a year. There was nothing he needed to hear from a man who treated his son no differently than the students in his mathematics classes at the gymnasium.

The portrait of Sylvia that Daniel carried in his memory for the rest of his life came at that moment; a beautiful newlywed, incubating a new life, with an expression of utter despondency, a sign that she really did care for him. As always, it was her imploring eyes that demanded a valid response from him, because if he didn't meet her standards, it risked her respect and her fraternal love, the only type she could offer and the one he had come to accept.

"It might be best if I went home. Ian cannot get back from France. There is no one left to look out for our father, and he is not the most practical man in the world." If only Ian could hear him say those words.

"That's south," Sylvia pointed out. "And now with Slovakia…"

Joseph spoke with a conviction he did not feel, quoting Marshal Rydz-Smigly that his million-man army could hold against any attack until the British and French arrived.

"That clinches it, then," Daniel said. "I'll go home and bring my father to Warsaw until this is settled." They sat together in their corner, and Daniel never remembered what else they spoke about, only that Joseph and Sylvia were leaving, and he was going to get his father, until Mieszko finally sent them out.

Nancy, 29 Aug 1939

Dear Father,

Greetings from France! After all the planning and arranging my affairs, it feels a little strange that I am actually arrived. Please know that I will always be grateful for your encouragement and support.

The train voyage was impressive. In a journey of over a fifteen hundred kilometers, we passed so many new bridges, overpasses, factories, and even stadia!

You will be pleased to know that I secured lodging in a well-reputed student boarding house here in Nancy. However, please use the Poste Restante address, as the landlady prefers not to act as a postmistress. I am registered with the police and enrolled in the University, a student in engineering! All that I saw from the train, not only in Germany and France but in Poland, make me confident that my choice is a good one for my future and that you and Daniel will be proud of what I do when I return in four years. As you predicted, the lectures at the University so far are like music to me.

Daniel looked well when I was in Warsaw, and he asked about you.

I believe that the amount we discussed will be sufficient to cover my necessities. Please send it as a draft to me in care of the Poste Restante in Nancy.

Your son,

Ian

Ian — Nancy, France, 30 August–1 September 1939

There was no wait for the bathroom now that two of Ian's fellow boarders were gone, called up in that last mobilization and probably now huddling inside a bunker on the Maginot Line sixty kilometers to the east. As a bonus, the creaking, whistling old pipes had sufficient hot water for him to finish what he needed to do, so long as he was quick. He dressed back in his little room under the sloping roof, and rechecked that he had his notebooks, slide rule, templates, and pencils, before locking the door behind him and carrying his bag and his shoes down the stairs toward the back door.

No use. Madame Jacquot was at the kitchen table, reading yesterday's newspaper as if that were the only reason she stationed herself there. Ian assumed that she washed her one housecoat every night, because it never looked stained, and she was not the sort who would pay for two identical ones.

"Good morning, Madame. I trust you had a good night's rest."

"Barely, Monsieur Ian," she said. She called all her student tenants by their first names. "You are, by far, the loudest borders I have ever had. I must remind you that I have a strict policy, all noises cease by nine p.m."

"Of course, Madame, but I was in bed by eight thirty. I do not know who would have made any noise, but I assure you it wasn't me," Ian said. In fact, the noisiest boarders were the ones who'd just left.

Madame Jacquot sniffed her skepticism, as if to say she hadn't caught him, yet. Ian took a step toward the door, but Madame was not finished.

"Monsieur Ian, I remind you that the rent is due in two days, on Friday."

"I will have it for you, Madame. You will find me a most reliable boarder." And that last assurance, reinforced with what he intended to be his best smile, got him out the door. At the corner, a moment's hesitation; through its door he saw several burly men in blue overalls standing at the zinc counter of his café, his because he had been inside twice. His budget permitted a coffee and a roll with butter, but only on Tuesdays, Thursdays, and Sundays, so on he moved to the open space they called Place Stanislaus. In no other corner of France would a Pole feel more welcome, dominated as it was by an equestrian statue dedicated to the man who lost the throne of Poland, only to gain the dukedom of Lorraine by marrying off his daughter to Louis XV. It was a tenuous way to feel closer to home in these first few weeks, yet he often chose to cross Place Stan on his way to and from the university. Also, the P.T.T., the main post office, stood around the corner from the square, which is where he lined up this morning at the Poste Restante wicket.

"*Oui*, yes?" the clerk barked, giving no indication that he recognized Ian from having served him the day before, and the day before that. The clerk made a show of comparing the photos in the French Identity Card and passport with Ian's face, got up, and disappeared through a door behind him. He was back too quickly.

"*Rien*, nothing," he said, pushing the documents back to Ian. "Next!" was a substantial woman, sporting a disproportionately small hat, around whom Ian maneuvered to return to the warm sun on Place Stan.

In a few more blocks, he was at the School of Engineering and settling into his usual spot near the back of the lecture hall, though it was early and almost all the seats were empty. He tore a page from his pad of graph-lined paper and, not for the first time, toted up his resources and his expenses. Tuition for the year was already paid; that substantial expense was gone. He had rent to pay, he needed to eat, and he might require another book or two. If he was careful, a few more weeks of mail disruption could be tolerated. Ian wondered if Herr Hitler ever analyzed the costs and benefits, the pros and cons, on a piece of scratch paper, or did he have his Nazi functionaries do it? Ambitions on one side and on the other, iron-clad promises from France and England, Poland's forty divisions on his eastern border, plus he had to consider France's ninety divisions on his other flank, and factor in England's navy.

Ian had a good ear and could follow all the lecture material. Soon he would try conversing with his fellow students, even the French ones. Then they could meet some evenings at a café or bar, and he wouldn't always be in bed by eight thirty. Assuming that his father's remittance came through.

Today, at least a third of the seats stayed empty. It was like a poultry farm selling off their chickens, starting with a few to a local restaurant, and now many

more to bigger markets, the result a steadily shrinking flock. The newspapers de-
bated the risks of further mobilization, how the other side would interpret it as a
declaration of war, yet it appeared as if everyone eligible was already gone. They
were saying that almost three million would be under arms by the end of the
month. Ian scribbled some more figures under his budget calculations; assuming
one armed soldier per square meter, if the whole French Army lined up along the
German border, they would create a formation eight soldiers deep. Ridiculous, of
course, armies weren't placed like that. As for Poland, the Marshal proclaimed they
did not need a Maginot Line. A million Poles, imbued with the spirit that beat the
Red Army in 1920, were just as good.

The professor entered, this time without crumbs in his beard, and commenced
to lecture. Ian wrote down everything. It was all he needed to do: listen, digest,
and transcribe, and the stresses, materials, equations, and constants filed themselves into what he sometimes imagined were slots in his brain already prepared to
accept these specific pieces of information. Another ridiculous thought. It was
merely the sense of validation that he was doing what he was meant to be doing.
Even these introductory classes were sparking ideas and tools that he would soon
use to construct huge dams, new Eiffel towers, tunnels under the English Channel.
Whether in lectures or at practicums, no thoughts of Poland, Germany, France,
armies, his father, or his self-centered brother intruded.

Walking back to his boarding house the next afternoon, Ian saw shopkeepers
boarding over their windows, and bakeries with sold out notices posted on their
doors far earlier than usual. No matter, he never shopped at any of them. The food
at the student cafeteria was cheap, if not good, and Ian filled himself up at his
midday meal. The primary reason he was early to bed, like a hibernating bear, was
to avoid being aware of his hunger.

He had the *francs* ready as he descended the stairs to the kitchen on the morning of the first of the month, but Madame was not at her usual place nor was a
cigarette burning in the ashtray. Ian heard voices toward the street side, and he
followed them to the open front door. Madame stood on the top step speaking
with the postman, her friend from next door, along with an elderly gentleman

whom Ian often saw walking along their street. Today he had a row of medals pinned to his jacket. Ian hung back in the shadows.

"We won't do it," Ian heard the old man say. "It is not our fight, we won't lose another generation, not for Danzig."

"*Bien sur*," Madame Jacquot agreed. "But will Hitler stop after Poland? When he finishes them, will he turn to us?"

All year, every week and now every day, the world had ricocheted from fear of the certainty of another war to relief that the leaders appeared to have stumbled onto the necessary requirements to avoid that certainty. Germany would want something, England and France would posture and dither, and then there was Russia and Romania and Poland and Slovakia and Mussolini and the Pope — it was like perpetually watching a juggler who used hand grenades rather than rubber balls. Had one dropped?

Madame Jacquot sighed as she turned to reenter her castle. More than one emotion crossed her face when she saw Ian before settling for her usual haughty scowl.

"Monsieur Ian, you have the payment for September?" she asked, closing the front door behind her.

"Of course, Madame, it is right here." He handed her the bills along with the few coins. Madame Jacquot took them to her little desk off the front parlor and counted it twice before putting it into the pocket of her housecoat. She carefully wrote the date, his name, his room number, and the amount in her account book, with the concentration of someone who did not write often. Madame put her book away in the desk, locking the drawer with a tiny key she kept in the same pocket as his rent money, and looked up to Ian.

"You are from Poland, no?"

She knew it, so why the question, Ian wondered, as he nodded at her.

"Have you not heard?" she asked. "The Germans invaded your country early this morning."

Perhaps his pupils dilated a little. A few hairs on his neck may have come erect. Nothing that Madame would notice.

"Whole divisions, the air force. Warsaw has been bombed," she continued. "I have heard this on the radio." She got up and walked over to a corner of the kitchen where she kept her stack of newspapers, access to which was not included in the rent. She handed the top one over to Ian. It was from yesterday. On the back page, the headline was about Poland's defeat of the Hungarian football team. It was the front page that held all the news he did not want to see. The border between France and Germany was now closed. A confusion of meetings between ambassadors, Hitler, cabinets, and generals, all as effective as a child playing with dress-up dolls in morning dress and military uniforms. Poland now claimed two and a half million men under arms, according to one headline. Daniel said that his perforated eardrum and heart murmur, buttressed by some impressive paperwork supplied by Joseph's family, made him ineligible. Would that matter now, Ian wondered. Was there fighting near his home?

"Madame?" Ian asked, pointing toward the front parlor where the Lemouzy radio console held pride of place on a side table; boarders were not permitted to use the front parlor. "Under the circumstances, could we listen to the news, perhaps, for a short time?"

The old woman looked, for a few seconds, as if she would consider whether the return of war was sufficient reason to change her rules. But she shook her head.

"*Mais non!*" She went on, "Monsieur Ian. It is not possible to know when there will be mail again between Poland and France. Did you bring all the money you need with you? You expected to get shipments, I believe." She rubbed the hairs on her chin.

"I am fine, Madame. You do not have to worry."

"Another thing, Monsieur Ian. I am afraid that I must increase the rent next month. Another, um, fourteen francs."

"That's not fair, Madame! We agreed a rate was to be for the year. You can't change it just like that," Ian protested.

"There is no choice. You are too young. I remember what happened to prices for coal, for food, for everything in the last war." She had another thought. "And people from Alsace are being evacuated from the border. There will be more, all needing rooms to stay."

Ian felt a hot wave flow out from his core into his chest, shoulders, and neck seize him for a few seconds. He willed it away by bidding a curt good day to his landlady, and deliberately walking past her to exit through the front door. Clots of people stood whispering to each other on the sidewalk and in doorways. He paused at the corner; he needed information, he needed to think. With sufficient information, he would find the solutions to these new problems he was confronting. He entered his café, schedule be damned!

The excited voices of the veterans vowing to do it again to the filthy Boches made it difficult to hear the radio broadcast. This café discouraged socialists and communists, who had their own gathering places, so there was unanimity in the comments. Luckily, it was too busy for the owner to notice him and insist that he order something. Ian wormed his way closer to the radio. He made out martial music and, as the church across the street tolled the hour, a news bulletin.

It was true. Well before dawn, the German Army had attacked, from the west, from Danzig, from East Prussia, from Slovakia. Warsaw bombed. There was no mention of Lodz, the closest city to Father. He understood something about heroic resistance, and then the announcer moved onto French Cabinet meetings, and General Staff meetings and meetings in London, as if meetings were the best way to stop an armed invasion. One patron loudly and repeatedly proclaimed that it would all be done before Christmas, that they just needed to repeat Marshal Foch's lessons from 1918, that the French Army was already preparing to cross the Rhine and wouldn't stop until Berlin.

Ian slipped out to the street, almost colliding with a buxom woman pulling along a waddling basset hound. "Excuse me, Madame," Ian apologized, and her answer was a snort that resembled Madame Jacquot's, before she and her dog continued on.

Ian followed, guided by the flow of the people towards Place Stanislaus. Strangers in the square would have no more information, but this was a time not to be alone in his rooms, a study carrel at the university library, or his place at the top of the lecture theater.

Would there even be a class today? Amidst the innumerable government and university regulations, was there one that said, "In the event of war, lectures will be rescheduled to the first Tuesday after the first month after an armistice...?" It would not surprise him. But since France had not actually declared war, as far as he knew, if such a rule even existed, it was not applicable yet. It didn't matter, he could not go to class today.

Instead, he found himself at the P.T.T. office, waiting in a long line at the Poste Restante. Still nothing for him, so he moved to the telegraph section and carefully composed messages on two forms.

To: Joseph Ciszek: Write when safe. Ian

He used the same words for the telegram to Daniel, to which he added, *Check Father please.*

Eleven words total; it would cost little and perhaps his plea would encourage Daniel to put aside his anger and bitterness towards their father, to remember life before their mother died. He took the forms to wait in another line and when it was his turn at the wicket, passed both under the grill to the well-dressed man, who looked like a manager reluctantly pressed into doing menial work far below his station. Quickly, the forms were pushed back.

"No telegrams to Poland today. Lines are blocked."

Ian looked into the man's face across the gilt grill. "When will they be reopened?" he asked.

"I do not know. Try again in a few days. Next!"

Ian turned to slowly make his way to the front door and into sunshine that no longer provided him any warmth.

Warsaw, 30 August 1939

Dear Father,

After discussion amongst several colleagues with insight, it is my considered opinion that it will be safer for you to move to Warsaw until this crisis is resolved.

Please inform me if you will arrange your own travel, or you prefer that I come and escort you back here. There is a private room for you next to my flat available due to the call up, and as I shall be at work during the day, it will be tranquil and quiet for you.

Your son,

Daniel

Henry — Queens, New York, 18 March 1961

Stories of parental mortification and amusement, when young children guilelessly say out loud what everyone else knows should not be mentioned, are common in almost all families. *Why does that lady have trouble getting up from her chair? Is that his real hair?*

Not in my family. From a preternaturally young age, I knew to say nothing. While learning my table manners, for example, I never called out one of my elders who had an elbow on the table, or who pretended not to have passed gas.

I was around six or seven when I waited until we were back home to ask my parents why my uncle always finished his food so much faster than everyone else. It didn't matter where — at their house, or ours, or at a restaurant — and it didn't matter what was on his plate. He was always waiting for the rest of us to finish. Except rice. My mother and aunt never served him rice, and if it appeared on his plate when we ate out, he left it untouched.

"So, you want to know...?" my father asked me.

"Why does he always eat so fast?"

"During the war..." my father began. I knew these words meant I would get limited information. "He lived for a time in a camp, far away, in Siberia. If you didn't finish your food there, someone might take it from you."

"And they mostly had rotten rice," my mother added. "He can't look at it now."

It was the first time I heard that my uncle spent time in the Russian Gulag.

Daniel – Warsaw and Eastern Poland, 8–17 September 1939

There was no light yet, not even in the east, as Daniel pulled the tarpaulin aside and pushed the motorcycle out of the shed. The air was irritatingly hot and acrid from the smoldering fires left unattended by the frantic old men of the Civil Guard, unable to keep up with bombs that fell like hail. He was one of the few young men left; a few days ago — he could not remember how many days — whatever civic authority remained urgently called for them to leave Warsaw and proceed east and south toward Romania. The motorcycle belonged to one of those young men, who fatalistically sold it to Daniel for very little money.

"Aren't you going?" he asked, suddenly suspicious.

"Soon," Daniel answered. He had to see to his father first and then he would be ready to join. The young man shrugged and handed over a leather jacket as well.

The motor roared, as Daniel took Jerozolimskie Street west toward Piastow, where the road south toward home began. In better times, he might be there by dinner, nightfall at the latest. Today, who knew? His letters and then his telegrams produced no responses. There were rumors of a large battle near Lodz. The air was as thick with rumors as with smoke. The occasional bulletins from Radio Warsaw, which vacillated between celebrations of smaller and smaller victories and increasingly desperate and contradictory orders, only fed the inchoate fear of the remaining residents.

Without streetlights, he almost crashed into a roadblock.

"Where are you going?" one soldier asked, as two others stood in the shadows with rifles pointing toward Daniel. "Papers?" He handed over his identity card and military exemption certification but when the soldier kept rereading it, he spoke up.

"I am not… the exemption, I am denying it. I am on my way to join. I am assigned to the Army Lodz. That's where I am going," he lied.

"No, you are not," came the sharp reply. "Lodz is gone, fell this morning. Their general is here in Warsaw."

Daniel looked devastated by this news. "What do I do?"

"You can try and find one of their units, maybe the 2nd Legion. There's talk that they are moving up to the Modlin Fortress." The soldier also appeared disappointed, as if he wished he were somewhere more important than a roadblock in Warsaw.

Daniel took a chance. "Look, I still need to go. My father, he's thirty kilometers from Lodz. He's alone and not equipped to handle this."

"Impossible. Maybe halfway, or who knows, maybe closer, there are thousands of Germans, tanks, artillery. It's changing every hour, where the front is and who controls what. Your town may already be gone. Go back, find another unit to join." Daniel knew this was an order. He took back the papers and turned the motorcycle around towards a horizontal streak of pink, segmented by many vertical plumes of smoke.

The tower of the new train station lay in several large pieces across the road. Hats off to the architecture critic of the Luftwaffe. But there were also craters and debris from other, better buildings that demonstrated the indiscriminate cruelty of aerially delivered explosives. The train station, factories, rail yards, even government buildings, these might have some military justification, but homes, schools, grocery stores also were in ruins, tombs for uncounted souls who thought themselves safe at home.

Surprisingly, the knots of soldiers at either end of the Poniatowski Bridge did nothing to prevent him from crossing the Vistula. He finally stopped near Zabki as the sun was coming up when, over his engine noise, he heard rising shrieks like angry eagles, and looked back toward Warsaw to see new blossoms of fire planted by the German dive bombers.

This road led in the wrong direction. He needed to turn south and west, to get around Warsaw to the town he'd left six years previously because there was nothing there, just soulless gray buildings thrown up between a forest and a river, filled with a people satisfied with themselves and their life, waiting like cows along a fence line for whatever modern life might come by, all its edges sanded and smoothed away. That was now his hope, that the town was too insignificant, and contained no one of note or threat, for the German Army to take notice of it at this stage of the war.

He was no longer alone. Others — city-dwellers, based on their clothes and shoes — trudged along both sides of the road, carrying valises, or pushing hand-carts, moving east. The rising sun painted the wheat fields on both sides gray then dusty green and finally yellow green. Daniel stopped and peered down many of the lanes that ran off south between the hedgerows and under the birch bowers edging the fields, trying to discern which might be more than a track to a farm-stead. At each major crossroads, he racked his memory to recognize if the town name to which a southward arrow pointed was one he might want, staring into its dust and haze as if to see if this was where he should turn. At the fifth one, for no logical reason, he chose the route toward a town called Lochow, but barely a half hour along, he came to a bridge over an unnamed river, now in ruins. An old man sitting in the sun nearby responded to his question about the next bridge with a complicated set of turns and landmarks, and no assurance that it was intact. In-stead, Daniel retraced his route back to the main road and continued northeast-ward. Each kilometer was one more between himself and his father, but he didn't know what else to do. He just hoped that if he got far enough from the capital, and found an open route back around, he could scoop up his father and transport him to safety with his mother's family in Romania. On the back of a motorcycle, no less. He imagined how his father would react to the indignity, and what argu-ments he would need to make to convince him.

Trucks now slowed his progress, most of them bleeding into the road from the north. When he had to stop for almost an hour at one crossroads to watch them cross over the wide Bug River, he realized that the army was planning to set their next defense line on the south bank. That meant that the Germans would arrive on this side soon. He pushed his motorcycle to the front of the line, but troops forbade him to cross. Only soldiers allowed on the other side, they told him. Or-ders were to hold the Germans until the 1st Division came to their aid. "Worst case, we turn south and regroup later." They couldn't or wouldn't tell him where there was another crossing point.

Perhaps the most basic and practical lesson in his architecture classes was that plans must account for placement, environment, and circumstances, not just wishes. The best buildings responded to and reflected their surroundings. The scope within which he could operate was rapidly narrowing. He needed to change his plans. First step: get across the Bug. Then he would find options for subsequent moves.

Daniel put the motorcycle under a tree and walked toward the nearest group of officers before a soldier stopped him from approaching too closely.

"What do you want?" he barked.

"To join. I had an exemption, just a perforated eardrum. I want to fight."

Daniel handed his papers over, and the trooper brought them to one of the officers. The man scanned them before waving Daniel over.

"You want to fight, Daniel Ciszek?" the officer asked.

"Yes, sir!" Daniel tried to approximate the soldier stances he'd seen in movies.

"Have you ever fired a rifle?"

"A little, sir."

The officer looked appropriately skeptical. "No matter, as long as you follow orders and shoot in the right direction. He's your responsibility, Sergeant." The officer went back to his compatriots.

Daniel took his papers back, except for the exemption form, which the sergeant tore into pieces in front of him.

"You think you picked a better time, eh Ciszek?" the sergeant said, as he walked Daniel over to a supply truck stocked with uniforms, boots and a used rifle. "You missed the party at Rozan and the one near Ciechnow, but you're in luck, tomorrow should be just as fun."

He left his leather jacket with the motorcycle on the north bank of the Bug, crossed over the bridge, and was quickly tasked to dig a foxhole for himself and the sergeant in the soft bottomland soil under a copse of Norway spruce. They were beautiful old trees, with compact root balls that did not interfere with his labors. If he ever could, Daniel fantasized, he would come back to cut one down so his luthier friend, Szymon, could make him a guitar.

"Hurry up there, Ciszek, we don't want to still be digging when the Panzers arrive," the sergeant said as he set off to deploy the rest of his men among the hedges and stone walls that, over time, had subdivided inheritances. He soon returned but every hour the sergeant grunted as he heaved himself out of the hole and, staying low, went off for something obviously military but what, Daniel did not know. This was an alien society, with unfamiliar roles, language, and culture.

The luminescent hands on Daniel's watch said it was a quarter to eleven when the sergeant returned from yet another sortie.

"Cover that! Or take it off," he hissed. "No light!"

Another rule to file, another mistake by which to anger the sergeant. Daniel was surprised, then, when the man passed over some bread and cheese, and a full canteen of water. After they finished, the sergeant pointed north to where he must keep watch, and Daniel settled in, determined to do well. He kept trying to distinguish between the obsidian, the ebony, the jet and the onyx, shadows that were either a projection of his fears or the harbingers of his death. He didn't realize he'd fallen asleep on the soft loamy ground until he awoke, alone, as the birds in the spruce branches above celebrated that they were still alive after another dark night. Stiff, cold, and thirsty, he stretched out and took a last long pull from the canteen. He really needed to urinate. He propped the tip of his rifle against his helmet it so it wouldn't get dirt into the mechanism. Daniel was proud he'd thought to do that. He stood up and walked over to the back of a tree a couple of meters away.

"Get down, you idiot!" The sergeant tackled him, and they both fell back into the foxhole, Daniel painfully rolling over his rifle. "I don't care if they shoot you, but you will not give away our position!"

Daniel was ashamed of his stupidity and embarrassed that he lay still exposed.

"You a yid?" the sergeant asked, pointing.

Daniel didn't know what to say.

"Put yourself away," the sergeant said, and Daniel buttoned up. "Haven't met many. Didn't like 'em." He thought about things for a few seconds. "Right now, it doesn't matter, as long as you are not a German. You do your job, you do what I tell you, we'll be fine." And he added, "But if I catch you trying to steal anything, I'll kill you before I do any Nazi." The sergeant lay down and fell asleep. Daniel figured that meant it was his turn to watch and prostrated himself against the north side of his hole, trying to see something besides the Polish countryside.

The battle, when it came the next day, was short, loud, and terrifying. Blast after blast made the earth tremble and heave as the men hugged her closer than any lover or mother. Shells sheared branches from the trees, turning them into deadly spears aimed at the soldiers below. The roar gave no respite, no opportunity for the brain to come to some accommodation, so it became more than noise because it felt as if it were coming from within the brain, displacing any capacity for rational thought and leaving only one primitive wish — to survive the onslaught. Then came machine guns and shells from the Polish side, more noise, now accompanied by some hope. The sergeant seemed to understand the language of the guns, which ones spoke Polish, and which were German. He kept his troops in place and functional, and when word came that the enemy had crossed upstream, they jumped out of their holes and followed him east, across open fields that would have made them easy targets had there been German airplanes about, and all his men were accounted for when they finally all joined up on a road. There was an officer, a lieutenant, from whom they sought directions. He consulted his map for a long time before he pointed right, and they walked away from the noise toward, they hoped, more of their comrades. Daniel no longer had a plan; south was better than north, and when the opportunity came, he would go due west.

They stopped, not long after noon, in the village called Treblinka, to rest by either side of the road. The country quiet finally penetrated and dampened the ringing inside Daniel's head, and he became aware that the air again smelled of grass and fir and earth. A knot of officers conferred in the shade of an old oak, deciding their destiny, then sent out their orders. The sergeant gathered his squad.

"The bridge," he said, thrusting his thumb over his shoulder. "It's still ours, both sides. They want us to set up on the north and hold. The 1st Division is not far from here."

From Daniel's eventual vantage point, back again on the wrong side of the span over the Bug and kneeling beside a too-thin railing, both the plan to defend the bridge and his — to join the army to get closer to his father — appeared increasingly wrong-headed, if not suicidal. The 1st Division hadn't arrived when they'd previously been expected, making this next promised rescue suspect. There was no chaos to allow him to slip away, if that had ever been a possibility. His position was between a murderous enemy bearing down on them and a summary execution for desertion. Stupid, he angrily judged himself. Stupid.

It took another night and half a day for the Germans to arrive. Daniel's squad quickly turned back two troop carriers and a staff car before they even reached the bridge, a victory as illusory as it was short. Several whooshes and booms from two German tanks, and the sergeant ordered the men back across the bridge to where two more undermanned Polish squads lay in wait with their anti-tank weapons. They shot the turret off the lead tank before it was halfway across, then the remaining tank scored a direct hit on the bridge-keepers hut, and Daniel saw his first dead people, their bodies coming to rest at angles that he knew could not be attained in life.

So it went, thrust and parry with black powder and steel, into a night which was the darkest he had ever experienced, even as he considered whether that was because he kept his eyes closed as much as possible. When morning light came, the land around him, from the bridge back a hundred meters, looked like the no man's land from movies about the Great War. On the other side of the river, more large dark mechanical shapes moved slowly toward them, belching fire, and the answers from his side were now more tentative, like from a debater who knew they were losing the argument. Even if the 1st Division miraculously arrived, their position was deteriorating, and soon word came to pull out. It wasn't orderly or pretty, and at least two men fell, shot in the back as they ran across the fields. The sergeant pulled Daniel up by his collar, and they moved to the right, along the bank, before striking inland through marshland and scrub. After three exhausting hours, their boots heavy with caked mud and their pants soaked to their thighs, the sergeant decided that they had to use the road. They went towards the line of trees that marked the roadside. Maybe, the sergeant hoped, some of his men might be there.

But it was a German patrol that was waiting, and Daniel became a prisoner of war of the Wehrmacht.

Daniel — Soviet-Occupied Poland, 17 September–10 November 1939

The moment the first mortar rounds fell around them, the sergeant and Daniel dove into the underbrush. Together with two other quick thinkers, they belly-crawled to a spot along the river where they hid under a tangle of black alder roots until dark, listening while German armor settled the issue of the mortars. Through the night they moved east along the river, avoiding houses and villages. The four men slogged across the countryside, and only ventured into abandoned and ran-sacked farmhouses to look for food, which netted only a couple of potatoes. Finally, they stood beside a road that looked to be the best chance of taking them to the 1st Division, if it still existed, or to the redoubt near Romania.

Even if it was the only choice that made sense for Daniel, he felt an almost paralyzing sense of guilt. He had left home soon after their mother died, which left Ian to deal with their father, and Ian had never said anything to him about that, never complained. Now it was his turn, and he was failing. Daniel kept his eyes down, knowing each step along the macadam increased the unbridgeable distance between him and his father. He only looked up when they stopped and once again faced the rifle barrels of another German company.

They spent two days bound and often blindfolded before their captors delivered them to a makeshift camp cleared from pine forest, just south of Bialystok: several hundred square meters enclosed by double rows of barbed wire and gray-coated victors. The compound already held a few hundred defeated Poles: officers, non-coms like the sergeant, and ordinary soldiers, standing, pacing, or sitting on the ground, unsheltered in a perpetual cold mist that penetrated and saturated whatever they had left to wear. There was no wood for fires, no blankets, only a misery as permeating as the rain, as dark as the black-green trees standing guard around them. It all seemed to exacerbate the effects of the wounds that many suffered, so that almost hourly another man died where he sat or lay. One of them was right next to Daniel.

"Hey, Yid," the sergeant whispered harshly to Daniel and reached over to rifle through the pockets of the dead man.

Disgusting, Daniel thought, how, even here, a peasant could act this way.

"Give me your papers!" the sergeant said.

"What?"

"Give me your papers. Take these." He thrust a leather wallet extracted from an inner pocket of the dead man towards Daniel. "Quick, before anyone sees. You want to be a Jew with these pigs?" he tilted his head toward the guards at the gate. "Memorize this guy's name."

This is how Daniel became Piotr, from a village near Brecsz, when all the surviving prisoners lined up to give their names and papers to two German Army officers. It was the name on the list they handed over to the Soviets a few days later, together with Daniel and half the men, though not the sergeant. This was how he came to be stuffed in a basement, trapped with the smells of dozens of unwashed bodies, of shit and piss, and of festering wounds, smells that kept hunger at bay, though it had minimal effect on thirst.

The first sign that they were not all going to die came when a Russian soldier brought four new buckets and took the full ones out. He likely did not understand Polish, but the soft laughter after somebody made a comment alerted him that he was being mocked. He quickly returned with another man, and they proceeded to ram their rifle butts into the heads of the closest prisoners. Everyone moved away into a crush against the opposite wall, except the officers. Daniel watched them slide and push until they stood, erect as green pickets, in the center and then, like a flower opening, parted to reveal an infantry colonel in a torn uniform, a red gash across his forehead, and an Adolphe Menjou mustache above his lips. The colonel approached to tell the two young Russians, in their language, his requirements: to speak to their commander, treatment for the wounded, food, water, and better conditions. Not an hour later, they came back for the colonel, and the spirit in the cellar rose as he was escorted out, until they heard a single gunshot. After that, whenever anyone appeared with new empty buckets, or with one filled with water, or on the third day, with bread and slices of sausage, no one said anything, not even "*Spasibo.*"

Daniel appreciated that the prisoners were from a dozen or more units, and he'd been in uniform for only two weeks, so no one knew him. Also, no one felt much like talking. He spent his time lining up for food, for water, for a turn at a bucket, and otherwise sat near a wall through which he could feel the cool foundation rocks that were covered with homemade concrete and a layer of what might have once been white paint. The best that could be said about the basement was that it kept everyone dry. As a heat trap, however, it failed.

Change finally came on a day in mid-October when new Russian soldiers appeared. The next morning, the prisoners finally were let outside into a courtyard to stand in rows. Low gray scalloped clouds raced across the sky, the wind felt cold, like it came from the north, but also wonderful on everyone's face. A Russian officer read out names. Daniel paid close attention so he could answer quickly when he heard Piotr's. At the conclusion of the roll call, officers were separated and marched off and the rest put back into the now roomier basement.

"I'll bet the officers, they're living above ground, eating real food now," one man said.

An older man spoke up. "Not me," he said. "I know these Communists. They do not like anyone who is not a farmer, a factory worker, a poor *chlop*."

To everyone's relief, the first man removed for interrogation the next morning was back in half an hour. Daniel's turn came on the fourth day. They brought him to an office off the courtyard — four bare walls, the door through which he'd entered and another one opposite, and two desks behind which sat an officer and an enlisted clerk. The officer took his time reading what was in the folder the clerk handed him.

"You are Piotr Milkowski?" he finally asked.

Daniel made a snap decision, based, he realized much later, on nothing except that he thought the officer looked a little like Joseph. "No, your honor."

Both Russian heads snapped up. "What do you mean?" The officer was indignant.

Daniel had to sell it or there would be trouble, maybe even terminal trouble.

"Your honor, I am…"

The Russian interrupted. "You will call me Comrade."

Daniel adjusted. "Comrade, I felt it would be unwise for the Germans to know my true identity." The officer stared at him for long seconds, as Daniel tried to think of a better story without success, before he saw the creases around the eyes relax ever so slightly. The man did not smile, yet Daniel felt a small amount of hope, like the beating of a bird's wings in his chest. He now offered his real name and the name of his hometown.

Fear exploded back when the officer announced that he was in the wrong place. His home was within German territory and by regulations he needed to be transferred to their custody. Thankfully, the terror did not last.

"This is not an optimal time to effect this re-exchange. But that is the last lie that the Soviet people will accept, Ciszek." The way Daniel stumbled back to his spot in the basement led some of his fellow prisoners to wonder if things weren't getting rougher.

Visits to the office off the courtyard continued even after all were processed. A large picture of Stalin now hung on the wall behind the desks. At his next visit, it was as if they'd not recorded the real information Daniel gave them the first time, likely looking to test the consistency of the answers. The next time, they demanded more details: parent's names, siblings, schooling. Week followed week as Soviet bureaucracy ground along, and the men, fed, rested and restless, now speculated and gossiped. Despite the order not to discuss what happened in the room, even the meekest Pole whispered their report upon their return to the basement. There was now a third inquisitor, a member of the NKVD, the state security service, and new questions came about work and professions, about memberships. Daniel worried again. How much did his fate rest on the spider-silk connection made with the first interrogator? This new interlocutor added a third side, and though triangles could be useful in, say roofing and bracing, no one constructed a complete building with them.

He could not plan, just react as he stood again in front of the desks.

"Comrade Ciszek," began the NKVD man, the first time Daniel had been so addressed. The clerk licked the end of his pencil, poised to write. "Which gymnasium did you graduate from? And what year was that?"

"I didn't graduate, Comrade," he responded. He knew his story by heart. "In fact, I never attended a gymnasium. My father sent me to be a bricklayer's helper with Pani Jaskowlak, at a brickyard in Czerniewice, a village about twenty kilometers from home." Jaskowlak, Czerniewice, Jaskowlak, Czerniewice, he kept repeating to himself. The NKVD man got up and came around the table, to grab Daniel's hands. He turned them upward and ran his thumb over the palms, while staring at Daniel, who willed himself to meet his gaze, just as he'd done with his father. He hoped that the cuts and scrapes acquired during his escape, and the callouses formed when he dug and dug into the soil of Poland before capture were satisfactory.

A week later, he was back in the office off the courtyard. Only the NKVD man remained.

"Comrade Ciszek, the Soviet Union welcomes workers of good character who want to build a new society. You may be one such man. We have just one more formality." Daniel said nothing, as nothing seemed required. The other man continued. "According to the Ministry Statement of 17 September 1939, reference P-32-K-907, the Polish state ceased to exist when its government left the country. Therefore, membership in any armed force subsequent to that date is insurrection and will be punished by trial and execution. Do you understand?"

Daniel's nod was not enough, and he had to say, "Yes."

"Furthermore, Soviet forces have reclaimed land stolen from our Ukrainian and Byelorussian republics in 1921 to protect the population from exploitation and murder. All residents within those territories are, therefore, considered to be Soviet citizens. Congratulations, Comrade Ciszek. You are now a citizen of the USSR. Sign here," and with that he thrust a paper toward Daniel covered in Cyrillic script, with a line on the bottom where his signature was expected.

He was eight when Poland became its own country again. He and his classmates were members of the first generation in centuries that knew themselves only as Polish. Without hesitation, though, he signed. The alternative hadn't been specified, but Daniel assumed that it was not good. Back in the basement, a few patriots tried to rally everyone to deny that Poland was gone, a little whispering cabal huddled in a corner.

It was a cold November evening when a new NKVD officer came to the bottom step and instructed those whose names he read off to gather their belongings and be prepared to move. A little over half the men, including all the cabal members, walked up the stairs, some marching smartly, a few glancing back as if to take one last mental snapshot. Two machine guns announced their fate ten minutes later. When the NKVD man came back to tell all those who remained to pack up and follow him, he brought with him a dozen armed men to prevent their fear and panic from detonating. The column marched out of the courtyard and continued until they reached the train station, and with each step Daniel became surer that this was not the night his life ended, especially when he saw the train waiting for them. It was not a passenger train. The cars were the kind used for cargo or cattle. Into each, the guards shoved as many as they could, and when full, they closed and locked the doors.

Ian — Paris, 3 March 1940

Ian's anxiety grew as he descended from Belleville, as it had every morning for the last two weeks, fueled in part by his lack of a destination. Yet as with all those other mornings, he eventually found himself maneuvering past sandbags and anti-aircraft gun emplacements to sit next to the gates of Les Invalides, where Napoleon's remains rested within their six nested caskets. In his bedroom at home was a small library dedicated to the Emperor, and he sometimes imagined how a boy from the provinces of Poland might someday also become recognized, or even famous, for uncommon intelligence and hidden valor. Napoleon would never have reneged on a sacred promise to defend Poland. Nor, he knew, would Napoleon have let his army sit and wait in bunkers along the border. When he worried that the police or guards might grow suspicious at his loitering, he proceeded around the corner to the Polish Embassy to ask if there was any way to get word about his father, or Daniel, or failing that, if he could leave his name and address, in case. Every day came the same answer. No.

By midday, his hunger could no longer be ignored, but his pockets held not even a *sou*. The tuition money reluctantly refunded by the university when he withdrew had been whittled away by inflated food prices and Madame Jacquot's ever-rising rent. Despite that, he stayed in Nancy because it was the last location his family knew him to be, but by December, he had to acknowledge that Paris was three hundred kilometers further from the armies at the border and likely to be more vigorously defended. Two high school mates, Paul and Christophe, had gone to Paris months before Ian came to Nancy. He wrote to them, explaining his situation.

"We don't have much either," Paul wrote back. "But we get by, and the more the merrier."

So Ian came to Paris, where he'd always dreamt of going. Nancy had merely been what he felt he deserved.

The walk back from communing with Napoleon took him past the golden-winged horses rearing over the Pont Alexandre III, under the leafless trees in the

Tuileries, and around the sandbagged Louvre, before he came to the market stalls filling the streets around Les Halles. By now, greengrocers, cheese merchants, fishmongers, and butchers, restaurateurs, chefs, and sous-chefs had already selected their aubergines and potatoes, eels and oysters, whole dressed lambs, and fresh milk, leaving the farmers to sell what remained to less selective and poorer shoppers. First, though, it was time for the farmers to cover their wares with tarps or gray bedsheets, and head to a local bistro for lunch, or alternatively, for a different sort of treat over on the rue St. Denis. Aimless men like Ian competed with small packs of lean dogs to sniff out what might have rolled off the pallets or been rejected and thrown out. The boldest or hungriest fellow might even risk a peek under a tarp. Ian was late today; there were few items left. He finally found some turnips, runted and bruised, to pocket.

On rue St. Denis, not so young women stood in front of doorways to buildings that looked as tired and resigned as they did. Ian chose to walk the extra block over to the Boulevard de Sebastopol and followed it up to where it widened in front of the Gare de L'Est. Streams of people, coming and going, flowed around soldiers guarding gun placements. On some days, such as today, he lingered to scan faces, even if the odds of seeing Daniel approached the definition of impossibility. Also, he liked being in the crowds, one little fish within a huge swirling bait ball, anonymous and safe, or at least safer.

Finally, as the day waned and being a sardine no longer appealed, he climbed the last blocks back to the apartment, six flights up a perpetually dark staircase on an unworthy street in a far corner of Paris. Christophe was at the little stove, stirring something. Paul sat at the table, rolling a cigarette. Upon hearing the front door, the fourth roommate, Gregor, leaned out from his room to grunt his approval before disappearing again. Ian heard a voice from behind Gregor's door. A female voice.

Paul caught Ian's look. "She's a friend of Gregor's. Alicia, I think. Might be staying. For dinner."

The three young men stared at Gregor's door. Paul lit his cigarette and blew out the smoke.

"Did you bring back anything?" Paul finally asked.

Ian took the two small turnips from his pocket. He felt their judgment. After almost two months, he was still not adept at finding work, money, or food.

"We seem to find a way to get a few francs every now and then, don't we, Christophe?" Paul asked.

"Ha-ha, today it was a box of doorknobs. Sitting outside a store, asking us to take it, that's what you said, Paul."

"Christophe and I took that box to a store in another arrondissement and left with ten francs, so a little bit of meat in the stew tonight, eh, and something left for tobacco. You don't smoke, do you Ian?"

Ian shook his head and flopped down on the mattress in the corner that was now his home. All day walking with only two turnips to show.

Christophe did not like silence. "Hey, you think your father would be proud that I can divide two turnips into five portions?" he asked Ian.

"I'm sure he would," Ian said. It wouldn't take much. His father judged Christophe to be one of his worst students ever, though at school, where he was careful, proper, and even imperious, Father said nothing. When home, though, he could never contain his frustration, and made regular brief, devastating judgments of various boys and girls. Maybe because this time it was a classmate, Ian took it upon himself to secretly tutor Christophe, and the boy managed to pass the mathematics exam, despite Father's prediction. Paul's name had come up once, after large rude caricatures of the teachers were found hanging in the school on a Monday morning. In Father's judgment, Paul was the only student with the 'temperament' to break in and install them. This was because whenever there was a burglary in town, the police would bring Paul's father in for inquiries. And if Paul instigated the prank, his friend and acolyte Christophe must have been involved too, Ian's father stated as fact. The culprits remained unidentified. The night of their graduation, though, Father predicted that both were likely to end up in jail one day.

Dinner time, Christophe announced. The three young men were at the table when Gregor came out of his room with an extra chair and a woman. Ian stood until the young lady settled into the chair Gregor offered and, for that, he received a soft smile and her brown-eyed gaze for several seconds, until he remembered to sit down himself.

Through quick glances over his spoon while he tried not to slurp his stew, Ian took in her deep brown hair, her carefully penciled eyebrows, her fashionable blouse, and cardigan, and how that smile modulated but never left her lips. Christophe announced there was a little left in the pot. Alicia demurred, as did Ian, so the other three divided and finished the stew. Paul rolled another thin cigarette and began the conversation.

"So, Miss, how do you know our Gregor?"

Ian leaned in to hear her voice, to add another color to the portrait he was painting in his mind. Instead, it was Gregor who answered the question.

"She is a comrade. That is what you need to know."

According to himself, Gregor was an important link between the Comintern and various groups in France. He intimated that he'd been at the Seventh Congress in Moscow five years earlier, which was possible, since the best guess had him somewhere between twenty-five and thirty-five. He was certainly mysterious. Several nights, Ian heard him leave the apartment after midnight or return right before dawn.

Paul and Christophe had been at a Popular Front workingman's café to get a hot meal — in exchange for sitting through a lecture — when they first met Gregor. The speaker was young like them, not one of the older, harder-looking workingmen and talked in platitudes and slogans. Christophe clapped when Paul did, who took his own cues from the audience. Watching so carefully, Paul noticed a man with a distinct mustache standing by the side of the small stage, surveying the crowd. He also saw three men in better quality coats standing against the back wall, men who never clapped at all. Paul told Christophe to be prepared.

"For what?"

"Don't know. Just be ready."

For his wind-up, the speaker exhorted the men to remember that they were all brothers to their class, that their strength came from their solidarity, and that together they could break the control of industrialists and their government lackeys. They were French, yes, but they were also one with workers, students and others who fought for the same rights in Marseille and Rheims, but also in Warsaw and

Moscow and even in Berlin. This war was not really their war, but it was their blood being spilled for the benefit of the bourgeoisie.

This is what triggered the men in the nice coats to blow their whistles to signal charging policemen to crash through the front doors. The noise of chairs falling over and plates and heads breaking accompanied the chaos. The front of the police phalanx closed in on the speaker, who stood like a male Joan of Arc, defiant and petrified. Paul thought him either foolish or brave. Then he saw the mustachioed man walking with deliberate speed towards a door half-hidden behind the stage.

"Come on!" he told Christophe, and they rushed through the door behind the man, to find themselves on a small landing. The man with the mustache, who turned out to be Gregor, judged them not to be cops, and gestured that they should shut the door and follow him down. Evidently, he had prepared this escape route, which took them through a storeroom, a closet and, after easily removing a grate, some sort of tunnel. Gregor lit a lantern someone (himself?) had left and led the way. The smell was bearable — it was not a sewer — but it was still dank and small sounds from the dark edges made Christophe worry about rats. Several meters along, Gregor went around a ladder that led up to a cover through which light leaked.

"It's a bank, likely guarded. We keep going," he whispered.

They eventually exited into an embankment within some overgrown shrubs behind a patch of small workshops, far enough from the lights and *heee-hooo* sirens. At the first open café, the three stood at the bar for one small drink each, and then another. By the end of the evening, Paul and Christophe had a Bulgarian roommate with whom to share the rent.

Alicia scanned the faces of the three boys, coming to rest on Ian. He quickly looked anywhere else.

"I don't believe we've been introduced. My name is Alicia. And yours?" Her French was native.

"I am Ian, Ian Ja uh…gowda."

"How do you do, Ian Ja-agowda," Alicia said, and got the flush she appeared to want.

"It's Ian Jagowda. It's like Jean Lebaie in French." His classmates did not challenge or correct him.

"Jean Fraise should be your name, to go with your hair." Her little laugh neutralized any sting. "How long have you been in Paris?"

"A while," Ian answered. Daniel's wise counsel: *Be polite and circumspect with strangers because one never knew if there was a malignant purpose behind their questions.*

Paul now took the opportunity to recount his success at finding the doorknobs and negotiating such a good deal, hence their fine dinner tonight. Christophe beamed at Gregor and Alicia's thanks. Ian did not mention his turnips.

"Did you hear about Madame Sikorska?" Gregor changed the subject to the wife of the commander of Polish forces now gathering in France. "She and her husband are living in a small palace, while workers, students and peasants enlist to fight in the name of a state of industrialists and militarists."

Each boy, in his own way, dealt with the guilt of not fighting while their country was carved up like a slaughtered hog, their hometown occupied, their families… who knew? Gregor's repeated attempts to place it all within a Marxist context, asserting that their non-combatant status was at the vanguard of the inevitable revolution, went over their heads, but nonetheless made them feel ashamed. On the other hand, he was the only one who somehow had his share of the rent on time every month.

"I heard a story," Alicia said. "It seems that two Belgian girls ran away from their convent school because they fell in love with some handsome Polish soldiers stationed along the French border. When General Sikorski heard, he made the soldiers marry the girls. Something about Polish soldiers is attractive for young innocent convent girls." She laughed. Its music drove any negative thoughts from Ian's mind.

Gregor pushed his plate away and asked Paul for a cigarette, which he accepted without thanks. He blew out a smoke ring before looking from one face to the other, much the way Ian's father did, standing at the front of the classroom until even the most rambunctious child stopped and gave attention.

"The rent is going up again," Gregor announced.

Christophe spluttered. "For this shithole? We're sharing our space with rats and roaches and pigeons and… I want to kill the Durands." He named the concierge, who lived with her unemployed husband and their four young children in a basement flat.

"No. They are also exploited by the landlords. One day they will have to choose." Gregor took another puff on his cigarette. "This is not the day. Comrade Stalin is waiting for the correct moment. But we have to be ready."

Alicia looked at him as a mother does when her child serves an imaginary dinner on pretend plates. "Yes, but how does that solve your rent problem? None of you, I believe, has a job, and I assume you even lack the papers to get one."

Only Gregor did not look down at the stained tabletop. He smiled. "I actually have a solution, one that works for the revolution and solves our immediate financial problem. Now, I do not need to say this, but we must all agree that we will keep it secret. It is not dangerous, far from it. That's the beauty of it. It's reclaiming what belongs to all. Still, the owner class will object, and they own the police. So, do we all agree, it's secret?" Paul nodded, and so did Christophe.

"How do I agree to something I don't know anything about?" Ian asked.

"He is only asking that whatever you hear, you keep it a secret. You do not need to agree to participate, Jutek." Paul answered for Gregor, invoking Ian's boyhood nickname. Ian nodded, reluctantly.

Gregor lowered his voice to force the others to lean in. "Alicia is the key. She works in the office that assigns storage sites for all the material the government is buying to line the pockets of the war capitalists." He went on about why this was immoral, counter to history, and so on.

Paul had to cut in. "What does this have to do with us?"

"I am coming to that. Action without thought violates the imperative…"

Alicia's voice was like syrup. "What we are talking about is not merely machine guns and armored cars. I get to know about anything moving in or out of the warehouses and where it is going. Things like nails. Cotton. Or cigarettes. "

It clicked for Paul first. "So, if a load of cigarettes is supposed to move from one warehouse to some other place, and it doesn't arrive…"

"There are so many shipments that if a truckload or two of cigarettes went missing, it will take a long time for anyone to think it was not merely a bookkeeping error," Alicia said.

Now Christophe got it, and grinned as he did the mental math to calculate what a truckload of good quality cigarettes, at current black-market rates, meant when split five ways.

"This is not dangerous? And what do you do with the cigarettes once you have them? Where do you put them?" Ian threw out the first concerns that occurred to him.

"Good questions, my dear Ian." Gregor gave him his full attention. "We replace the driver with one of us. He drives the truck to a garage owned by people I know who will pay us for the cigarettes, and — this is the best part — for the truck, too. We walk away with the money for the revolution. And rent, of course."

Ian heard excited voices speculating about thousands of francs, what the truck might fetch, where they would celebrate, what district they might move to. Alicia stayed quiet, watching Ian's struggle play across his face.

She spoke directly to him. "This is not a normal world or a normal time, Ian. Circumstance makes us consider whether to act in new ways. That is no one's fault. And, Ian, we are not talking bullets or helmets or food for the soldiers. I know, for a fact, that few cigarettes reach the troops because the corruption is so deep."

Taking Ian's silence for agreement to not report the plan, they went into more detail, fleshing out tasks, proposing alternatives, and Ian could not help contributing solutions to potential problems. By the end of the evening, they agreed on all the detail but so long as it stayed an idea, Ian refused to worry about it.

Daniel – Bira, Siberia, 16–17 March 1940

Three weeks in that cattle car, sitting for hours on a siding waiting for more important trains to pass, or hurtling along with bruising speed, formed bonds between the forty-five or so men who survived the voyage. It started a few hours in, for the most prosaic of reasons. With each bounce, the regular ones and the ones that threw him into the man standing next to him, Daniel's bladder sent increasingly desperate signals to his brain. To distract himself, he began to bounce on the balls of his feet, which is how he noticed that the floorboard under his left foot felt different. Softer. Chips flew when he slammed the heel of his boot into it. He and some of his neighbors opened a hole through which they saw the rail bed flash past, and they organized a slow rotation of bodies around the car to give every man a turn at the hole, privacy be damned.

Almost a full day passed before the door slid open for the first time to let in light and fresh air, and every man looked out desperately for any indication of where they were going and what was to be their fate. Daniel, the nearest to the door, accepted two large loaves of bread, and felt water slosh onto his feet from a bucket lifted into the car. But the door closed and locked again too quickly for anyone to learn anything. The frustration fueled a surge of movement toward the door, and him.

"Wait!" he yelled and held up his hand. "We need to... We can't spill any of this water or lose a piece of this bread. We will distribute it fairly; everyone will get some."

Much later, he wondered how that car came to contain, for the most part, civilized men, or whether it was too soon for fear and desperation to manifest themselves. Whichever the reason, all benefited and suffered equally from the semi-random delivery of food and water. Over twenty days locked in that car, stutter-stepping across Russia, permitted each man to know whatever the others were willing to share, starting with names and hometowns. Even without officers, they could organize into something more than a cattle car full of the injured and intact, the coherent and shell-shocked, the resolute and the frightened, although all harbored these feelings in variable proportions. Even during the five-day march through thick woods after their debarkation at the end of the line, sleeping on the snow-covered ground and going without food for the final two days, many took a turn to help those whose injuries made it difficult to keep the pace the guards demanded. Nothing was known yet, and if they continued to look out for one another, they were not lost.

Four months now since they arrived in the camp. Four months of a cold no human was meant to live in. A cold that superseded every other organic and inorganic fact. A cold that ignored the small stove in the middle of the barracks. A cold that found all the gaps and chinks in the wooden walls. Four months on a diet deficient in what a body needed in this environment, not to mention what they expended cutting down trees six long days a week. Four months of lice and bedbugs that thrived on meals made of prisoners' blood. Over a hundred days and nights in this cold stretched and tore the bonds among the forty-five, as if what had held them together had been but a single strand of spider silk.

The first one died quickly. He was older. He'd been an accountant and then paymaster for his Polish regiment when the 'liberating' — as they called themselves — Russian Army overran it. He spoke little of his life before, as if he'd not had much. In any event, the story went, one morning after his brigade arrived to the small section of forest from which they were assigned to harvest timber, he dropped his axe and walked out past the rope that marked their boundary. A guard yelled once and then calmly shot him dead. Daniel no longer remembered his name. The next one, a week later, appeared to be from a heart attack. Then came a surprise. A young man, strong enough to be in a carnival sideshow bending iron bars, whom everyone expected would have no trouble doing all the work. But after doing well initially, he progressively weakened. As his work output fell, so did his food ration, despite efforts by others from the cattle car to shift some of their production to his ledger or to slip him some of their food. Even though he was moved to easier camp duty cleaning toilets, he died one night in late December. A windless night, Daniel remembered, when the stove hadn't seemed so inadequate, yet he died. For another, it was a saw blade which snapped and cut a major blood vessel in his neck.

They were six kilometers from camp and any medical help. He bled to death before they were even a third of the way there.

Daniel no longer knew how many of those he'd come to know in the cattle car were gone. Maybe one or two transferred to other camps, the rest were likely dead. He lay on his wooden berth, not daring to move and anger the man sleeping next to him, and thought of the growing pile of frozen bodies stacked like logs inside the barbed wire fence under the northeast guard tower, waiting until the ground thawed sufficiently so they could be buried in what would probably be a mass grave. They had been men, and now they were frozen logs. He'd known the men, not the frozen logs, which might explain why he had no reaction, not sorrow or anger or even resignation. Feeling nothing made sense, as nothing was his life now. To be aware of or even think beyond that was an unnecessary expenditure of psychological calories, an effort that would only diminish what he needed to conserve and use to survive. Thinking that the fourth from the top of the pile of might look a little like Jan Dzinkowski or that fellow with the bad eye from Lublin — what was his name ? — contributed nothing to putting one foot in front of the other on the march to and from the work site or to making sure he received and consumed all the food he could or to grabbing a piece of the blanket of a dead prisoner with which to patch one of the holes on his coat.

Daniel could see similar changes in almost all the others. At first, small secret gestures of defiance helped many to maintain a bit of individual dignity, but standing outside overnight as punishment made those little gestures first feel childish and then irrational. All retreated into the numbing routine of waking in the dark, lining up for inspection, lining up for a piece of hard coarse black bread and a cup of soup, whose only virtue was that it was hot, lining up to march through the snow and into the trees, cutting down some of those trees — never making the forest appear to notice — then lining up to march back, lining up for inspection, lining up for another inadequate meal, finally collapsing into a wooden berth to huddle next to another stinking body for warmth, doing it day after day after day after day of monotonous cold, of monotonous snow, except on days when there were skies so blue, it hurt the eyes.

The telltale sign that it had finally become too much was when a man stopped looking up. He no longer needed to see what time it was, or what the weather might be, or where he was, or who was with him. It didn't matter. He knew that it would be the same for days until the inevitable end, so stopped trying to prevent the cold from finally penetrating to his soul. A few days or a few weeks later, he would lie down in the snow, or not get up from his berth, and his body was added to the pile.

Daniel shrank further under the shared blanket and moved a little closer to his neighbor. What was his name? It did not come to him. Instead, he willed his mind to move to his nightly reverie, the manifesto. He recited it, internally, from the introduction and charge, through the critique of current Modernism, until he came to where he'd left it last night, adding several more paragraphs before he could finally sleep.

Ian — Paris, 2 May 1940

Another tense evening of waiting. Ian sat at the table, jotting things along the margins of a piece of graphing paper. Alicia tilted the lampshade so she could read a week-old sports newspaper listing the horses running at St. Cloud two days from now. The other three were out, working a scheme to gain a few francs or plotting the worker's utopia.

"What are you writing?" Alicia asked.

"Nothing, just scribbling," Ian answered.

"You are anything but a scribbler, Ian. Behind those glasses, you are always turning things over, looking at them from all angles to make sure you haven't missed something crucial."

He'd lost count of how many blushes she'd elicited by her words. Even without prompts, his face often betrayed his thoughts about her.

"Gregor, he gets so carried away with his revolutionizing, and the other two are… simpler. Without you, I might be long gone," she said.

This new compliment triggered another facial flush. "Any legitimate analysis would conclude that this is a foolish idea. Yet we are still planning to do it," he ventured.

"Why?" Alicia challenged him.

He assumed she asked about the foolishness. "First, because it is wrong. All our laws, our codes prohibit it. And even if the risks are as low as Gregor claims, though I doubt they are, the consequences were something unexpected to happen are significant."

Alicia turned to give him her complete attention. "The nuns in school would agree that the commandment not to steal is inviolable, but they would say it is because those laws come from God. Do you believe that?"

"Not really," Ian answered carefully.

"I never accepted it either. Those nuns, though, they had an unpleasant reaction to a little girl saying there was no lawgiver God," she said, her gaze steady with the memory.

Ian remembered the arguments around the dinner table at home when he criticized what Father Klimecki taught in Moral Philosophy class. His own analysis of those lessons, plus defending his conclusions against his father's criticisms, helped to create who he knew himself to be — a man of knowledge, now under siege because of this ridiculous plan. "No matter the source, when humans are in groups, they need universal rules. Society would not function if everyone was stealing from each other all the time," Ian said.

"Certainly." Alicia answered. "I am sure even the Soviet Union has laws against stealing, at least until the workers rule. But if it is a fundamental maxim for social life, why are you helping plan a robbery?" Was there a slight upward curve at one corner of her rouged lips?

"It's a question I ask myself almost hourly," Ian said, and ticked off the potential reasons on his fingers. "Because I have no other place to live? Because we need the money? That it will only hurt a faceless corrupt state entity? Out of some sort of affiliation with Christophe and Paul? Because I worry how Gregor might react if I pulled out?" He paused, then added, "I am not proud of myself."

No judgment, no dismissal from her. Instead, she said, "Those nuns, their threats to my soul or to my knuckles did nothing to convince me they were speaking for God, but I learned all those rules. I saw my parents try to live them, as did most everyone in my town. Anyway, it generally worked. But, Ian, what happens when the world is gone completely mad, and people, leaders, even whole countries are violating any or all rules, starting with 'Thou shalt not kill'? What happens then? Is that a time when you can make selective exceptions? I am not proud either, I have a conscience, but I think the world has thrown away the rules, and I have to make up my own to survive."

Ian looked at this beautiful, worldly woman, who was engaging with him as a peer. Maybe he could agree with her, a little, without slipping further from who he thought himself to be. It was, after all, only theoretical. Before he could formulate an adequate response, she went on.

"It must be very difficult for you. You are cut off from home, from family. Christophe and Paul mentioned your father, the math professor, and your brother, what was his name?"

"Daniel."

"What about your mother?"

"She died when I was thirteen. Cancer, I think. My father never said.

"I have a younger brother, and my parents were alive when I left home," she said.

"You don't know if they still are?" Telegraph and mail were still functioning in France.

"I did not leave with their blessing, let's say."

It was another tile for his mosaic of her and he treasured it, but he didn't know how to keep discovering more, so he returned to their first subject.

"I suppose I am a rule follower." He laughed at himself. "But now, you are right, I feel like I am unmoored, lost at sea, and I don't know what direction to sail. You know, to keep from going in circles or running into rocks."

"Have you ever stolen anything before, Ian? Have you felt defiled, as St. Mark informs us?" she asked him.

She must see his blush, as he recalled how, when he was around six or seven, he had taken a piece of halvah from Daniel's drawer. He began to wonder if she was mocking him. He picked up the pencil again and turned his attention to his paper.

"Come on, I don't believe you draw flowers on the margins of your paper." Alicia got up from the old horsehair sofa to snatch up the sheet before he could react.

"A letter? To Daniel?" she sounded relieved.

"It was his birthday yesterday." His voice was low.

"He is back in Poland? When was the last time you had any contact with him?"

"We saw each other when I left. Last summer. Nothing since."

"You never talk about it," she repeated. "It's like it's another planet."

Almost every night, in that time before he fell asleep, his mind went back to the town in Poland where there was no war, and every evening Father presided over the table, sometimes with Daniel present.

"It wouldn't do any good to talk about it," Ian told Alicia.

"And would be painful. I am sorry, Ian. I should have realized this. Forgive me." She looked so in need of absolution; Ian immediately assured her there was nothing to forgive.

Alicia continued. "What a terrible thing no information is. The imagination has no boundaries then." She was sitting closer now, in the chair next to him, one elbow on the table, the hand cupping her chin, those brown eyes aimed at his face.

He told her about the details he did remember, of what the apartment smelled like when the maid cooked his favorite, *bigos* stew, of how their little dachshund would lie still while he fell asleep playing with her tail. He bragged a little about how well he did on the national examinations. Nancy, in his telling, was an affirmative decision, an opportunity too good to pass up.

"Why engineering, although I think I can guess?" she gently teased.

He told her how a drawing was only scribbling on a piece of paper unless someone could make it happen. Daniel could draw fantastic homes, homes that filled every human need. Ian admired their logic and beauty, and at the same time, thought of them as no more than dreams. He wanted to be the person who made sure that all the pieces fit and did their job well, so the train could cross the bridge over the river, the aqueducts and tunnels could bring the water from the mountains to the city, or a new auditorium unlike any seen before could actually stand.

He stopped, embarrassed once more for monopolizing the conversation. "What about you?" he asked. "How did you come to Paris?" She smiled without answering, so he asked about anything, from where she'd gone to school to the name of her sibling until he ended with what was her favorite animal.

She laughed. "OK, stop, stop. I'll tell you."

She'd grown up hundreds of kilometers to the southwest, near Pau, with memories of swimming in the river and picking wild blueberries in the summer, but Spain and its war came, a lopsided dress rehearsal for what was happening now, involving many of the same participants. Her father was an official in the local communist party, which meant long, loud debates at home about anti-fascist coalitions, and it also meant squirrely knocks on the back door late at night, bringing Republican refugees to hide and pass on to the next safe house. She wanted desperately to help, but her father's dedication to Mr. Stalin did not extend to permitting his only daughter to contribute to the coming people's revolution, only to fetching food and drink. One night, though, because the police were becoming much better at arresting those challenging Prime Minister Daladier's cowardly prohibitions, no one else could take a young — and admittedly handsome — man named Rodrigo on to the next rescuer. Before they reached the next safe house, the pressures building up inside her about life in Pau burst, and she ran with Rodrigo all the way to Paris.

"Where is Rodrigo now?" Ian had to ask.

"He got careless, arrested in December. I waited, but it seems he did not betray me," Alicia said. "The education my father insisted upon helped me get the job at the Ministry, so everything turned out okay."

"What is okay?" Gregor banged the door open, startling Alicia and Ian. Alicia went quickly to place a kiss on his cheek.

"What did you bring, Gregor?" she asked brightly.

Gregor revealed his food purchases the way a hunter pulls his catch from his bag, one by one, except it wasn't pigeon or boar, it was potatoes, some cheese and a sausage that Ian remembered tasted of iron and oatmeal, made from the blood of a slaughtered animal.

Alicia had made it clear she was not their cook or maid, but tonight she sliced, chopped, and fried while Ian moved to his mattress to get out of the way. Gregor stood by the table, chewing on the ends of his mustache. Previously, as soon he arrived, Gregor asked Alicia about her day, or shared some news from the central committee, then nonchalantly asked if the date for moving the cigarettes was set. Now, though, it was the first thing he said to her each evening with increasing urgency. He wouldn't say who was putting the screws to him to produce the cigarettes or the money, but it was clear that pressure was being applied. Without anything definitive, Alicia could only say 'soon,' and Ian imagined that Gregor's bosses were increasingly dissatisfied with 'soon.' The last few nights, it felt like one wrong word might trigger something, like brushing up against a pod of touch-me-not impatiens.

"Why have they not moved the cigarettes yet?" Gregor asked, loud enough that Ian worried someone would hear.

"Because there is a war on!" she answered.

"Have they given you a date?"

"Of course not, otherwise I would have told you."

Alicia brought three plates of food to the table, and an unspoken truce allowed them to eat. When they finished, Alicia turned down Ian's offer to clean up, as she deftly cleared the table while staying out of the reach of the Bulgarian, who sat, unmoving, watching her. Ian moved back to his mattress.

When she finished putting away the dishes, though, he sprang up and grabbed her roughly by the upper arm, to pull her into their room and slam the door. Gregor's voice, tight like a fist, was clear. "When is the shipment?"

Ian imagined more than heard her say, "I don't know yet."

"When is the shipment?" His voice made Ian think of a cocked gun.

"I don't know yet." This was clear.

"When is the shipment?" followed by the sound of a hand slapping a face. Close after that Ian heard a suppressed cry. He sprang up from his mattress, straining to confirm what he knew was happening.

"You know, you know…" Gregor was menacingly mad now. "You know for a while. You are not telling me what you know." Slap.

"Gregor, don't!" said Alicia.

"You tell me when shipment moves. You tell me the route. You tell me now!"

"I can't! I don't know yet. I can't tell you what I don't know!"

Slap. Something fell to the floor. Ian tensed, knees bent, preparing, yet at a loss about what to do.

"You know. I know you know. You were telling that pimple face Polack the information. I know this, I see it on your faces when I come in. You are trying to do this without me, to cut me out."

Now it was only sounds like laundry flapping onto a rock by the river, wet and heavy. Ian burst through the door. Alicia was curled into the furthest corner of the bed, staring up at Gregor standing over her.

Gregor was shorter but stockier than Ian. The surprise of Ian's assault overcame any differences, sending Gregor crashing into the space between the wall, the bed, and the armoire. Gregor looked confused for maybe a second or two before he scrambled up to reassert his authority over this young and stupid student.

"Stop, Gregor." Alicia's voice was strong and calm, unaffected by Gregor's violence, her confidence clearly derived from the small pistol which Ian saw in her hand, steady and pointed at Gregor's chest. From this distance, she would not miss.

"What is this? Alicia, what is this?" Gregor looked from the gun to her face to Ian's face and back again. This was not what Gregor had planned, assembling this team to strike a blow at the corrupters and exploiters. Ian wondered what Gregor's masters were promising him to make him so desperate. Reassignment to Sofia? Or maybe even England.

Gregor forced his body to relax and aimed a rueful smile at the other two, as if to ask how there could be any discord among friends. Ian stood panting, his heart racing, questions popping. Why did Alicia have a gun? Would she shoot Gregor? Would she shoot both of them? Who was she?

Alicia's voice was cold. "No one hits me, Gregor."

"I am sorry, *cherie*. I don't know what happened. It is the importance of what we are doing, of our plans. Being ready, waiting, it got to me. I am sorry. It will not happen again."

The gun did not drop even a millimeter. "No one hits me," she repeated. "There is no pretending like it never happened. Once is already over the line. You do not get a chance to lose control again."

Gregor's eyes darted around the room, looking for something to distract or to anchor an argument, or reconnect him to the woman, anything that might change the trajectory of what was happening. Alicia interrupted his search.

"Get out." Alicia waved the gun in the direction of the door, but no one moved. "Get out, Gregor. If you do not, I will kill you. You tried to rape me. Ian is a witness. If you want to fight for your workers again, get out."

Gregor's face went into an angry twist. He hesitated, appearing to weigh and reweigh his choices. Something, finally, made the decision for him. Perhaps, like Ian, he realized he did not know enough about Alicia to predict with sufficient confidence what she was capable of doing, or maybe the fact that she had a gun meant she was more dangerous than he had considered. Turning his back to her, he opened the armoire door.

Ian reached out to put a hand onto Gregor's arm, which Gregor easily shook off. "Leave me alone, pup. I am only getting my clothes." Two handfuls of shirts, socks, and underwear went into a cloth bag. Gregor turned to face the two mutineers, like he wanted to either punch one and slap the other or give them a lecture. Instead he shoved past Ian and headed toward the front door, throwing the epithet, "*Bourgeois!*" over his shoulder as his exit line.

Ian heard Alicia laugh. That laughter, together with the pistol still in her hand, raised his fear even higher, relieved only when Alicia reached under the bed to pull out a small leather bag into which she deposited her gun.

"We live in a crazy world, Ian. I don't have to tell you. You see how it is full of crazy people. They develop these grandiose theories to explain everything and convince others to believe them. And anything that doesn't fit, they either squeeze it to fit, or they try and destroy. You understand what I mean?" Alicia asked him.

"I think so," he offered, even though he didn't.

"Well, take Gregor. Not a terrible man, born and raised within a family and culture like most. Maybe just not a complete man. Then he hears about Marx and Lenin and Stalin, and he loses that part of Gregor that was human, that could connect him to another person. To him, we all become mere tools for the proletariat revolution."

Ian leaned against the opposite wall, trying to appear nonplussed, even if he'd never seen a woman with a blackening eye and bruised cheek before.

Alicia continued. "I met them in Pau, Republicans from Spain who would not accept that they lost, that they were now in France. So, they would plot and drink and sing sad songs and vomit and fall asleep. It was pathetic."

"Did any of them hit you?" Ian asked, tentatively.

"No, my father did that, and the nuns," she answered. "But you could ask if, since I already knew Gregor's type, why would I connect with a zealot like him?"

"I did not think that."

"Well, you should! It's too dangerous not to, Ian. You can't be a piece of driftwood anymore, or you will be smashed into a million pieces by the tidal wave that is our world right now."

Ian felt like he could make out the edges of what she was saying, but not the whole picture. All he could do was nod.

"After I lost Rodrigo, I was alone and I could not survive on my own, and Gregor offered some… I don't know, support? He got use from me, as I did from him. But he crossed the line. And you sprang to my rescue."

Ian did not care if she saw how red this made his face.

She started to laugh again. Was it at him?

"Poor guy. The cigarettes are moving up the queue, the transfer will be soon. He was so close." She got up and walked directly to Ian, getting close to him up against the wall. "We don't need him, Ian. You can do this, you and those other two. The four of us can do this. What do you say?"

Ian — Paris, 2 May–3 June 1940

Paul looked at Christophe, shrugged, and that was that. Gregor was no longer part of the plan.

"The shipment is moving soon," Alicia told them. "We need to be ready to do this on short notice."

Paul had a thought. "What about the buyer? Gregor found him, right?"

"I went with Gregor once to meet him. His name is Zemmour. Works out of a bar in the 13th. I can set something up," Alicia said.

"I'll go with you," Ian said, which prompted stares from everyone else. "One is risky, four makes us look like amateurs," he explained. He did not mention that he based this judgment on gangster movies.

This was how Ian found himself standing with Alicia on the rue de la Butte aux Cailles, across from the Le Diamant bar. He felt a shiver under his shoulder blades as cold as the blue glow shining weakly from the streetlamps. Once more he noted that this was not the way he'd imagined Spring in the City of Light.

The unspoken but clear message greeting them upon entry was, *You have walked into the wrong place.* Additional messages of menace, mixed with lascivious invitations, came through the looks directed at Alicia. Like Mowgli did to the wolves, she stared them all down as she led Ian toward a small man sitting in a dark corner near the back, until two big men blocked their advance. Ian was gruffly patted down, and Alicia's little handbag searched before the bodyguards let them within conversational distance. Ian thought of Napoleon.

"You were here with Gregor," the man said to Alicia. "Where is he?"

"There have been changes," Alicia said. "Johan here has replaced him."

So, Ian told himself, I am Johan.

"Mmm." The little man slathered butter onto each tranche of a generous ham sandwich, slapped the two halves together and took a crocodile mouthful. He wiped his lips on the back of his hand rather than the napkin tucked into the vee of his vest, before nodding toward two chairs. Ian hadn't ever seen ham in Paris. It was rationed.

"I don't care who," the little man said. "As long as the goods are delivered." Small bits of food escaped his mouth as he spoke.

"Nothing else has changed," Alicia said. "French cigarettes, ten thousand packs. Stamped."

"Do you know what to do?"

"Call the number and give the delivery time, at which point we will be given the address. We arrive, you take the truck and merchandise, and pay us 100,000 francs."

The little man took another meaningful bite of his sandwich, chewing and swallowing before he went on.

"Well, there have been changes at this end as well. The attack on Belgium and Holland, the news from the fronts, it has created a whole new situation, pressures from the authorities, the curfews … you know. I can buy the cigarettes, but not the truck."

"What would we do with the truck?" Ian protested.

"Exactly. It is a problem." The small man looked over at one of his associates, as if seeking a solution. "I suppose we could try and find something to do with it, but that is a new and rather considerable expense, you see this, of course. In that case, I could only offer you fifty thousand francs." Zemmour's lips curled into the sort of smile delivered to someone who has stepped in dog shit.

Ian stood up, and they all stared at him. "It was just courtesy that we thought we would try and honor the original deal. Come on, Esther." His revenge for Johan.

The man looked up at Ian and laughed. "I had to try, you understand," he said. He reached across the table to shake Ian's hand and bestow a kiss on the back of Alicia's, then directed one of his Praetorian guards to gift them a package of Player's English cigarettes. Immediately after, they were out and walking through the gloom toward the Place D'Italie metro station. Alicia linked her arm into Ian's and all the way back to the apartment, he only knew that her soft breast pressed into his bicep, which became the center of his existence.

The boys were out. Ian stepped ahead to find the chain for the light bulb above the table.

"Wait," Alicia said. Ian turned, and felt her hands grasp both sides of his face, and one beat later, her lips were on his. The kiss was unlike any he'd ever had, either of them. Soft, searching, and expressive in ways he had not known possible. He wanted it to continue indefinitely, yet he was the one to break away.

"What about Paul and Christophe?"

"They aren't here," she whispered, so close he could feel the words on her breath. She took his hand to lead him into her room, closing the door against Paul, Christophe, the little gangster and his ham sandwich, Gregor's ghost, the German offensive, and wherever Dunkerque was. Ian spun between two poles — desire and the realization that he was going to do what he had dreamed of, versus fear of not knowing what to do and of failing. A powerful magnet, spinning inside his tightly coiled mind, generated currents that sent increasingly powerful electric pulses to explode in his heart and brain.

Alicia pulled him down to sit by her on the bed. She removed her blouse, and the movements caused small shifts in the mattress that felt like earthquakes. He sat completely still despite how uncomfortable his erection was becoming. She leaned in toward him.

"Alicia," he felt compelled to say. "I don't think I should take advantage…"

Her finger was on his lips. "Don't think. And I have been doing what I choose since I was eighteen."

A seed of panic grew in his gut because he did not know what to think and then because he couldn't think. Finally, he didn't think, and the panic disappeared.

Naked, under covers, exploring with lips and fingers, smell and taste, listening for little noises that told him what was desired and what was appreciated. It was over, too quickly, and then came a slower and more satisfying round. No monuments to Victor Hugo, no philosophical discussions in the café, no absinthe —

but lying next to her in the dark made Ian feel that he had arrived, that he was now a member of the club of young men who come to Paris to find deeper meaning in wine and oysters, in study and thought, and in making love.

Alicia reached over and lit one of their new English cigarettes. He stared up at where he knew the ceiling to be, aware of her hip against his. He marveled that a naked woman wanted to be there. He wondered if they would ever make love again. They heard a truck convoy outside. Maybe new conscripts for the front, or maybe cigarettes. Alicia shifted onto her side, and he ran the backs of his fingers gently over smooth skin that felt cool yet also warm, and she did not withdraw from his touch. He knew he would not sleep tonight.

Except morning sunlight was the next thing he became aware of. Was it normal to fall asleep so easily? Would she be offended, or disappointed? No, she was still there, still naked next to him. He lay completely still so he would not wake her, even though he ached to see her body, which he knew only by touch. Also, he needed to pee. What if she woke up and misunderstood his erection?

"Good morning," Alicia said. She turned towards him, leaning forward to kiss him. Ian shifted onto his side and tried to concentrate on her eyes and not the breasts in plain sight.

"That was marvelous," she said. "I had forgotten that making love involves two people."

Ian didn't understand but assumed it referred, negatively, to Gregor.

"Good morning. Yes, marvelous. That doesn't feel like the right word. It's much more. I don't know..." Ian said.

"How about nice?"

"You're mocking me!" Ian pretended to be offended, and it worked. Alicia tried to apologize and when she realized she was the object of the joke, pushed away the hand on which Ian supported his head, which flopped onto the pillow, and they laughed together. She moved over to rest her head on his chest, draping her leg over his and making electric contacts again.

"Alicia," Ian began.

"What?"

He took a deep breath to organize his thoughts. "We don't need... I am wondering if..." His point refused to be made.

She whispered, "What?" again.

"What if we... What I mean is... We don't have to go through with this. We can leave, go to Pau. You know people there who could get us across the border. I hear that if we get to Gibraltar, we could go on to England. Or Lisbon, we could get a boat to... to... an island in the Caribbean. We could find a little cabin on a beach somewhere so far from this war and..." It hadn't felt as silly and juvenile when he thought of it as when he said it aloud.

Alicia did not move from his chest. "Oh, Ian. What a sweet dream."

And then she proceeded to shoot his vision out of the sky like one of those anti-aircraft batteries in the Tuileries. The French and British were being pushed out of the north and rumors were growing that the army was not going to defend Paris. Refugees told frightening stories of planes machine-gunning civilians on the road. Their wish to find a slice through a rapidly narrowing world by which they could escape was as beautiful as it was impossible. She politely did not call it naive. What she did say, though, was that the proceeds from a truckload of cigarettes would significantly enhance their options. As she spoke, Ian felt like he was fifteen, and not a man in bed with a woman.

Her eyes looked hazel in the morning light. "After we complete the job, if things look too hot here, we can consider your Caribbean island." She got up to prepare for work at the Ministry.

This became their new routine; each day the same monotony, each night a new discovery. The boys sat around the apartment until one had to get some air. They now confined themselves to the immediate neighborhood, what with the right-wing papers screaming about spies and saboteurs hiding out among all those foreigners. Any military victories that made the front pages diverged from what witnesses arriving to Paris from the north described. Plus, there were increasingly frequent sweeps looking for draft evaders.

The monotony almost destroyed their plan. One evening before dinner, Paul and Christophe could only talk about how Poles were fighting in France, refugees like them in Polish battalions flying Polish flags.

"You could join us, Ian, you are a patriot, too," Christophe and Paul told Ian. "We could fight together, not sit here, waiting for the Germans to march into Paris."

Ian heard the call. His father acted more Polish than most of their neighbors, and Ian proudly marched in all the school celebrations of nationhood. On the other hand, it was a country that denied him a place in her universities and preached he was a Christ-killer every Sunday to pews filled with the young men he would be fighting beside. This was the scene Alicia found when she rushed in, quivering like a plucked guitar string.

"I have the date. It's in three days, June third," she announced, instantly banishing all other plans. "One truck, going to the army depot in Roissy, with cigarettes for troops on the eastern front. Leaving the warehouse at four in the afternoon."

Days before, Christophe had found the car they needed near the Porte de la Villette. Based on the layers of dirt, dust, and pollen, no one had used it in months. Early one morning, he and Paul pulled the door lock open, wired the starter and drove it to a previously scouted spot in the Javel quartier.

The only variable Ian did not feel he had fully analyzed was the driver.

"The driver is an old man; he has no loyalty to the cigarettes or the Ministry. He sees Paul on one side and you on the other, he will just get down from the truck." She secured the reassurance with a kiss.

Ian did not want to make love the night before the hijacking, but Alicia did. Later, when he thought about it, that night's encounter ranked near the bottom. In the morning, Alicia followed her normal routine, and then Christophe and Paul left to get the stolen car into position. Ian stayed behind, lying on the bed, sitting at the table, looking out the window for any signs that the police were onto them. It was a thirty-five-minute walk to his assigned position. He left the apartment at one. He imagined how Alicia would appreciate his foresight in considering unexpected contingencies.

Sure enough, air raid sirens began to wail before he was halfway. To not follow the other pedestrians could arouse suspicions, so he walked to a shelter under an old apartment building, quickly filling with women, children, and old men. Ian leaned against the wall in a corner, away from any suspicious stares, but when the tattoo of anti-aircraft guns began, all eyes moved up, as if trying to judge if there was enough cobblestones, bricks, and soil between ceiling and street, while children buried their heads into their mothers' bosoms.

A very loud boom shook everything, including courage. Now looks turned to strangers as well as loved ones, eyes asking, *What was it? Is it a bomb? Where did it land? Will there be another one? Will it hit the building on top of us?* And mostly, *I want to run away. Where should I go? Should I stay here? If you run, I will run.*

The next two booms were softer, like thunder from a receding summer storm against a background of continued anti-aircraft gunfire. Everyone stayed quiet, even when the all-clear sounded. Ian emerged into the bright light, and when his eyes adjusted, was surprised to see nothing different. It had sounded so loud, but it wasn't even close.

His first bomb.

He was on post by two thirty, looking like another indolent Frenchman, he hoped, leaning against a wall, smoking a cigarette, reading and rereading a newspaper. He resisted looking at his watch too frequently, in case someone might see, but with only warehouses and workshops nearby, few were even around to take any notice of him. One fellow in a blue apron and a slouch cap passed him twice, mumbling to himself each time with such animation that Ian was certain the movie playing in his head was more engrossing than anything in the neighborhood,

When he finally checked, it was already three forty but there was no sign of the car or of Paul and Christophe. The plan depended on precision. Where were they? He looked toward the gate from where the cigarette truck would emerge, where he knew Alicia was finalizing the paperwork and consigning the load to the driver. Should he try to contact her, ask her what they should do?

Finally, an old gray Citroen Avant arrived, and Paul stepped out. He leaned in to say something to the driver — Ian presumed it was Christophe — and the car moved up and around the corner, out of Ian's sight, as Paul put up a detour sign in the middle of the road with an arrow pointing toward the rue Varet, the road on which Ian would enter a new life with a new set of rules. He was not completely certain he was there of his own volition, yet he could point to no external coercion or threat, so it must be by his own choice. Paul waved toward where Ian was standing, and Ian's hand gave a little acknowledgment back. All was ready.

Daniel — Bira, Siberia, 3 June 1940

The camp commander had selected Monday as the 'day without work.' It was a mandate from the central authorities meant to maintain the pretense that the Gulag was a state business and the prisoners merely proletarian workers. Monday, not Sunday, to rub it in the noses of those who still harbored old religious superstitions. Daniel only cared that it came with a blessed extra hour in bed. It was also bath day. At the appointed hour, everyone in the barracks who could marched to the bathhouse, where they stripped immediately upon entering and stood in a line so slow-moving that the mosquitos had plenty of time to select which piece of fresh flesh to feed upon. Finally, the men stood for a few minutes under rusty showerheads dribbling out cold water. Each man used their sliver of soap to wash, then rinsed and proceeded via another slow walk to the next room. In winter, bone cracking cold on wet naked bodies replaced the biting insects of summer. Thousands of bites versus frostbite, depending on the season.

While the prisoners shuffled through the showers, their coats, shirts, pants, underpants, and socks took their own journey through a space under the bathhouse, hung on a wire which passed them through an oven, which was supposed to heat them to a temperature lethal for lice and bedbugs. The warm clothes ascended through a hole in the floor to drop into a pile at the end of the last room, to be reclaimed by their dripping naked owners, all supervised by one of Kortnev's men.

Kortnev ruled the camp as much as its commandant. Along with captured Poles, ethnics who were living where Stalin did not want them, and Russians banished for political transgressions, the camp housed a core of true criminals — feral brutes who ruled these isolated semi-societies by intimidation and force despite being outnumbered, often fifty to one. The man in charge of the sublayer in Bira was a Russian named Kortnev, a big man with a shaved head and rumors of a murderous past both inside and out of the Gulag. He was always accompanied by two men who looked, to Daniel, as if they belonged in the primate cages at the Warsaw Zoo. When he first arrived to this clearing in the Siberian forest, eight thousand kilometers from civilization and order, Daniel couldn't imagine what sort of booty or benefits these Urka sought. It turned out to be survival, first and foremost. By using their intimidation, they placed themselves in charge of food distribution, meaning they always ate first and best. They ran a small black market in paper, useful for wrapping the coarse tobacco that they also had the monopoly on, or for writing letters home. Most importantly, they became brigade leaders.

The brigade was how the prisoners were organized and through which the Gulag worked. Each brigade had a work quota that needed to be fulfilled daily and weekly, which was the sum of the quotas of the individual prisoners who comprised the brigade. The brigade leader could not only assign tasks, he also recorded each man's work. If he chose to undercount the work, that prisoner would see their food ration cut — a powerful weapon. Those on good terms with the brigade leader could even stay in camp doing easy work and still get credit for a full quota, but those who made him angry or did not give him what he demanded marched to the furthest site, did the hardest, most dangerous work, and were marked as failing to measure up. The central office reported — and maybe even believed — that they shipped sufficient food for the prisoner count at each camp, choosing to ignore the transportation captains, the truck drivers, camp commanders, officers, non-coms, and the Urka, who each took their cut. What was left was never enough, especially in winter. If a brigade leader reduced it even more, it was slow murder.

Daniel stood naked in line, slapping at the bugs. The Urka in charge of the pile of warm clothes had a stick with which he rooted around, every once in a while tossing what was clearly a better specimen into a smaller pile next to him. If a prisoner took too long to find his own things, the Urka shoved the nearest items from the large general pile over, then shoved the man away. No one said anything.

Sometimes a man has had enough, and today it was the fellow just in front of Daniel, someone he thought he might recognize from the cattle car, who'd been an auto mechanic from Wroclaw before joining the army. On the train, he looked as solid as an engine block. Now, Daniel saw, he was ribs and sticks. The man quickly found his pants, shirt, and hat, but then started pulling clothing aside, searching for more. Daniel wished he'd hurry up. The longer he stood, the more likely someone might notice his circumcision. The mechanic stopped when he saw his jacket in the small stack of reserved clothes. He moved to pick it up.

"Hey, what do you think you're doing?" the Urka demanded, putting his arm in front of the mechanic.

"That's my coat!" The mechanic pointed.

"No, it's not!" came the response.

"It is, I tell you, I can identify it, it has…"

"It's not yours. Not now. Here, take this one, and get going." The overseer pushed the one he picked up from the top of the large pile into the arms of the mechanic. As if that finally made the armful too heavy, the mechanic dropped all the clothes onto the floor and shouted, "That's my coat. I demand to have my coat!"

Several high-pressure systems were colliding: the mechanic's anger at the theft, the Urka's anger, or maybe fear, at the challenge to his authority, and from everyone else, dependence on the smooth movement of the line. Daniel felt the gathering force at his back as he watched the confrontation in front of him. In Warsaw, his choice would have been automatic. After he and Joseph finalized their manifesto, everyone would understand that the individual had value equal to or greater than the group, and honoring that value would, naturally, produce humanistic choices and progress. This was not the place or circumstances to invoke those principles.

"Get going, hurry up!" he yelled, which sparked even more and nastier cries from the other waiting men. The mechanic looked up at Daniel. Over a few seconds, those eyes went from recognition to resignation. He picked up the clothes he'd dropped and moved to the dressing area to search for his own boots.

Daniel took only a few seconds to locate his shirt and pants from near the bottom, so they still held a little heat. What he couldn't locate, however, were his socks.

"Enough. Here take these," said the overseer, and handed Daniel a pair far less threadbare than his own. Daniel said nothing about it, to himself or to his benefactor.

6 July 1940

Dear Father,

It has been, I believe, over ten months since I last wrote, and much has happened to me since then, the details of which are not important. The circumstances that have landed me here have also, I am certain, impacted our town and you. I sincerely wish that you are as well as might be hoped, given these circumstances.

It is both strange to be writing to you and comforting at the same time. I don't know where my friends are, and Ian is unlikely to be in Nancy anymore. You are the closest that I have to a constant, a base in the natural world around which we can create a new home. Ever the architect, eh?

One thing that I do not lack for now is time. With that time, I have been thinking about my past, and I have been thinking about you and us, and you and me.

This is not easy to write, but I want you to know that I am sorry for being such a difficult son. I had no right to question your motives. You only wanted what you thought was best for me and for all of us. I think I misplaced my anger at Mother's death and was too immature to realize that you were hurting as well. What I have come to appreciate is that you provided us with the safety to imagine widely, maybe wildly, compared to what you knew from when you grew up. No matter what happens, I want you to know that I am grateful for the opportunities to pursue ambitious dreams, if only for a short time.

Love,

Daniel

Ian — Paris, 3–7 June 1940

Finally, the gate opened, and Alicia led what had to be their truck out onto the narrow street, ensuring the driver turned left in the direction of their trap. Ian signaled to Paul at the next corner. The driver ground the gears as the truck approached, which made Ian worry if he was an inexperienced kid and not an old man. Ian was on the wrong side to see. Diesel smoke perfumed the air as the truck passed the utility pole behind which Ian stood, after which he stepped out into the middle of the road close behind the tarpaulin-covered rear. The narrow road, the unfamiliar controls, or maybe the driver's age, kept the truck at a pace Ian could match. A yard dog jumped up to make a run at him, but only as far as his chain allowed. Ian couldn't peer around the truck to see if Christophe was moving the old Citroen across the top of the road, to create the roadblock so he and Paul could bracket each back corner and appear in the rearview mirror when the old driver thought about backing up. Alicia assured them that the driver would not do that just to protect someone else's cigarettes.

Paul now ran past Ian and up along the driver's side, and the truck came to a sudden stop. This was not part of the plan. They were the net, holding their prey until Alicia arrived to tell the driver that his assignment was done.

A loud shot came from somewhere in the front. Ian squeezed between the wall and the right side of the truck until he could hoist himself up to look into the cab and saw Paul standing on the other running board. Between them, the old driver sat with his hands on the wheel and his head turned toward Paul, not moving. Not breathing. Ian smelled the cordite before he saw the pistol in Paul's hand.

"What the hell!" Ian yelled. "What are you doing? Why did you shoot him? Who the hell told you to bring a gun?"

Although his eyes were very blue and his nostrils flared a little, Paul looked as calm as when he rolled a cigarette at the apartment table. There was no quaver in his voice.

"He looked like he was going to fight."

"He's an old, old man, too old to be called up, probably gassed in the War and… Ah shit, ah shit." Ian got down and paced in the little space between the truck and the blockading Avant. He had never stolen anything except for that piece of halvah. Why had he not insisted that this was a terrible idea?

Paul got down, and Christophe came to stand beside him. They watched Ian walk his circle, until Alicia arrived.

"They shot the driver! They shot the damn driver," Ian announced. Murderers were guillotined in France. Ian assumed that Alicia knew that.

Alicia drew herself up to survey the cab. Without taking the time Ian would need to process facts, implications, reactions, emotions, she began issuing instructions.

"Give me the gun. Christophe, you and Paul get the driver, put him in the car boot. Don't take it back to Javel, go to the Meudon Forest. It's closed, but about two kilometers along its south side, there is an entrance — you can lift the chain and get in. Drive up to the lake and drown the car, together with the body and your overalls. They have blood. Then, walk to the train station at Chaville. Ian and I will go quickly, before Zemmour hears anything, and we will meet you back at the apartment with the money."

It was like she'd anticipated this. No one moved.

"Go, Paul, go," she said. "If we wait, all we will have is a murder charge, not even 100,000 francs to show for it."

Paul did not like the new plan. However, since even he had to acknowledge his responsibility, he was in no position to argue. He grunted at Christophe, and together they moved the body into the Avant. Alicia tore out the blood-stained driver's seat and found an armful of Le Matin newspapers to put over the post to create a new one. She threw the seat into the Avant and pushed the gun deep within the cartons stacked in the back of the truck.

She had to shove Ian up into the passenger side before she went around and got behind the wheel, throwing the truck into gear as soon as the car departed. Ian looked out the windscreen, seeing nothing. He was an accomplice in a murder. In Paris, which had just been bombed. Random death or specific death, take your pick. If the truck was hit by one of those bombs, or buried under the debris of a collapsing building, the pilot would know nothing and feel nothing. Was a pilot as responsible as Paul? Ian knew he was as responsible as the crewman who'd loaded the bomb into the plane.

"Ian," Alicia called his name three times before he indicated he was listening. "What time is it?"

Seventeen minutes past four. They were on schedule for a plan that no longer resembled what anyone had actually planned.

"What do we do now?" Ian asked.

"Nothing changes, Ian. We stay together, we don't fall apart. The police are busy today, with the bombing and the damage and the panic." She geared down to take a corner. "We stop at a café, call Zemmour, go to the rendezvous, exchange the truck and cigarettes for the 100,000 francs. We should have kept Christophe with us. Christophe would look like muscle."

She was so focused, so logical. Ian's mind, in contrast, was an uncontrolled conflagration of monologues, conversations, and accusations. He could not imagine what he would say to his father or Daniel, if they ever spoke again. He wondered if Alicia's body would metamorphose into something as angular, hard-edged, flinty as her new behavior, and if so, would it ever return to yielding and sinuous and inviting? Sure, the Caribbean island was schoolboy's talk, but maybe they could go to Spain or Portugal. Which were further from home and family than Paris. The war be damned, this sealed it. He would never see home or anyone he knew ever again. He would be a fugitive, not the silly engineer which had been his adolescent dream.

She suddenly pulled the truck over near the Volontaires Metro station and ran into a café with a telephone disc above its door. She came back in less than two minutes.

"As I suspected, it's behind the Gare d'Austerlitz," she announced.

They stayed within their own thoughts. Alicia drove carefully so as to attract no attention to the nondescript unmarked truck, until they were paralleling the railway tracks that fanned out southward from the station, named, Ian knew, for Napoleon's great victory over two emperors.

"There," Ian pointed. Alicia stopped centimeters from the metal gate and honked once. Two of the big men from Le Diamant pushed the doors open, then closed them like a sprung trap after the truck lurched into the courtyard. Zemmour was there, in a black jacket despite the summer heat. The little man moved like a dancer, all balls of his feet, as he came to Alicia's door to offer his hand as she descended from the cab. Ian joined them at the back where one of the men untied and pulled back the tarpaulin to reveal boxes, all labeled *cigarettes*. Zemmour ordered four random packs brought to him and confirmed that each was complete. Ian took note of this, in case he needed to know how to be a successful criminal in the new life he was now destined to lead. Zemmour took one of the cigarettes for himself before offering the pack around to his goons. He spoke only after exhaling his first drag.

"Well done. Marcel will bring the money. You may count it but once I make an agreement, I honor it, and I expect the same from whomever I deal with, as everyone knows. When they do what they are supposed to, there is no need for anything further. Come inside, I have some special cognac."

Ian spoke up, his voice deep and calm. "Thank you, but I am afraid we cannot. We have friends who are expecting us. They may get nervous if we are delayed."

"Of course, you also keep your promises. Good. I wish we could do more business, but I suspect that this war will disrupt things for some time. If I may offer some advice, you might think about leaving Paris soon. My sources indicate that the city will not be stable for a while."

"Will you be leaving?" Alicia asked.

"Well, it is a little complicated for me. I have so many people who depend on me and my business. And some chaos can be beneficial for people like me, no? But that is not a situation for everybody."

Ian wanted to walk away, to never see Zemmour again. He wanted to flee Paris, and to consider whether Alicia was included in that desire.

Marcel returned with a canvas bag, which he swung over to Alicia. She opened it and showed Ian that it appeared full of francs. Ian took charge of the bag, and Alicia held out her hand to Zemmour. "Monsieur, our business is done. Yes, I believe we will be leaving Paris, so we are unlikely to see each other again. *Bonne chance.*"

They went out the gate and joined the flow of other couples, families, old men, and mothers with children, most carrying bags and moving as quickly as possible in the direction of the railroad station. Ian remembered that trains from Austerlitz went south. Probably to Pau.

"Alicia, listen." He tried to keep his voice low, the street was thick with would-be refugees. "He is right. And we don't know if the police are waiting for us at the apartment. We can buy tickets at the station for Pau, and wire Paul and Christophe their share as soon as we get there."

Alicia stopped in the middle of the road and started to laugh.

"Ian, Ian. Oh, my poor Ian. What have we done to you? First, we turned you into a thief, and now you even think about deserting your comrades."

His face made her laugh harder. He also noted that she had omitted the greater crime.

"No," she continued. "You don't mean to cheat them, but that is what they will think when they get back to the rue Chevreau and we are not there. I can't do that to you, Ian." She pulled him by a wall surrounding a garden, out of the tide of humans.

"Let me tell you why we cannot go to Pau. The truth this time. My parents aren't in Pau, they died four years ago, of nothing except age and poverty. My father was a farm worker, we moved between various villages around Pau. Often, I lived with my grandparents in Gurs, so I could attend school while my parents went wherever the work was. You have heard of Gurs?"

Ian shook his head.

"The government has a camp there for people fleeing Spain, the ones who have lost. It is a horrible place: people packed together, open sewers, little food. I, uh… I had been helping, during the civil war, moving people, and sometimes even guns, across the mountains. I belonged to an anti-fascist group, on my own. Anyway, we started trying to help our comrades in the camp, and the Gendarmerie, they found us. There was a policeman, Etienne Aubert. I knew him from school. I think he may have liked me. Anyway, he led the arrests. Most of my friends were taken to jail or worse, and, well, my group, they all thought I had something to do with it, because I wasn't arrested."

Ian's body flushed with confusion except where his shoulders leaned against the cool wall. He had so many questions, like what should he do now or whether she had betrayed her little Communist band, or which story was the truth, or whether anything she had told him, verbally or physically, was true. Was he a fool, as well as a thief and an accomplice to murder? The roar in his head competed with cars honking to get by, voices from pedestrians urgently moving toward what they hoped was a route to a safer place, the cries of children, a train whistle nearby. He noticed that the trees in the garden were full of berries, yet devoid of birds. He heard no bird song.

"I didn't do anything. I was away, but you understand, I can't go back there, they won't believe me." She stared into his face. "The Ministry is staffed by cheats and conscription dodgers and a boss who keeps offering me stockings to sleep with him, the fat pig. Gregor, I won't talk about. But you, you are always looking for what is the right thing to do even when it is stupid, now, to do the right thing. It is what I am coming to love about you. But we can't run away to Pau. And you need to bring the money to your friends. You can't lose any more of what you are."

He heard her words; he could not process their meaning.

Alicia hooked her arm into his and navigated them through the mass of people pressing toward the front of the station, while avoiding the police working to control the chaos, and then they were past, looking like any young Parisian couple walking along and over the Seine. They kept to the smaller side streets leading up to the 20th arrondissement. It was unusually dark when they finally reached their corner because the authorities, fearing a night attack from the German air force, kept the blue streetlights off. They stood for a few minutes and watched, trying to detect any police waiting to pounce. Finally, hungry, footsore, and exhausted, they wordlessly agreed to cross the street and enter their building, tensing in anticipation of a nightstick blow as they reached the door to their apartment.

The hallway bulb only threw a few centimeters of light past the door, leaving most of the apartment dark, so when someone inside switched on the lamp, Ian jumped almost a meter in the air. This was, somehow, the most hilarious thing any of them had ever seen, and all four were convulsed by laughter, which only subsided when Alicia put the bag on the table and pulled out stacks of franc notes. They sat in front of their four equal stacks as if they were seated for dinner at the Ritz.

"We all came back," Paul said.

Ian let this statement, evidence of some sort of honor, temporarily soothe the unease he kept feeling.

"What do we do now?" Christophe asked.

"We keep it in the one bag until we get three more?" Paul offered.

Alicia repacked the money as the boys recounted how the roads were clotted with cars, carts, families, dogs, caged birds, and trucks piled with mattresses and grandmothers, all trying to move west. When they stopped, as happened often, they heard rumors about the army redeploying away from Paris to create a redoubt in Brittany. At one point, Christophe scouted ahead on foot and discovered an unused track which, it turned out, led into the Meudon forest. They saw no one, including when they reached the lake, and they did what they needed to do. The train back from Chaville to the Gare Saint-Lazare was empty.

"We were here only about thirty minutes before you two arrived," Paul said. "Not enough time to worry."

Ian, in turn, described the drive to Zemmour, the transaction and their return to the apartment, leaving out the advice to leave Paris and what that had prompted him to propose.

What had surged through their bloodstreams — to galvanize their senses, to fuel their efforts, to clear their thinking, to propel them past whatever might impede their necessary actions — disappeared almost simultaneously from all four, as they fell silent, too exhausted to speak further. Alicia trudged to her room, with a quick look over her shoulder at Ian, and a whispered 'good night' to the other two. Paul and Christophe were next, and finally Ian dragged his body to the bedroom. The bag containing what they had hoped and planned, sacrificed and feared, and now killed for, remained on the table.

He lay down next to her expecting to fall as deeply and instantly asleep, but his mind would not cooperate. It caromed from place to place, trying to isolate the variables, to assign them weight, and arrange them in a manner by which he could construct a path out of an unrecognizable landscape marked by signs he could not interpret, as if they were in a foreign language in this foreign land. Finally, mercifully, his exhaustion overwhelmed his panic.

They were all awake soon after a gray dawn. Alicia insisted she should go to work. "If we do not arouse suspicion, continue as before, the war will distract them and give us a few days," she said.

Ian was dead set against it. "People are leaving Paris at every hour of the day and night. They will assume you are one of them," he argued. "And if they suspect, that will be where they will be waiting for you."

They went back and forth as Alicia dressed. Ian looked fruitlessly for support to Paul and Christophe, who were at the table drinking their first coffees. She gave him a quick kiss on the cheek and left.

Christophe took a few francs from the bag to go buy some food and any newspapers still being printed. "Don't flash it around," Paul told him.

"I know," Christophe said.

He returned with bread, cheese, coffee, the papers, and cigarettes. Two hours later, the detritus of their breakfast lay scattered amongst the newspapers, and a light blue haze hovered over the table. That was what Alicia found when she walked in.

Ian jumped up. "What happened, why are you back?"

"They sent us home. The minister is in meetings. They are in a panic. Everyone was crying because they worry that it means the Germans are going to be in Paris any day now, or angry because they will not have a paycheck."

A different individual went out each of the next three mornings for food and, critically, for newspapers, which they searched meticulously, thankfully finding no reference to a truck hijacking, a missing driver, or a murder. That task was completed by lunchtime, which left the rest of the day to pass, and they waited, but they did not know what for. Each noted that fewer police could be seen trying to keep order among the multiple streams of refugees coming in from the north and of Parisians trying to flee to the south and west. Rumors flew like leaves in the fall. Alicia came back with word that, despite the war about to engulf Paris, Gregor had been arrested in one of the continuing roundups of Communists..

Christophe appeared to crack first, which manifested as an inability to sit still. Paul took him into their room to distract him and not bother Ian and Alicia. They could be heard whispering and staying up late to whisper more. When Ian returned with their breakfasts on the fourth day, the two came out and stood by the table to announce that they had decided to join the Polish Army.

"Why?" Ian and Alicia both asked.

Paul shrugged. "It sort of makes sense, and it doesn't. We can't just stay here waiting, you know. If we run, where to? I mean since there is a war on, eh? So we thought they wouldn't look for us there. I mean, why would anyone who just got so rich join the army?"

"Besides, we always planned to go back home, and what would we say when we got there, and people asked us what we did?" Christophe added.

"Here's the thing," Paul continued. "In the army, they'll give us a uniform, food, maybe not a house, but a tent at least. We won't need all the money, so Christophe and me were thinking, we'll take some, and leave the rest, 'cause you guys are going to need it."

Ian did not know what to say. He walked over to embrace each one in turn. Alicia did the same. When she stepped back, Alicia said, "Your share is a loan. When this is over, we will find you and pay you back." Ian nodded. Everyone knew how fantastical this promise was.

The boys put a few personal effects, toiletries and the like, along with a larger bundle of franc notes than they originally intended, at the insistence of Ian, into the new bags they'd bought the day before and, after more hugs, they left into the morning sunlight. His father would have to reconsider his assessment of Paul and Christophe, Ian thought. How would he judge Ian and his choices, he wondered. Ian imagined the scene that Christophe described, all three back and only Ian not in uniform. He knew that his decision about whether to fight was not as simple as theirs. They would not have to lie and hide their background from birthright anti-Semites. Unlike him, they were naturally adventurous, and even brave. Also, their equation did not include the variable called Alicia.

All the while Paul and Christophe had been whispering and deciding, Ian was trying to come to terms with who Alicia was and how he felt about her. There were probably bits of truth in each of her two stories, but it was also possible that neither was actually the truth. The salient fact was that there were two stories. Had she run to Paris with Rodrigo for romantic reasons or to continue working for the communist underground, a kind of promotion? Gregor's relationship to her... maybe it meant she was a member, too. If that were true, would she keep the money for herself, to give to the cause?

The apartment echoed, emptier with only two. They barely spoke to one an-other. Summer heat penetrated the roof to cook them, and they kept all the windows open, which brought in noises from the street far below mixed with the chirping of birds nesting in the elm trees. The heat did not dissipate as the day waned, as Ian stood at the window trying to catch any faint airflow. Today, he noticed, there were no bird noises. There was something else he could sense. It was more a low vibration in his abdomen than a sound, and as he listened, it became a hint, then a confusion; finally, the birds had enough and flew off from where they'd hidden amongst the leaves to escape the sound of artillery guns firing again and again from north of Paris.

Ian went back to the table on which their money bag sat and faced Alicia. "We can't stay. Zemmour is right," he said.

The Gestapo had a deserved reputation for finding and cruelly dispatching those whom they deemed enemies. They would find out about her past, whatever it was, and the consequences were unthinkable. Even before the Germans came, he risked being swept up by the police corralling young men as deserters and mo-bilization dodgers. Looming over all but centered in the pit of his stomach was the hijacking and its horrible complication. He listed all these reasons out loud as she sat, passive, and now he talked about how they needed to persevere together, about how he wanted to protect her. He stopped there. The words were in his voice, but he did know from where they sprang.

Alicia smiled at him and then stood up. Ian reached for her, and she buried her head into his neck while he inhaled the clean smell of her hair and the light lavender of her perfume. They held each other until the rumble in the distance broke through into their consciousness.

"Okay, okay," she laughed. That she could laugh at this moment when he could not bring himself to search for a thought that might prompt a smile, and that her laugh was large enough to embrace him, meant everything. "We will go together. We will go to Pau; I think maybe there are people there who will help us. Thank you, thank you Ian."

He wanted to leave immediately. She insisted that there were some essential tasks she must do. If the Ministry reopened, her absence could connect her to the hijacking, so she would meet a coworker to arrange for a good cover story. She would also procure the permits and papers that would ensure that their escape would be successful.

"I will be an hour, two tops. I will meet you at three o'clock, at the tobacconist in front of the Gare d'Austerlitz. Give me the bag, I think my friend will need some persuasion." She went into their room and came out with clothes, a little jewelry case, some brushes and toiletries. "Go and buy another bag and put these items in it, with yours. Meet me at three. Don't get caught by any police. Please be careful, Ian."

"You be careful, Alicia. I will be there. I love you," he repeated.

Henry — Garden City, New York, 24 June 1963

My parents knew the names of the many children who lived on our block and always stopped to exchange a few words with their parents. My mother regularly brought potato salad or a chocolate cake to school events. What they never did was place themselves into situations where someone could ask questions, starting with where they were from. Into their true social circle, they only accepted fellow refugees. There was only one without an accent, a man who'd gone to boarding school in England before the War. I loved his voice, but never dared to leave my parents' side and search for him when they brought me along, which was pretty much always because leaving me with a local teenager for a few hours was an unthinkable risk to my mother.

One summer weekend, we attended an outdoor gathering of these same people and after seeing how the others dressed, my mother permitted me to remove my clip-on tie and my jacket. She drew the line at me rolling down the knee-high gray wool socks, but they soon pooled around my ankles anyway. My parents, wearing their best, must have envied their hosts — she looked elegant and cool in a peach sleeveless blouse and he was in a baby blue and white polo shirt. I don't believe I had ever seen any of the refugee adults dressed so casually. I tried not to stare though, because whenever the man in the blue shirt met me, he pinched my cheek, hard.

We returned home and I waited until my parents finished changing back to how they normally looked.

"Mama?" I asked.

"What is it?" she blew the smoke from her cigarette away from my face.

"Mr. and Mrs. Fischer... on their arm, there was something blue. It looked like some numbers. Mr. Silberman has one too. What is that?"

That shadow I sometimes noticed passed over her face, and she didn't answer. It was my father who told me, "It's not time to discuss that, son. Let's wait until you're a little older and then you can ask again."

When I felt old enough to ask again, I knew not to.

Daniel — Bira, Siberia, 5-18 June 1940

Marching out to work was easier now that the ice and snow were gone, and any berries the bears left on the bushes provided a welcome snack. On the other hand, the melt turned the ground to mud, making the footing treacherous when manning two-handed saws, swinging sharp axes, or scrambling out of the way of a falling tree. This was also the season for every insect to emerge, feed — preferably on a blood meal — fuck and die.

Ergorov, another of Kortnev's crew, was now Daniel's brigade chief. For his first act, the Urka reassigned a sick old man from barracks cleaning duty to a death sentence on the forest crew to gift the lighter duty to one of his friends. The daily payment for being on 'the trim' went from ten to fifteen kopecks. The trim was easier and safer than being on the saw or wrapping chains around the trunks to drag them to the head of the road, where the lowliest brigade members lifted them, using hands, arms, backs, and ropes, up and onto trucks. In accordance with Stalinist theory, what remained after subtracting the cost of food, was deposited into each prisoner's account, with which he could purchase small comforts like tobacco or paper. Or bribes. The latter was not in accordance with what Stalin, the *Vozhd* of the proletariat, espoused, merely its practical application.

One of the four men with whom Daniel shared a bunk was Dmitri Yakimchuk, a man so slight, the other three could imagine he wasn't there each night. His size made him wary around people; he preferred to stay at the periphery. His invitation to the Gulag came after a gang planned to rob a factory office just prior to payday and needed someone who could fit through a narrow window to open the door from the inside. Once in, though, he was no match for the heavyweight guard. Production quotas were not adjusted by weight so Yakimchuk had to perform at the same level as men twice or more his size. His shortcomings and the resultant food and calorie deficit made his destiny clear and brought out his survival talents. He became adept at finding favors to do for the men. "Hey, Pavel, I will carry your saw for a while!" or "Oleg, I can write that letter to your wife, she will love how beautifully you have learned to say those special things!" for which he would accept a piece of bread or a few kopecks. These, together with rare gestures of generosity from men who felt for the little guy, were enough to get him through the long winter and the short spring.

A change came one night when a far heavier man heaved himself onto the bed, next to Daniel.

"That's Yakimchuk's spot," Daniel informed him,

"Not anymore. Ergorov moved the little weasel closer to his own billet."

A week later, Yakimchuk walked as if he had grown a few centimeters. He no longer carried any heavy tools on the long trek to the timber site. During the day, he stood next to Ergorov making little notations on a clipboard, yet he received a full portion at each meal. Resentful mutterings and jealous snipes bubbled, quietly so they would not come to the attention of Ergorov or his minions. Daniel ignored it all. If this was a way for the little guy to get through this hell alive, it was his business.

He knew most of the other two hundred men in the barracks by sight, and a few even by name, but he kept his relationships limited generally to being at the other end of the two-handed saw. When a commotion started at the other side of the barrack room before lights out, he didn't bother to look to identify who was involved. Probably a couple of Joes settling a debt or an insult or challenge, basically a release of pressures stoked by frustration and impotence. Eventually he noted that he was alone, everyone else clustered around where the noise and emotions were erupting. He stood up on a table to see over all the bodies and still couldn't understand the scene.

"What's going on?" Daniel asked another man on the table.

"Guy called Urbancyzk. Seems that he's been doing favors for the bosses. A few of Ergorov's friends were caught, you know, *tufta*." Tufta was a generic term for the numerous ways one could cheat or falsify the work quota. Daniel now saw Ergorov, along with three of his goons, looking down at the spot where, he assumed, Urbancyzk was unlucky enough to be. Yakimchuk was probably somewhere nearby, hidden among all the larger men.

What was first a murmur rose to no more than a low-pitched rumble, but when the lights extinguished, it grew to a cacophony of loud voices until Daniel heard a higher-pitched scream that was suddenly choked off. Silent men brushed past Daniel on the way back to their assigned spaces. Even in the dark, the way they moved, loose limbed and slow-gaited, demonstrated their catharsis. Bumps and grunts accompanied the body's disposal somewhere outside the barracks, and then everyone was silent.

The next day was one more in the endless line of identical days. Urbancyzk was gone from both the physical world and from the consciousness of his fellow prisoners, like a rock sinking into a muddy pond, making a few ripples, then leaving no evidence that it ever existed. If there were people back in Poland who knew or longed to see him again and who held out whatever hope irrational humans cling to, they would continue to do so, his death notwithstanding.

It wasn't until the third day that it became clear that Urbancyzk was a human being, not a rock, and the ripples would not disappear so easily. Kortnev had the optimal combination of ruthlessness and intelligence, and while Ergorov matched him in cruelty, he wasn't as smart. Even he, though, could see that something wasn't right when he was summoned that evening to the production office to face accusations of more tufta and threatened with the loss of his barracks leadership position if he let it continue. As Daniel later heard the story, Ergorov went straight from the office to Kortnev. The chief gangster barely looked up from his chicken dinner as he told Ergorov to clean up his barracks, or he, Kortnev, would find someone else to do so.

"What do you mean, clean up?" Ergorov purportedly asked.

"It obviously wasn't that Polack you killed the other night," was all that Kortnev said.

Ergorov's paranoia was a noxious gas affecting everyone he came near, except Yakimchuk. Before the brigade marched out to the work site the morning after, the little man busied himself as usual, assigning tasks, moving men around, recording things on his clipboard and making his little financial 'arrangements.' But that evening, as he stood near Daniel's bunk collecting on one of those arrangements, Ergorov, who had almost a meter of height on him, appeared. Yakimchuk covered any surprise or fear well as he handed a small bag up to his boss. He either didn't notice the two huge men who'd accompanied Ergorov or figured there was no percentage in acknowledging their presence. Daniel had a front row seat this time.

"*Suka! Pizda!* You little cocksucker. It was you!" Spit flew from Ergorov's lips as the epithets flew out. Impossible as it seemed, the accusations further shrank Yakimchuk.

"What are you talking about, Boss?" the pitch of his voice a little higher than usual.

"Don't play me, you little insect. I know what you did, you fuckin' canary."

Concentric circles of men formed around them as Ergorov's words stoked a fire underneath the tightly lidded pot of water that was their anger that what happened to Urbancyzk was a waste. Yakimchuk looked around with frantic eyes, trying to find a place to alight that might provide succor, or even some small hope. He held Daniel's gaze until Daniel looked down. No need to watch the inevitable.

His previous failure with Urbancyzk as prosecutor, judge, and executioner had no effect on Ergorov. He announced that it was Yakimchuk who'd betrayed them to the guards and the camp bosses, who put his own skin above any other's. He was the lowest of the low, undeserving and ungrateful for all that Ergorov had done for him, only using it to feather his own nest. To Daniel's ear, the personal betrayal sounded far more significant to Ergorov than anything else, more than Yakimchuk's violation of the fundamental rule of their underworld society — as if there were rules this far from any civil society. Maybe when survival was a given, constitutions and laws could exist. Here, the sole imperative was to live, which could mean actions one might not consider in Moscow or Warsaw or any of the towns and villages and farmhouses these men came from. Daniel believed there were things he would never do, lines he could not cross and continue to live with himself. He also knew that he hadn't yet tested those lines.

The crowd, and its rising noise, pressed in around where Yakimchuk knelt, looking up from Ergorov to his two hulking enforcers to any of the surrounding eyes, including Daniel's.

"Wait," Daniel heard his own voice, as if it came from someone else.

"What?" Ergorov searched to find who had interrupted his justice.

Daniel's mind raced to find something plausible. "Wait. If we kill him, there could be trouble, you know," he rushed on with the sapling he found to pull Yakimchuk from his quicksand grave. "I mean, they are going to be suspicious, you know, if two bodies from this barrack come in so short a time."

In the new silence from Ergorov and the mob, Daniel wondered if he'd foolishly cast his fate with Yakimchuk.

"Maybe. Let me think about this," Ergorov finally said. "You," he pointed to the informant on the floor. "We will be with you every minute, when you sleep, when you shit, so don't think about running to your masters for help."

And so Yakimchuk waited under constant guard for almost a week before his end finally came. It was in the forest, not the barracks. He was now part of the crew assigned to lift trunks onto the trucks. He tried, pulling his rope with all the strength he possessed, and it appeared as if it might work, as each day he received full credit for meeting his quota. His last afternoon, he was trying to raise the last medium sized spruce up on top, when one already loaded suddenly rolled out, followed by all the logs, crushing him. They managed to save the load, the daily quota met, before they recovered his body.

That night, someone he did not know stopped by Daniel's berth and whispered, "Better be careful." He caught Ergorov looking at him a few times. He started failing to make quota, first, every once in a while, and then almost every other day. Before falling into his usual exhausted deep sleep, he lay awake trying to think of a way to redeem himself, but nothing came to him.

Rescue arrived via a flier tacked up on the barracks door. The commandant, a man more rumor than real, announced that he was leaving to a new camp. It was not a timber operation. Rather, they had the glorious opportunity to punch a tunnel through for a new rail line, and he was looking for men with useful skills to go with him. Daniel lined up early the next morning to reclaim his identity and emphasize the engineering classes that were foundational to the architecture curriculum. The following day, he was excused from work, and then came another cattle car train ride, this one for only a day and half, and escape to a new camp in the Sikhote-Alin mountains, wherever the hell that was.

Ian — Paris, 7 June 1940

In the plaza fronting the Gare d'Austerlitz train station, murmurations of people flowed around stationary families and waiting soldiers searching for the magic door that would lead them out of Paris. Others stood patiently in lines, to advance a meter or two before they stopped to sit on their bundles and suitcases and stand again to advance another meter. On the roads leading to and from the station, the important cars of important men, who could not believe they were being forced to leave Paris — but if they were, they had to leave immediately, ahead of the less-important — kept up a cacophony of ineffective horns. Pigeons roosted on the roof line, alert to the sudden appearance of a patch of pavement clear enough to let them swoop up any crumbs the children might drop, until a shift in the wind brought the low rumble. This set the birds off, and further agitated the Brownian motion of the people within the plaza.

It was already past two when Ian fought his way to the front of the tobacconist kiosk, where a hand-lettered sign announced that cigarettes were available only to those with ration cards. For a few anxious minutes, he considered if her changing stories meant she would not show, and then they saw each other, and his fear dissipated like a puff of smoke on a windy day. Their embrace made him, for a moment, forget there were others all around. Alicia took him by the hand to tug him in the direction away from the ticket counters. Perhaps she knew another way into the station? But when they left the Belle-Époque façades of the plaza and kept going south past the Square Marie-Curie, where others waited impatiently for their chance to approach the train station, he had to ask, "Where are we going?"

She appeared not to hear him amid the commotion, even when he twice repeated his question, louder each time. She did turn every few minutes to smile, her smile like a mechanical rabbit for him, a greyhound engaged in a strange kind of race, or like a salmon running against the current of humanity. Finally, they passed the front of the Grand Arts et Metiers Paris — the acme of engineering schools — which Ian never dared to dream of attending, and he pulled her into a side street relatively free of anxious people. Ian put the valise down and, almost like a petulant child, refused to go further.

"Alicia, wait. We need to get to a train, to go to Pau, now."

"Ian, do you trust me?" she asked.

An unexpected and unwelcome question. You trusted the builders of the elevator that lifted you up the Eiffel Tower, or the bridge that took you over the Seine. Relationships, he was learning, were not physical objects subject to well-defined laws, their behavior consistent and predictable. But trust, he knew, was critical in relationships, so he said yes, and felt momentarily better for having done so.

She promised that she would explain everything in a few minutes and resumed leading him across one street and down another until she knocked on the door of the shuttered Café Le Diamant. One of Zemmour's thugs ushered them in to where the little gangster stood talking with a man wearing a French Army greatcoat despite the heat.

Ian ignored it all. "What is going on?" he asked Alicia.

Zemmour answered for her. "You, my friend, are fortunate. Everyone seems to be looking out for themselves, but your lady friend is only worried about your safety."

"What is he talking about?" Ian looked from Zemmour to Alicia. Once again, she stood calmly while he felt his heart beating from his chest up into his head. Zemmour politely turned away, but the tall stranger continued to study them.

"Ian. Listen to me, carefully." Alicia held his shoulders. "I cannot go with you. I am sorry, I am really sorry, but I can't go. There is no time to explain all of it, but Pau is not a place I can be."

A vortex in his brain blocked Ian's ability to absorb and interpret her words. He forced a single thought through the maelstrom, which emerged as, "What about us?"

"Ian. I have never met a man like you. I am so afraid that this war, this world, it will ruin you."

The stranger's voice was deep, his accent indistinguishable. "It will be kinder to make it quick." Alicia stole a glance at him.

"The calculation is simple," she continued. "Fundamentally, it's an inequality. On one side, it is too dangerous for you here. On the other, it is too dangerous for me anywhere else."

Ian interrupted. "It doesn't have to be Pau. We can go to Marseille. Or to our Caribbean."

She shook her head as if to remove any visions of tropical beaches. "My best chances are here in Paris. If the Germans take over, I can reappear with a name that is different than Alicia, or my birth name. Zemmour here will provide me with a new identity."

"Not *gratis*, but yes," the little man said.

Her name wasn't Alicia? The floor underneath his feet was the only thing Ian could be certain of.

She continued. "There are several organizations, besides the police, who are interested in my location. It's okay; it was by my choice. But I cannot endanger you anymore. I know how to hide in Paris, but not with you, because for you, Paris means death and I would constantly be scared for you. You must go, Ian. Anything else I cannot live with."

Zemmour took over, because more talk was unnecessary and expensive. He led Ian behind a curtain to put him into the uniform of a private in the French Army. Ian never remembered taking off or putting on anything. Zemmour handed him a passbook and an identity card.

"You are Private Claude Pronovost, born in Algeria. You were with the 12th Zouaves of the 3rd North African, most recently up near Verdun. You were messengers, now reassigned. Put your own papers inside this oilskin in your boot." He pointed to the other man. "This is your comrade, Corporal Lachance. He has orders for both of you to report to a Sergeant Bricasse, attached to the President of the Council, on the rue de Varenne. You need to get there very quickly."

Ian only wanted to go to Alicia, or whatever her name was, to hold on to her body and to stop whatever was happening from happening. It was too much, too fast, unclassifiable, non-linear. Instead, so-called Corporal Lachance pushed him into a chair and stuffed his feet into a new pair of boots. There was something inside each. One was probably the oilskin. Lachance pulled Ian up and with curt thanks in the direction of Zemmour, pushed Ian out the door. The last thing Ian saw was Alicia handing the rest of their money over to Zemmour.

"Keep walking, my friend," Lachance said. "Look ahead, not behind."

"I am not your friend."

"At this moment, I am the only friend you have in this world. But understand this: if you do anything that jeopardizes our escape from this quickly closing trap, I will abandon you to whatever fate you choose or is chosen for you."

He was an automaton following Lachance, who sliced through the despairing masses like a surgeon dissecting through skin, fat, muscle, and sinew to get to his goal. Ian had no idea how long it took them to arrive, bruised and out of breath, to the Hotel Matignon. As at the train station, bedlam ruled there, the center of government. Big cars honking their horns to get into or out of the courtyard. Civil servants in their formal clothes running from building to building holding boxes and stacks of record books. Young women standing under a chestnut tree, smoking, hugging, and crying. The smell assaulting Ian's nose came from the black smoke billowing from all the chimneys.

"Hey, what's going on?" Lachance grabbed a young army private by the lapel before he ran by.

"We are evacuating. Haven't you heard? To Tours." And he rushed off to do something important for one so young.

"Perfect!" Lachance muttered and dragged Ian along until they located Sergeant Bricasse in an office near the stable where big ministerial cars were being packed, emptied, and repacked with presumably critical papers and even more important personal effects.

Bricasse deftly accepted the envelope that Lachance produced from an inside pocket of his coat. He glanced at their papers. "Lachance, eh?" he sniffed. "As good a name as any, I suppose. And who is your slovenly companion, Lachance? If you want to stay assigned here, he is going to need to learn to stand, salute, and look smart at all times."

"Pronovost, Sergeant," Lachance answered for Ian. "He has a little, uh, shell shock from the fighting up by the Somme, but he will be fine, I promise."

"He had better be," said Bricasse. "Talbot, Bouchard! You are reassigned. Go to the third floor and report to Lieutenant Angers. He needs you to destroy some radios." Turning back to Ian and his companion, he said, "You take their place, drive the car over there, it belongs to the new Minister of Finance, Bouthillier. New, so he doesn't know everyone yet. You can drive?"

"Of course, Sergeant," Lachance answered and jabbed Ian hard in the ribs as a prompt to march over to the car.

"Can you drive?" Lachance asked Ian, with such urgency that Ian had to break his silence.

"Yes, a little."

"How about maps? Can you navigate?"

"Yes. For sure." At home, he loved his collection of maps describing Napoleon's battles.

"Good. I drive, you navigate. Your French is pretty passable, plus they will ignore us. We are like furniture and from Algeria to boot. Still, try not to speak too much," Lachance said, as he lifted up the hood and checked the oil.

Ian tried to remember how a soldier acted. Who do you salute, which side does the kit bag go on? He needed to concentrate, and to start, he listed what he knew. He knew that he was leaving Paris, in someone else's uniform, tied to a stranger who would abandon him as soon as it suited him, who was not Lachance, even as his own name and history were not his own. Most shockingly, it was without Alicia, who had paid for him to leave. He told himself that it was a time for action, that analyzing had to be postponed. He found a rag and started polishing the car with a circular motion that matched his state of mind.

A commotion near the doorway announced the arrival of an entourage surrounding a man the way young girls might ring a movie star promenading down the Champs-Élysées. In panicked Paris, though, this was no matinee idol. He appeared to be in his forties, his middle wider than his shoulders, round glasses pinching his nose, hair borrowed from various constituencies to provide cover. Functionaries pushed papers at him to sign, after which they peeled away like geese leaving a vee formation.

Bricasse came running. "This minister, he is yours!" he yelled at Ian and his companion. "Snap to it!"

Ian ran to one side and Lachance, after closing the motor cover, to the other, opening the doors for two of the officials who thought themselves worthy to leave Paris, who turned out to be the minister and his most important deputy. Both continued to yell orders and receive more papers through the open windows, even after Ian and Lachance closed the doors and took their places in the front. Bricasse leaned in on Ian's side, handing him a map. "The Porte D'Orleans is being kept open for official business only. Take it towards Villejuif then turn south, you'll be directed to the road to Tours."

This was how Ian was tossed out of Paris.

Ian — Tours to Bordeaux, 9–19 June 1940

"She was your first?" Lachance asked Ian. The Tours Hotel de Ville was now the Ministry of Finance of France, and they were in the basement, getting a hot dinner. Their minister was in swankier rooms somewhere upstairs.

"Never mind," Lachance continued when Ian gave no response. "It is better to say less to friends but especially to strangers."

"And you are which, exactly?" Ian almost never spoke so rudely. But he was speaking with a man on the run who knew Zemmour, with all that implied.

"A fair point," Lachance said, not visibly offended. "Three days ago, you became Private Claude Pronovost and that is how I know you. Similarly, I am Corporal Lachance to you. Only the soles of our feet know who we really are. What a strange, strange world, isn't it?"

"Yes," Ian agreed, and went back to his beans. Lachance clearly did not want to stop talking.

"Are you familiar with Kierkegaard? No? You should read him one day. He speaks of alienation, of being lost because faith in universal truths is disappearing as the Church loses its centrality. I think about what that means now, when everything is chaos. What are the rules, what is the roadmap now for an individual to make decisions with? What do we use to construct a definition of who we are?"

This was as unlikely a conversation as Ian could remember ever having, and he needed to be careful. "There are some rules that cannot change, Monsieur. Gravity does not turn off and on randomly," he ventured.

"God doesn't have a switch to play with, then? Mmm, perhaps. Perhaps, though, he wants us to go mad every generation or two," Lachance took a long draught from the bottle of wine they shared. "You don't strike me as an aspiring poet or painter who's come to Paris to find inspiration and love, though you seem to have had some luck on that score. What were you studying?"

Ian only admitted to being a student, without specifying the field. He needed to change the subject. "What about you?" he asked.

"What? Am I a poet or a painter?" Lachance laughed with his whole body. "No, I was a minor administrator for a charity. Probably gone now." He paused. "My name is Avigot, by the way. Claude is my name, but I lend it to you, and will keep Yves for now."

Truth? Or maintain his false identity? "Ian. Ian Ciszek," he finally said. He did not see any percentage in adding a third identity. They shook hands and decided that was enough for this evening.

They bivouacked in the garage next to the Minister's car. Ian lay on his blanket using his greatcoat as his pillow but remained awake, worrying. Daniel was probably dead, entombed in the ruins of Warsaw pictured in so many newspapers and newsreels. Next, what was going on in his hometown, and to his father? His dutiful thoughts done, he moved to Alicia, or whatever her name was. He wanted to believe that it was as she'd stated, that the calculus of their situation made buying his escape from Zemmour the best, maybe even the only solution. But he also wanted to believe that, had she consulted him, he'd have assigned enough value to his feelings for her that they would have had to stay together. Finally, as he knew would happen, he remembered the truck driver, who, until their crime unfolded, probably thought himself safe from the risks of war, but in those last seconds, must have felt a terror like none Ian had ever experienced. Lachance always fell asleep quickly, a sign of a clear conscience, according to Ian's father.

The next morning, the summer sky was blue and the sun bright, but the air felt charged, as if a storm was imminent, except it was the agitated buzz from a hornet nest in an unreachable upper corner of the garage. Not long after lunch, their minister needed to be driven to a meeting. Bouthillier was apologetic.

"I am sorry to call on you again," he said. "Events are moving swiftly, I am afraid." Both knew that no answer was expected.

There were even more private cars, trucks and carts, families, individuals, and even groups of nuns and students filling the road today. By the time they arrived to the bridge over the Cher, they could barely inch forward. The Minister considered abandoning the car and walking through the mix of refugees, taking Ian as a guard, before a route to the Chateau de Cange finally appeared.

"A few hours are likely necessary to resolve our questions, so get some food, requisition supplies for our Ministry, whatever you can think of, and make sure the petrol tank is full," the Minister told them before he walked, with a dignity that belied his stature, toward two men standing at the garden entrance.

"That's Petain," Ian recognized him from newspaper photos.

"Yes, and Weygand," Lachance said. He turned away, uninterested, to mix with the other drivers and guards which Ian knew was smart because it looked more natural than hiding by yourself, but Lachance had twenty years more experience from which to curate a plausible false persona. Ian had not completed the process of metamorphosing from child to adult. He was still testing out new parts, on top of which, he was supposed to be Claude Pronovost, a confusion that made the risk of revealing the wrong fact at the wrong time quite real.

They quickly finished their work, and then sat together on the grass in the summer warmth to eat their evening meal and try not to listen for any indication of German artillery. Lachance quietly shared that the word around the motor pool was not good. Mussolini had conveniently declared war on a reeling France. Paris was now an open city, and some said it was already in German hands, while others claimed that Maurice Thorez had engineered a Communist takeover, a new Commune. The older man took out his pack of army-issued cigarettes. He'd learned not to offer one to Ian. After lighting up and enjoying the first lungful, he lay back on his elbows.

"Do you wish you were up there, listening to the discussion?" he asked Ian. He meant inside the Chateau.

"Being responsible for decisions like that? No thank you." Ian answered.

"We all need to make decisions, Claude." They'd agreed to use their pseudonyms as often as possible. "Certainly, history books will record their decisions, where ours will only matter to our families."

"If there is any family left to care," Ian said. He waited while Lachance took another drag. "Are you... Are you afraid of being captured by the Germans or is it something else, with the police? I don't mean to pry."

"Best not to. We were both at Zemmour's because we needed to leave before the Nazis came. That's enough to know."

"Sorry, Yves," Ian said and, embarrassed, lay back on the grass.

Lachance shrugged at the apology. "As I said, there may be no framework for right and wrong anymore. There are frightful pressures from multiple directions. The only thing, I believe, one can do is to prepare to act, quickly if necessary, even when the information you normally would need for such decisions is inadequate. Like those ministers up there."

"That is very depressing," Ian observed. "I can certainly accept that this might be true for you and me, but they have maps, reports, spies, generals."

Lachance gave a condescending chuckle. "These are the heirs of the men who led us to so many deaths twenty years ago. Some are actually the same men."

Ian couldn't help but ask. "Were you in the Great War?"

Lachance let the question go unanswered. "Have you considered what you will do if the Germans continue to smash their way over France. If you are captured? Or if the French decide we belong at the front? We haven't tested Zemmour's papers yet. What if they aren't good enough?

Ian sat up to face Lachance. "No, not really," he confessed.

"At this moment, we are in a good place, and functioning as a team. Of course, that may not always be true," Lachance added.

The reassurance, so quickly whipped away, did nothing for Ian's state of mind. He looked to gauge the threat and saw a man, calm and self-contained. Ian wanted to light up one of those cigarettes, look out at something in the middle distance, and appear as imperturbable as Charles Boyer, in the hope that this exterior would create a template for his interior, as he had done back at the apartment with Alicia.

Despite the risk of aerial attack, courtyard lights came on to allow the ministers to find their cars, and Ian noted how ashen their man looked. Bouthillier stayed silent at first, working on something deep and important, he assumed. After a few minutes, though, whatever the Minister was trying to digest would not stay down.

"Fools! Traitors! They actually proposed that France surrender itself to England!" he said loud enough for the two to hear. "Petain is correct. On our present path, it is only anarchy."

Lachance was driving. He finally spoke, softly. "There are difficulties, Minister?"

"Difficulties? No! Disasters. The army is decimated. And what do the traitors want to do? Agree to have England take over. They re-conquer France, and four hundred years of our history is wiped out. And if not that, some are suggesting we run away and fight for France from a *souk* in Algiers. Cowards. True Frenchmen will not run. I will not run. Campinchi, or that Jew Mandel, they will not be allowed to destroy France!" Realizing he'd revealed too much to men he considered had neither ears nor brains, he stayed silent for the rest of the drive.

The Hotel de Ville was in chaos because the government was moving once more, to Bordeaux. An hour past dawn, they were back on the road, together with all those who'd been swept ahead of the German Army as if they were flotsam pushed up the beach by the incoming tide. It took over eighteen hours, and when they arrived the streets of Bordeaux were impassable. Lachance played indignant and officious, the way he knew his Minister felt, to force a beleaguered military policeman to reveal that government space was being allocated by the mayor's office; an hour later, Bouthillier had the address of their hotel. He must have heard some news at the same time because he almost skipped out of the car and up to his rooms, with lan and Lachance dragging his luggage along after him. Their billet at the back was tiny, but it had real beds and a sink with hot and cold running water. Ian felt giddy at this luxury, until Lachance passed on what he'd heard while parking the car. "Tours is gone. Le Mans, too. At this rate, they should be here in no more than a week." But Ian was too exhausted to consider what this meant or to think of family, Poland, or Alicia.

The Minister shared nothing more over the next days, only issued orders to drive to the mayor's office or the Grand Hotel or to Council sessions at the Police Prefecture, leaving Ian and Lachance with nothing but rumors for their own personal deliberations. The sum of it all never strayed far from zero, except the military news was always negative. By Monday, Brittany hung in the balance and the

Maginot line was fully surrounded. What started as whispered comments about the waste of sacrifice in the face of an overwhelming enemy began to be heard in the open, and there were other signs: shoulders no longer square and back, a dirty boot, an unbuttoned tunic. Few raised questions about the honor of France and or answered those who asked what if there would be no one left to remember the honor. On the first day with rain in a month, the men in the motor pool gathered around a radio to hear Petain, the Hero of Verdun, announce to the nation that, with a heavy heart, he had opened talks with the enemy to bring an end to the fighting. A small cheer followed, from soldiers celebrating their reprieve.

Lachance and Ian slipped out quickly.

"This can't be good," Ian said.

"The Germans will do to France what they have done to Czechoslovakia, Austria, Poland, Belgium. Complete control. We need to consider, my friend, that within weeks we will be under a Nazi government."

Ian did nothing except consider it, while they drove Bouthillier around Bordeaux, or were back in their little room at the hotel. From the way Lachance now tossed in his bed, it was the same for him. Late one rainy night, while waiting on the Minister, who was in a cabinet meeting, they heard reports that put the German Army sooner in Bordeaux. When they finally returned to their room, Ian had to speak.

"The way I see it, if France falls, and French files become Nazi files, I don't know how well these false papers will work."

"That is reasonable," Lachance answered.

"There are several major problems with any other choice, though." Ian spoke aloud to himself. "First, are there any better places to be? Another, even more fundamental, is what better actually means, and then what are the risks of getting there, since it would look like desertion. Damn, it feels as if these are all careening around my brain like a hundred billiard balls."

"No, it's good, these are my thoughts, too."

"France is so much larger than any of the other conquered countries. So maybe it's not a Nazi takeover. Even so, the French will put their bureaucrats and offices back together, and they will no longer be distracted by this chaos of war."

"The Germans will want access to all the organs of government, either directly or indirectly. The chaos will not last, as helpful as it is for you," Lachance said.

"And not for you?" Ian shot back. Lachance shrugged as if to agree, and maybe apologize and they ended their discussion without conclusion. What Ian noted and did not say was that in all of his scenarios now, Lachance was present. He needed to consider this wild card as another variable.

The weather cleared the next day, but Lachance stayed quiet and walked with a slower and heavier step and with an expression of resignation on his face.

"Melancholia, I am afraid," the older man said when he noticed Ian's worried gaze. "It is an affliction that I am not unfamiliar with."

"Is there anything I can do?" Ian asked.

"Your asking is truly a balm to my mood. One of its manifestations is disconnection, which is reinforced by the mood itself. Someone breaking through my wall, as you are doing, can disrupt the cycle and hasten its resolution. Of course, this time it is also circumstantial. We have not found a solution to our problem."

Ian noted the pronoun. "Perhaps today we will get something more substantial."

"Let's hope so!" Lachance clapped Ian on the back.

They did. Rumor crystallized into an announcement that the central authority of the government would move to French North Africa, to regroup and reinvigorate the fight. Perpignan, a city less than thirty-five kilometers from neutral Spain and across the Mediterranean from Algiers, was the embarkation point for the majority of leaders, most to Algeria, some to Morocco. Petain announced he would not leave French soil, but Ian and Lachance did not care. Perpignan was hundreds of kilometers from the advancing panzers, which gave them more time to figure out what to do.

Ian — Bordeaux to Toulouse, 20–22 June 1940

Two more feckless days passed. Waiting by the car from early morning until after dark allowed their concerns to escalate to confusion, then consternation, and ultimately, fear. Finally, Lachance returned from another trip to reconnoiter, looking disgusted.

"They are useless ditherers. Even now, when it is all going to shit, they are circulating reports and discussing options, as if there are so many they might choose from. Really, they only search for the best way to continue going from their mistress' bed on Saturday night to Mass with their wives and children on Sunday morning. They want to go back to being village mayors, arbitrating disputes about hayfields between pure wool Frenchman and to hell with anyone else. They deserve the boot that will descend upon their necks," he said, his melancholia clearly gone.

"Our Bouthillier as well?" Ian asked.

"Word is he is with Petain. No matter how much they try to lie to us and to themselves about an armistice, it is a capitulation, and the Nazis will have their way with us soon enough."

Ian started the car.

"What are you doing?" Lachance asked.

Ian felt an unfamiliar bolt of action meet and then slip past his standard spasm of fear. "I don't want to be sitting here when the Germans arrive, and I am sure you don't, either."

Lachance gave him a soft smile. "What is your plan?"

Ian was dizzy with the thrill of improvisation. He thought and spoke quickly. They would claim they were tasked with preparing the transfer to Perpignan, and that it was such an emergency, there was no time for orders. The car, the latest 4-liter Renault Vivestella saloon, might not be impressive enough to intimidate everyone but however far they got, it would be closer to Spain. Lachance approved and Ian felt proud.

There were no checkpoints, no demands for orders or papers, on the way out of Bordeaux, security seemingly overwhelmed by the masses seeking safety somewhere southeast. It took them three hours to reach Langon, barely fifty kilometers on, where they halted at the crossroads. According to the signs, straight on was the way to Perpignan via Toulouse. Off to their right, the bridge across the Garonne began the main route to Pau. Ian stared, as if somewhere along the way he might resolve the contradictions between what he knew and what he felt.

"She is not there," said Lachance.

"I know," Ian sighed. "I am tired, can you drive?" He crawled into the capacious rear and fell into restless sleep as Lachance drove on. The tendrils of whatever he was dreaming evaporated when Lachance finally woke him up to ask for directions.

"I don't like being north of the river, we need to cross," Lachance said. It took a few minutes for Ian to orient himself and identify where the nearest bridge lay. Still no roadblocks or authorities. To Lachance, this was another indicator of the failing French war effort, even if it was to their benefit, and it revalidated their decision to make a dash to Spain.

The needle on the fuel gauge moved steadily towards empty. Ian and Lachance, after much discussion, decided that they had to risk entering Toulouse to replenish their supplies, despite the likelihood that there would be officers who might be unconvinced that a corporal and a private should be driving such a motorcar to Perpignan without orders; their story and its presentation, however, got them through two roadblocks. Across a canal from the train station, they secured space in a garage for their car, and some fuel, for two hundred of Ian's francs, split between a sergeant and the mechanic. By now it was night, and they opted to sleep in the car, oblivious to what was happening outside the garage doors.

Ian went out to scrounge in the morning. Like Bordeaux, Toulouse was bursting with refugees, but here there were far more soldiers, in a variety of uniforms. Ian noted this, and something else that made these men appear different, something that took him some time wandering amongst them to define. Most of these men moved with purpose. They still carried themselves as soldiers.

He moved aside to assess where he might have the best chance of getting food when he heard what sounded like Polish coming from a passing band of French soldiers. Curious, he followed them. In a small square centered around the bust of someone of unknown import, Ian's group joined with others dressed in a variety of French uniforms, all definitely speaking Polish.

"Ian, Ian!" A voice called, just before he was embraced.

"Oh my God, Christophe!" Ian was almost moved to tears. "What are you doing here?" Ian finally managed to ask.

"I should ask you the same," Christophe answered. "I see you decided to enlist too, eh? Hope your outfit was better than ours. We were supposed to join the 4th Infantry but at the last minute they sent us to a French unit someplace near Saumur." He stopped.

"Where is Paul?" Ian asked, looking around.

Christophe looked down. "He was getting some food when they started firing, Panzers and artillery… when I got to him… he…" Christophe reached into his pocket and showed Paul's mud-stained identity papers. There were scorch marks on the edges.

Ian absorbed this news. He needed to change the subject. "How did you get here?"

"Not sure. There was a lot of walking, we were bombed a few times. Then, a few days ago, we heard that Sikorski wanted us to get to the coast and go to England. I only want to, you know, go back home to my family and to see Paul's family. And your dad." Christophe managed a little chuckle at that.

"Me too," said Ian.

Christophe offered Ian a government-issued cigarette, which Ian politely declined.

"The lieutenant, he heard that the consulate here was arranging for Polish soldiers to go through Spain and then on to England. Would mean a boat ride. Never been on one. I mean, Paul and I joked about using our money to buy a fishing boat once, but that was just talk," he laughed.

He took a drag on his cigarette. Ian noted new layers applied on top of the boy Ian knew.

"We've been here two days now. It's chaos. My lieutenant still wants to try for Spain, and one of our guys speaks Spanish. Others say the route is blocked now. I'm not sure what to do, but you're here now, Ian."

They sat together on a step, both gaining an intangible strength from the familiar presence of the other. Ian assessed what he knew. The armistice, or surrender, was likely, it was all anyone spoke about. They had no more than a few days and maybe only a few hours to decide on a course of action. And for whom? Himself, and maybe Christophe. What about Lachance? He needed more data and time, and right now, food. He promised Christophe that he would meet him at that exact spot in four hours, with a better idea of what to do. They embraced, like long-lost brothers reluctant to part again, and Ian hurried off.

He found food to bring back with his news, but as he approached the garage, he could hear shouting, and words like "No!" and "*Batard!*"

Their bribed sergeant stumbled out the door. He smelled drunk.

"What was that?" Ian asked Lachance, who stood panting near the car.

"The bastard got it into his head to get more money from us. Like he thinks we have a large supply."

Ian honored Lachance's need for time to calm down while they ate the bread and cheese and drank some of the cider he'd brought. The only other sounds came when the mechanic swore at the one-eyed garage cat for pushing something loud and metallic off a shelf. Finally, Lachance spoke up.

"Probably not a great idea to sit here, waiting." Ian nodded in agreement.

Lachance appeared to be talking to himself. "Got to figure that Nazis will be in charge, one way or another, soon. Egypt under Pharaoh or forty years to reach Canaan?" Lachance looked directly at Ian. "Maybe we should have taken that turn in Langon, unrelated to your personal reasons."

Ian smiled back. He now recounted what he'd picked up in his ramble around Toulouse, without mentioning Christophe. At a make-shift commissary where he had lined up for the cheese and cider, a non-commissioned officer shared with his companions how he'd barely escaped after walking into a Spanish police trap set up by the guides they'd hired to take them over the mountains.

"With papers like ours, I fear Spain is especially risky," Ian now said.

Lachance pondered this, then asked. "Perhaps your real, your Polish papers would be better?"

Ian wasn't sure. He told Lachance about Christophe. "I promised to meet him soon. Maybe he has learned more. Want to come with me?" Ian asked for no reason he could specify, except that sitting here was a clear dead end.

Lachance, seeing the genuineness in the offer, accepted. At the appointed hour and corner, they found Christophe smoking and waiting. He shrugged, which Ian took for acceptance, at the introduction of Lachance. Ian then repeated what he'd overheard about the Spanish border.

Christophe nodded. "My lieutenant, his name's Maszieveski, told us about a new plan. We are supposed to get to Marseille. There's folks there arranging evacuations to Gibraltar by boat. Anyone who wants to go to Spain can still go, but he thinks Marseille is a better bet. I am sure there would be no problem with you joining us." Christophe said this, hopefully, to Ian.

"It's only for Poles?" Ian asked.

"Well, yes, as far as I know," Christophe answered.

Lachance spoke up right away. "If this means you can get away, you must go."

Ian thought for a moment, fingering the forged documents in his pocket that made him, at this moment, Claude Pronovost.

"Christophe, I have something to ask." Ian dropped his voice to a conspiratorial whisper. Why did he have to make what, in any other time, would be a monstrous request?

"What?"

"Lachance here... we have made it this far together. Without him, I am not sure I could have. If we put his photo on Paul's papers, and said that he was brought to France as a baby so he didn't know much Polish, could he come with us?"

"I don't know, Ian." Christophe looked as stricken as Ian felt, except Yves Lachance, who was really Claude Avigot, was standing with them — and Ian believed he deserved a chance. Paul was now only a memory to honor.

"It would be temporary," Ian continued. "When we get to England, he'll be able to claim his real name, and we will put back Paul's picture. And I promise, if we can, I will go with you to give everything to his parents, and you can tell them about how brave he was."

Christophe turned it over in his mind. He made Ian repeat his promise to accompany him to Paul's home before he finally gave a small nod. In a shed behind the square, they carefully transferred Lachance's picture and made their way to the Place du Salin, where the lieutenant was gathering his orphans. Ian, with his fluent Polish, was no problem. Lachance's story took a little longer to successfully pass.

"No more!" Lieutenant Maszieveski ordered later that afternoon. Ian and Lachance plus one or two others, minus those who still wanted to chance the Spanish border, equaled exactly one truckload to leave the next morning for Marseille. Ian and the new 'Paul' stayed with the other Poles, not chancing a return to the car. The odious sergeant could have it and good luck to him. Christophe moved his cot next to Ian and Lachance on the periphery of the hall, a little removed from the others. He and Ian fell asleep quickly, soon after dinner. Lachance stayed awake. He kept examining Paul's papers, holding them in his palms delicately, like the Host.

Daniel — Kenada, Khabarovsk Krai, 19–25 July 1940

The Gulag had what Russia has always had: an endless supply of humans. When it needed more, Moscow merely defined a new crime to pump a new cohort of criminals into the flow.

The Gulag was impatient. Unlike a river, Moscow demanded that the Kuzetovsky Tunnel under the Sikhote-Alin Mountains be completed in ten months; water would take thousands of years. As determined by the Gulag accountants, a single man removed two centimeters of rock each day using picks, hammers, chisels, wedges, powered by whatever their muscles could still generate. Multiply that by dozens of men in three shifts, and you had the timetable set by local offices in Svobodny and stamped acceptable in Moscow.

Daniel stood, naked from the waist up, bathed in sweat from the heat and his exertions while his feet froze in the water runoff. He was indistinguishable from all the others working the tunnel. His task was to use his hands to pick up the rocks and gravel freed by others from the rock face and place them into his canvas sac and, when it was full, lift it onto his back and loop the handle over his forehead. It was three hundred meters to the dazzling afternoon light. Rock now, wood before, the work was steadily leaching muscle, kilograms, and life from his body. Rock or wood, he still slept next to men steadily losing their civility, humanity, identity, or minds. Rock or wood, he still lived in guarded compounds surrounded by wire. There was even another Kortnev here, in charge of this distant metastasis of the Urka, and a brigade leader stupider even than Ergorov named Lyadov.

That he had left the previous camp because he was really Daniel, someone who claimed to have valuable engineering skills, turned out to be irrelevant. Those in authority only saw another body for tunnel work. Every day he asked to see the Commandant whom he'd followed from the forest, until yesterday the sergeant in charge of the guards spat into his face and said, "If you ask again, I will kill you myself."

The whistle blew three times to end the shift, to his relief. He wasn't sure if his legs or back would withstand another trip in the tunnel. The men found their shirts and shoes and struggled back to the camp, to deposit their tools inside the gate and wait in rows in front of their barrack while the inventory of tools and men was checked and double-checked. Lyadov stood in his usual spot at the door, holding the food tickets. A red ticket entitled you to a full, though still inadequate, ration. Blue meant one would be hungrier than usual, while more than a few days of brown tickets equaled a death sentence. Daniel scuffled up the three stone steps in front of his barrack. The men in line in front of him got red tickets but the ticket in Lyadov's hand when it was his turn was blue. Daniel glanced at Lyadov's broad grinning face, which was wordlessly saying, "I dare you." He took the ticket and moved on.

In the time before the evening meal, Daniel sat on a corner of the pallet he shared with three others and tried to discern the meaning of the blue ticket. His trip count was the same as yesterday's, each haul a full load. He remembered no announced changes in work quotas. It was likely a random cruelty, maybe Lyadov probing for weakness or trying to provoke a challenge. Yet it continued the next morning. He received a new assignment, chiseling, but when he went to get a sledgehammer from the tool room, one of Lyadov's men laughed and handed him two iron wedges. Camp wisdom said that it took no more than five days as a wedge man before your finger, hand, or wrist was crushed. Luckily his partner today was a hefty Tartar, who not only struck solid blows, but, as Daniel gratefully confirmed at the rock face, never missed. To show his appreciation, he carried the heavy sledgehammer back to camp, and let the man step in front to get his red ticket. Lyadov held up a blue one again for Daniel.

"That's not fair!" Daniel protested. "I did the same work as him!" pointing to the Tartar.

"And who will you complain to?" Lyadov laughed.

He was right. Guards left the prisoners to their own sociology so long as they stayed on schedule and caused no trouble. Daniel barely slept, from hunger and from taking the situation apart in multiple ways to understand why he was being singled out. He asked the Tartar the next day as they walked to the tunnel, but the big man knew nothing. The third day, it became worse. After finishing his small morning square of dry hard bread and cupful of thin broth, he walked to the tool area to pick up his wedges, only to be handed two pails.

"You're on shit detail," Lyadov announced, to the amusement of all gathered around. It meant walking the buckets out of the tunnel after the men filled them to the top, causing a generous portion to slop over the sides and onto his legs, hence the name *kareechnivye nogi* or 'brown legs' for the shit detail man. The brigade boss sat with his crew in shade near the tunnel entrance, laughing whenever someone said 'brown legs' as Daniel passed. Only when he heard Lyadov add the word *'suka'* did it finally become clear.

He was stupid. An idiot. When he'd spoken up for Yakimchuk, the little weasel, he too became a bitch and that label had traveled with him to this camp, passed on from one outpost of the criminal subculture to the other. Hell, they probably all had the same mother, spawned by hundreds of Neanderthal fathers. Dark, angry thoughts that solved nothing.

He was on his way out for the fifth time, no longer caring what was coating his legs because a knife in his ribs was likely to come soon, when the cave-in occurred. A deafening roar behind him followed by a roiling rolling cloud of rock dust which raced around and ahead of him. He stumbled out, coughing, heaving, bent at the waist, gratefully inhaling large gulps of air. He finally looked back at the hole he'd just been deep inside. He was standing outside only because someone wanted to demean him before ordering his murder. Yakimchuk was going to be the cause of his death, and now he was why he was alive. Also because the toilet pails happened to be full at that moment! It was all a cosmic joke, and as injured men cried out, and guards and overseers ran around shouting contradictory orders, Daniel laughed.

He now joined the tide of people rushing back into the tunnel. Near the halfway point, a new wall of boulders and dirt confronted them. Torrents of water poured out from two places in the top half, which made Daniel realize he was submerged up to his thighs. Only a few oil lamps remained lit, the air was full of dust and water mist, and dozens of men screamed the names of those who might be on the other side.

"Wait, wait!" Daniel yelled repeatedly until he had everyone's attention. "We need to listen." He pointed at three men, "You there, you. Yell and hit the rocks, one two three then stop and listen. No one else."

By the time a captain and two engineers from the construction office arrived, Daniel had organized an assembly line of prisoners working desperately to remove the blockage. The inspectors stood where their boots wouldn't get wet and watched, wrote things down onto papers on their clipboards, put their heads together and whispered, then left.

"What if it's the whole tunnel up to the end?" one of the men ventured, hours into the rescue effort. All their work appeared to be having no impact.

"More likely it was one area that was weakened by the water, and they are in a pocket behind this stuff," Daniel said.

He had no idea if that was true, only that it helped make them work until they were past exhaustion. No inventory tonight. An accounting of tools and men lost would be for another time. Lyadov tried to look solemn as he handed out full quota red tickets to all the survivors, even Daniel, who so quickly fell into a deep undreaming sleep that he couldn't ask himself whether the extra exertions today might have hastened his end.

The announcement that work was suspended upset many of the men, especially those who had friends or even brothers buried in the mountain, and they tried to volunteer to continue the rescue efforts. The Commandant, standing with the chief engineer, would have none of it.

"We estimate," he said, "that up to fifty meters of tunnel collapsed. It will take weeks to clear," and left the implications unstated.

"Hey, citizen." Lyadov appeared in front of Daniel later in the afternoon. He was alone. "I heard what you did at the cave in. It didn't help, that was God's will, but you tried to help."

Daniel considered his response carefully. "It's Daniel. My name. It's Daniel."

An angry look passed across Lyadov's face, transiently. He left Daniel alone. It was a good time to write a letter, Daniel considered. Maybe a final one. To whom, though? His father? Ian? Joseph? And what would he tell them? That he is fine, that the weather is mild, that the accommodations are adequate? Or to inform them that he knew and accepted that he would never see them again, that he was a piece of dirt from civilization, brought to this place by forces greater than any one person might control, and that his death would only register on a piece of paper in a file in an office somewhere. He decided that this was nothing anyone would want to read, so he went to sit outside in the sun.

They roused them an hour earlier than usual the next morning and shortened the morning meal and count. The men were organized into larger brigades which caused enough confusion that the guards needed to count them three times, so the early start was for nothing. The dogs, normally heard barking from their kennel outside camp, now guarded the route to the tunnel, signaling the imminent arrival of Moscow inspectors. The thousand or so men stood or sat around the tunnel entrance while the chief engineer and his minions, and the Commandant and his junior officers, inspected and discussed and then argued and yelled about fault — always the other's — and ridiculous solutions. Finally, the two groups drove away, separately, and a few minutes later the prisoners were marched back to camp. The inspectors came the next day and left with the Commandant and chief engineer. There was little time to cheer, if any felt the urge to celebrate the loss of one op-pressor, because their replacements arrived within twenty-four hours. The new engineer had the sallow look of a former prisoner. The new commandant filled out his uniform and had better posture and complexion than the previous one. He addressed the prisoners right away.

"Citizens. I do not have to tell you about our setback. What I can and must tell you is that this temporary impediment will not cause us to shrink from our goal. Comrade Stalin himself has said that the completion of our rail line is of greatest necessity for the Soviet people, and our tunnel is the most critical part of that rail line. Eyes are on us. I repeat that, eyes are on us." He paused for effect. "We must now redouble our efforts. Your friends and coworkers who sacrificed themselves, they demand it. The people demand it. Comrade Stalin demands it, so I demand it. We will not rest until we are back on schedule, and you will be proud to tell your children what you accomplished."

"As if any of us will live to have children." The unspoken thought occurred simultaneously to many of the prisoners standing in formation, including Daniel.

His punishment for such thoughts was to be selected the next morning for the small brigade, no more than two hundred men, that followed the new managers into the tunnel, to do their bidding as they formulated the plans needed to get back on that schedule. This turned out to mean that all of them, including the engineer and Commandant, stood in knee-deep water looking at the caved-in rockfall, chilled by mist from the streaming mountain springs, yet this Commandant listened carefully and asked insightful and relevant questions of the chief engineer. They pointed, they nodded, they shook heads, wrote and calculated, determined to have a solution before they left the tunnel, even if it took hours.

Which it did. Guards and prisoners shivered. If the Commandant had the capacity to sense cold, he did not show it. What he did begin to show was increasing frustration and he finally directed his anger at the engineer, "You are useless, worse than these men who at least will move a train through a mountain for me. I don't care how you want to dig, if we don't do something about this water, moving all the rock in the world will make no difference."

The Commandant turned from the engineer to make his way toward the entrance. As he passed close by, Daniel forced his teeth to stop chattering and spoke.

"Excuse me, Excellency," he said. The closest guard raised his rifle butt and made to crack Daniel's head, but the Commandant stopped him.

"It is Citizen," he corrected Daniel. "What do you want to say?"

"Well, uh, Citizen Commandant, I couldn't help but notice that the water is entering at what must be several hundred liters per minute."

"Yes. So?" The Commandant was clearly not a patient man, so Daniel made his point.

"Well, sir. It's been four days and the water level is similar to what was here the day after the uh, incident." Daniel saw the understanding of what this implied proclaim itself on the Commandant's face, so he hurried on to claim credit. "That must mean that there is an egress for the water, or several, at floor level. We could drill into some fractures further down. It would be more efficient, more likely to be a permanent solution than pumps or buckets."

"Who are you?" The Commandant now came close to Daniel, face to face. Daniel stated his name and, for the second time, that he was a university graduate with an engineering background.

22 August 1940, Marseille, France

Daniel,

Even if you never read this, you are the only person I can talk to.

You remember Christophe, from our school? He is here! Even war and displacement does not change him. He still sees every day as overall good. There is another, a Frenchman, I think. In other circumstances he could be a good friend. He just keeps too much hidden to justify complete trust. And he is the perfect counterweight to Christophe's optimism!

Six weeks ago, we arrived to the British Merchant Seamen's Hospital, which we now see is a prison without bars, locks, or guards. Each day is hotter than the last and all we can do is play cards, nap, eat, argue, and stare through the haze to the harbor. A few 'patriots' tried to rouse us to storm out and hijack an old blue freighter which never moved from a place just off the old port, and either sail it to the Baltic or up to the Black Sea. The Vichy Navy is preventing ships from unauthorized departures from Marseille, and the German Navy and Air Force would sink it before they reached the Dardanelles. Plus, it turned out no one knew how to pilot or navigate a large ship.

All things considered, though, I am safe. I hope you too are alive, far from the fighting, and have food. After the pay the officers received before the Armistice ran out, we were asked to pool our money. I was proud to contribute my small share. With that, plus scrounging and begging, we are in reasonable condition. Some evenings, Christophe, Paul, and I take our rations and sit in the inner garden and convince ourselves it is a degree or two cooler there. A family of field mice is becoming dependent on us for their supper!

The worst thing about being here is that there is no far horizon anymore. Do you have the same? Can you see beyond today? All our news and rumor sources disappeared so all I know is that tomorrow is very likely to be the same as today. I can't stand it, except I have no choice. The longer we languish here, the more I lie in my room and stare at the cracks in the ceiling, or sleep. I have calculated how much plaster would fix the ceiling multiple times.

Each day, a few of the men decide to leave and either head for Spain or disappear into France. The two priests we have are enough, so far, to prevent anyone from permanently leaving, you know what I mean. Don't worry, my friends and I buoy each other up, and hope for a new tide to come.

I wish I knew where you were and how you are faring, so I could talk less about me.

Until tomorrow!

Ian

Ian — Marseille, 25 August–1 September 1940

They sat on a bench in the inner garden because the night was still too hot for sleep. His older companion took a breath.

"Do you believe in fate, Ian?"

"If you are asking, do I think Germany decided to conquer Poland, and then invade Belgium and France just to ruin my plans, then no." This kind of questions was from Lachance. He needed to remember to call him Paul.

"I know one thing. This wall," Lachance patted it, "I can see that it stands. Save for an earthquake, or a bomb, we can discern the rules to ensure it stands. It is what you came here to study, no? And that scientific knowledge is just our understanding of God's laws."

Aside from the references to God, these were words Ian would have used with Daniel in Warsaw, had he asked. Understand, and then harness that understanding to create. As he'd learned in school and at the dinner table, he pushed the argument. "So, Hitler, this war, are all part of God's plan?"

"No. Yes. I don't know. No one can know because we do not possess sufficient intelligence or maybe vision to encompass something as vast as the universe. But I believe there is an order, at some level." Lachance intercepted Ian's next challenge. "Why, then, don't we just sit back and let the rules, the fate, take us where it is meant to, you want to ask? I used to tell my boys that God sets the boundaries of the field, and the rules of the game, and even provides the ball. How we play, though, is up to us."

Ian let the reference to teaching in the man's past go. They sat in the silent dark, sharing a cigarette.

"Paul?" Ian used the name.

"What?"

"Do you remember details of your life from before? If I try to picture what my room at home looked like, or my father's classroom, I can't anymore."

"You are too young to have filled your memory library," 'Paul' laughed, softly and gently. "Too much is occupying your foremind, and that weight and noise prevents your memories from floating up into your consciousness. Don't worry, the important ones, the ones that are branded into your soul, they are still there."

Ian tried once more to test this and failed. "So, you remember details of your life before this?" he repeated.

"Oh, yes." 'Paul' threw the butt away and went to his bed.

Another set of rumors started first thing in the morning but this time they coalesced by mid-afternoon into a reality. The *Marie-Therese*, a type of fishing trawler out of a port called Sete, two hundred kilometers south, had owners willing, for a pretty steep price, to take up to two hundred Poles to Gibraltar. At the after-dinner all hands meeting, officers detailed how groups of ten to twenty would travel by train to Sete and board the *Marie-Therese* when the moon would be new, in six nights. Because the English Merchant Seamen's Hospital was set back in a park, no Frenchman heard two hundred men loudly singing, '*Poland Has Not Yet Perished*' at the conclusion of their meeting.

Ian, Christophe, and 'Paul' were in the fourth group to leave. After supper, they put on civilian clothes but kept their papers, as demobilized Poles were permitted to move about in Vichy France. The officer who handed them their third-class train tickets gave them their final instructions.

"You are to proceed to the station in small groups. Talk to no one unless you must. Take train number 8093 at 21:17 to Montpellier, then change to train 6344 at 23:45. It's only three stops to Sete; you will arrive just after midnight. Walk to the address on the paper. God willing, you will be in Gibraltar in three days and England soon after. God willing, we will meet again in a free Poland!"

Apparently, what France wanted most of all was blessed ordinariness, without shooting or bombs falling from unmolested planes. By streetlight, Marseille looked undamaged and ready to get on with its life. They found their train, boarded, sat down, and had their tickets punched. Ian and his companions stared out at the passing darkness, and as promised, a few minutes after midnight they knocked and were admitted to the safe house in Sete.

The officers in charge were a sapper captain named Wysoczanski and a Polish Navy sub-lieutenant who never gave his name. They were quite organized. Two hundred men squeezed into a house meant for three generations of one family, now filled with discipline, morale, and hope.

On the night of the new moon Wysoczanski began at sunset to send the men out in pairs and quartets to navigate through the streets of Sete toward the corniche road west of the town lights. The sub-lieutenant popped up at the rendezvous point to catch the men and distribute them among the vegetation growing between road and shore. The first time a passing patrol boat scoured that beach with its searchlight, all stayed hidden. "He will be back in a couple of hours," the sub-lieutenant said to no one in particular. "We need the *Marie-Therese* now," as he looked to the east, but almost an hour passed before they heard an engine and saw the running lights directly off their beach. The sub-lieutenant stood up to give the signal with his flashlight, and all the men exhaled when it was returned. A small boat rowed by two men came out of the low surf. The sub-lieutenant waded out to catch the rope and pull the boat up on the sand. He and the men from the boat talked for many minutes before the sub-lieutenant came back.

"Pigs. They want more money, of course. A hundred thousand francs. I asked him where he thought we were hiding that much here on a beach in the dark."

Ian felt his chest constrict around his heart. He had at least half that. Would he have to use it to save all these men but risk having his horrible crime come to light? Perhaps doing good could cancel his culpability in the driver's death and restore who he'd thought he was meant to be.

The sub-lieutenant continued. "I managed to convince him that we would pay it when we arrive in Gibraltar." Ian's thoughts lightened. "Okay. That boat holds ten, which means twenty trips. The *Marie-Therese* is about fifty meters offshore but the tide is going out so it will probably need to move at some point. You'll row out to the far side, climb aboard, and go down into the hold. No talking. The boat has papers saying it is on its way to Perpignan to exchange fish for oranges. They have racks of fish to cover us."

"What about the patrol boat?" one man asked.

"I know, I know. I am going a hundred meters east and when I see the patrol boat I will signal. All activity stops. We wait until it passes, and when I signal again, we finish loading."

At that moment, the lights on the *Marie-Therese* extinguished, and it was as if it disappeared. Ian felt 'Paul' on one side and Christophe on his other and heard the gentle slap of the waves — no other sound, touch, or sight except he thought a tribe of crabs skittered past them. Finally, a man from the boat sent out a guttural "*Allons-y, vite!*" and the first group crunched across the sand. He heard the boat's bottom scrape off the beach and then oars in the water, or maybe he just imagined it. He, his friends, and the other remaining soldiers stayed as still as statues until the rowboat was back for the next cohort.

The warning signal came immediately after the fourth load was launched and once again the waiting men held their breaths and strained to hear in the darkness, until the distinct thrum of an offshore diesel engine became clear enough to seize their breaths. If it changed its rhythm or even stopped, each man would need to consider the consequences of the plan failing and decide what to do. But the bass note of the patrol boat faded off to the left, the sub-lieutenant came back, and somehow his presence accelerated the embarkation so that within the hour, Ian and his two friends left in the last boat, the sailors rowing with confidence into the empty sea. Ian feared they might miss the *Marie-Therese* and row out into the Mediterranean, that nightmare evaporating only when a black steel hull materialized in front of them. On the far side, a rope ladder awaited, soaked and slippery, and then they were up on the deck and down into a large square steel cavern, illuminated by one weak bulb and smelling of oil, seawater, fish, and two hundred nervous men in close quarters. The engines started right up to get them underway to Gibraltar. Captain Wysoczanski left to confer with the ship's captain, and when he came back, he stood on a step to address the men.

"Congratulations! We have successfully embarked two hundred and three Polish fighters to rejoin the fight, with no losses. Well done!" Some started to cheer, and someone started singing '*Poland Has Not Yet Perished,*' but the captain ordered it stopped.

"We are not out of danger, and there are rules we must follow. The captain of this boat is, to be honest, nervous. He risks confiscation of his boat or even jail. Still, he is making more money than I suspect a full season of oranges or fish gives him. So, the rules: no one is to go on deck except twice a day we get an hour for everyone, all two zero three of us, to use the toilet. For emergencies, we'll put a bucket under these stairs. Next, they will give us food for three days. Most important, three loud bangs on the hatch, and everyone has to stop and stay completely silent. It could mean a patrol boat or even an inspection. Oh, and one last thing, for you smokers, sorry. You will have to do without till we land."

Christophe groaned.

"So, settle down and when we see daylight, it will be the last stop before England and the Free Polish Army," Wysoczanski finished.

The first day was bearable. The men were good, they spoke in low, mostly deep tones unlikely to break through the frequencies of the engines, and calm seas meant few became sick. Ian stretched out on his coat, with the man they called 'Paul' sandwiched between him and Christophe. They helped this new 'Paul' solidify his story by pretending to reminisce, "Hey, remember the time the river ice on the Pilica wasn't as frozen as we thought, and Ryszard fell in, but we all pulled him out and wrapped him in our coats?" or "What did you get on the final essay on *Pan Tadeuz* in old man Wojcik's Polish literature class?" By day two, heat and boredom let an incipient fear slip into the hold. They stayed quiet yet their nerves vibrated at a pitch that was almost perceptible. To distract himself, Ian lay back and tried to reconstruct a memory picture of his father and their home. It was not easy, which fed his worry. Thinking of Daniel was more successful. He didn't understand why. Clearest of all was Alicia. Was she, because of him, not safe? Was she in trouble? In the long darkness, he imagined a scenario where, upon arriving to England, he'd volunteer to return to Paris as a spy or a saboteur. When he knocked, she would open the door, and seeing him, fold into his arms. Then Gestapo agents would appear, and he would kill them all and they would escape to Switzerland. After that, he slept.

On the second night, when it was their turn on deck, Ian and 'Paul' leaned against the rail at the stern, watching the wake the ship was creating in the Mediterranean, out of earshot of anyone else for the first time since boarding.

"Paul?" Ian whispered.

"*Quoi?*" the answer came.

Ian continued in French. "Have you… well, I mean I am very thankful I escaped from France. But you know, where we are going… well, I have never been a soldier. Have you?"

This pause was so long that Ian wondered if he had even been heard.

"Yes, I was. Not a soldier, a sailor. This is not my first boat. I am from Alsace, and during the last war, many of us joined the German Navy rather than get drafted into the Army. We thought it would reduce the chances that we would have to fight the French, you know what I mean? It was 1917 when I enlisted, and, thankfully, I did not see much action. Mostly scrubbed things on ships parked in Wilhelmshaven. How well do you know your history, Ian? October 1918, for example?"

Ian dug into his memory. "Kiel Mutiny?" he ventured.

"Yes, the Kiel Mutiny. The war was essentially over, but that did not matter to those who wanted to go out in a blaze of glory, no matter how many of us it would kill. We stopped them, the ships did not leave Kiel, but… they arrested many and intended to execute them. I participated in the march to stop them. The admirals set up machine guns on the roof of the barracks and the man next to me, he took a bullet through his eye. Killed him, of course, after he screamed. I never was in battle, not in the trenches or even on a ship, but that was my war. Death for sure, and just as useless."

Ian stared out at where the horizon was supposed to be. He was sorting through the many questions that came to mind when 'Paul' stretched himself to his full height and pointed outward.

"Is that a ship?"

Ian strained his eyes to see what his friend was seeing when a member of the ship's crew came up behind them.

"Everyone get below and stay very quiet. Hurry!"

Ian and 'Paul' rushed to their hold and arranged themselves in positions that minimized the need to uncramp legs or take pressure off bones no longer protected by fat.

"Do you think it's French or German?" Ian couldn't help but whisper to 'Paul,' "Or maybe British if we are nearing Gibraltar?"

"Shhh." In the dark it was impossible to see who ordered the silence. 'Paul' put his hand on Ian's arm and gave a slight squeeze of reassurance.

Residual evening heat added to what two hundred men generated to make it especially oppressive. Only changes in the engine song provided any information. How many minutes passed was impossible to tell. Ian tried to breathe shallowly, to make less noise, to suck less heat into his lungs. Finally, the hatch opened and Captain Wysoczanski was ordered out. Now everyone was restless, sharing their anxieties and looking for courage from their comrades. Ian heard words like Gibraltar and Sikorski, and others he did not recognize — Lagarde, Narvik, Montbard. He wondered what Claude had done between Wilhelmshaven and Kiel in 1918, and Zemmour's warehouse in 1940. He wondered if he should believe this story as easily as he'd accepted Alicia's first tale.

Wysoczanski called them together around the stairway when he got back. He looked as drained as they all felt.

"The crew is refusing to go to Gibraltar," he spat out. "They think that the boat was a Vichy patrol boat. The captain says that if they are suspected of heading to or coming from there, the boat will be confiscated. They refuse to accept that risk, no matter how much money we offer."

He allowed the murmurings of the men to rise and fall before going on.

"The captain wanted to let us off near Perpignan, close to the Spanish border. I told him that was unacceptable. He might as well take us directly to an internment camp."

The murmurings became a more coherent chorus of, "No!"

"We have settled on an alternative plan. He will bypass Gibraltar and take us to Casablanca. That is acceptable to him because it is still part of France. It is not as good as Gibraltar for us, but it is still good. We have an active network there and we will only need to spend maybe another day on board this dump, and maybe an additional week or two in Casablanca before we can go on to England. I am sorry for this detour, but be assured, we are still on our way to rejoin the fight."

Christophe grabbed Ian's sleeve. They were going to set foot in Africa! On the other side, 'Paul' said nothing. He probably was also hating the feeling that he was a jellyfish directed by the current or the fear of small men.

Ian — Casablanca, 3 September–25 October 1940

All Ian knew about Africa came from reading Edgar Rice Burroughs' books about an English baby raised by jungle apes and from watching Johnny Weissmuller swing through the trees during repeated visits to his local movie palace. The only time Burroughs mentioned dust, he recalled, was when Tantor the elephant led a stampede. Yet here in Morocco, dust was everywhere, while trees, vines, and shade were all absent. If they had sweltered in Marseille, they baked here in Casablanca. A cooling breeze never appeared, neither at dawn nor dusk.

The problem presented to the local Vichy authorities by the *Marie-Therese*'s human cargo was that these men had recently fought valiantly for France, but now they sought to join with the enemy of their ally — or was it their master? Their short-term solution: add them to the Czechs, Belgians, Dutch, and Norwegians already interned in a camp set up on the less desirable eastern side of the city. Three to four men to a tent, basic food and running water, enclosed by perimeter fencing but with a gate that was only locked after ten p.m. when, it was assumed, all the men were back in their tents.

Soon after their arrival, 'Paul' made one of his presumptive declarations. Soldiers and sailors, he informed Ian and Christophe, have three needs, and two desires. They need a place to sleep, food and water, and women, in flesh or fantasy. What they desire is a way to escape, at least temporarily, from their situation or their fears, and an occasional connection to home and mothers. The camp fulfilled the first two needs. Escape through alcohol was available to those able to buy it. The rest had to make do with betting on fights between pairs of captured scorpions. Most surprisingly, a Vichy postman brought letters from home weekly to many of them, though none to Ian. On his third visit, after the postman finished mangling the names on the envelopes and was turning to leave, Ian tapped him on the shoulder and asked if he took outgoing mail.

"*Bien sur!*" the official straightened up to his full though unimpressive height. Ian thrust his envelope over, addressed to one Daniel Ciszek in Warsaw, but before the postman could hand it back because it lacked postage, 'Paul' stepped up to put a handful of coins on top. The man sniffed, pocketed the coins, and stuffed the envelope into his messenger bag before he turned on his heel and walked out the gate.

"You didn't have to do that. I just forgot," Ian said.

"I know," said 'Paul.' They walked together towards their tent. "We hardly talk anymore. Is it something I said?"

"No," Ian admitted. "It's this place. If we are really going to be here forever, there is nothing worth talking about."

"Hmm," 'Paul' said. "With no destination, our relationship has no purpose? How utilitarian. I would point out that it is unlikely that being solitary makes it any more bearable." Ian recognized the truth in this. The distance between them closed, immeasurably but palpably, by the time they reached their tent.

Mutinous murmurings began to bubble up by the end of the third week of rice mixed with a few pieces of unidentifiable meat and the occasional insect. Major (he'd been promoted) Wysoczanski's promise to address this with their 'hosts' changed nothing. Christophe, of all people, became the first to take matters in his own hands. One morning, he handed his plate of gray food to a surprised Ian and walked out the gate. Four hours later, he returned with a loaf of bread, three oranges, a leek, and a tin of sardines, which he shared with his friends. Thereafter, he left every other morning and came back sometime later with a different set of welcomed, if exotic, foodstuffs. Within a day or two, Ian's feelings of what 'Paul' termed melancholia evaporated. He even found himself daydreaming of what he would order if he and Alicia could meet to dine at the best restaurant in Paris. Here and now, though, they enjoyed dinners of lamb and couscous, and even a little wine and talk, leading to laughter and a flush of camaraderie Ian surprisingly welcomed. Afterward, though, as he lay on his cot in the tent, Ian remembered that he had no right to any contentment and like a stink bomb that releases its noxious sulfurous gas when pricked, guilt permeated all his thoughts.

He slept badly one night, disturbed, he knew, by dreams that he could not quite capture upon awakening. By the light from over the dining hall door, he saw 'Paul' up on his elbow, looking at him.

"What?" Ian asked.

"There may come a time when you or I need to leave here, if you know what I mean. I think we really need to convince Christophe to take us with him the next time he goes into Casablanca."

Ian was embarrassed he hadn't already thought of something so obvious. He whispered that he would ask Christophe in the morning. 'Paul,' satisfied, rolled over and quickly was back to sleep. Ian considered what he knew about him. Four months in each other's daily company and the only facts were that the man claimed to be from Alsace, had been in the German Navy at the end of the last war, participated in the Kiel mutiny, and he had taught boys at some point, before he became a charity administrator. The man was deliberately opaque.

'Paul' and Ian watched Christophe wash up, go for his breakfast tea and bread, and chat amiably with a few friends. Only when he was back in their tent, lacing up his boots did Ian finally speak.

"Hey there, Christophe." Christophe stopped to look up at the other two. "What are you up to?"

"Nothing much. Well, you know, maybe get some more goodies."

"Paul and I, we were talking about that. You know how grateful we are for all these… well, these goodies. And we were wondering, you know, if we could help…"

The smile narrowed, though not quite completely. "I don't know," Christophe said. "It's a little complicated."

"You are probably dealing with people who aren't exactly model citizens. It would be good to have some support. Not many, just me and 'Paul' here," Ian said

Christophe chewed over the thought. "There's always been someone, you know, the real Paul. This is the first time I've done anything on my own. But it could maybe scare off the men I do business with."

"Look Christophe," 'Paul' said. "We do not want to interfere with your business. You are the best, no one else in the camp does what you do. The truth is, though, we feel trapped in this camp, in Casablanca. And if we wait for someone to do something, well, who knows how long it will be? And what if Vichy decides to return us to France, or fight England? We are worried about that."

"Me too," Christophe agreed.

"We just want to go to find out what is possible, perhaps a boat to Gibraltar or to Freetown, see who can help, who we can trust, you know?"

Christophe became excited. "Yes! Okay, we could start doing this. Maybe get Novotny to help." Novotny was a Czech navy man.

'Paul' put up his hand. "For now, let's just keep this to the three of us. Once we have an idea of what could be arranged, we can enlist others."

They left camp individually to rendezvous where Christophe specified, a half kilometer up the road to the city center, at the edge of a grove of citrus trees behind a low stone wall. A few meters along, Christophe suddenly stopped, checked whether anyone paid them any attention, and stepped over the wall to crouch on the other side. Ian heard stones scraping and when the young man stood up, he triumphantly displayed a one-thousand-franc note. Ian knew its source, but 'Paul' had to ask, "Where did you get that? Do you have more?"

Christophe looked to Ian, as if to say, *Answering is your responsibility.* Two thousand kilometers from Paris, in a barren desert camp, with only a reed of hope of ever leaving: for Ian, it didn't matter anymore. He told 'Paul' of the cigarette truck hijack, omitting mention of the fate of the driver. 'Paul' displayed neither surprise nor judgment.

"No wonder you looked white as a ghost before your meeting with the police and Gestapo," 'Paul' said to Ian, referring to what happened after they arrived to Morocco. "They clearly don't know yet. That doesn't mean we shouldn't try and leave this place; we just don't have to be desperate and rush into something stupid." He had another thought. "It was your share that bought your papers from Zemmour."

"Worse," Ian said quietly. "It was Alicia's share. I still have most of mine." He took off his left boot and used a nail file to pry open a hole in the instep to bring out three ten-thousand-franc notes.

"Put it away for now. Maybe a time will come where we need to buy three passages. For now, we forget it is there." 'Paul' patted Ian's shoulder.

Ian's boot back on, they made for the *souk*, a claustrophobic warren of narrow passages and blind alleys packed with tiny shops. Some were just a mat over an open spot of dirt, others had doors and walls that defined spaces subdivided over the years into their smallest functional dimensions. Christophe led them left and right and left in what felt like a random manner, to finally stop in front of a shop that looked like virtually every other one they'd passed. Christophe ordered the other two to wait and disappeared into the dark interior.

"They don't like it," he announced when he came back out. "I explained that you are my friends from when we were boys, but still. They will definitely raise their prices, for sure." But he led them in.

One weak oil lamp, supplemented by the light sneaking through chinks in the corrugated tin roof, provided enough illumination for them to see two bearded men in dirty djellabas, clicking their beads nervously. 'Paul' raised his hand. "*As-salāmu ʿalaykum.*" The two Moroccans murmured their response, clearly not reassured by a foreigner intoning a few words of formal Arabic. Christophe broke the ice by picking up an item, asking its price, and then making a ridiculous counter-offer, to which the merchants shook their heads with such a tragic expression on their faces, wordlessly saying that with such a price, they and their children would starve and die. Ian could not believe Christophe's French or his bargaining skills. The three finally agreed on amounts that satisfied everyone's needs, for some butter, a cantaloupe and a piece of lamb for supper. This was when the meeting usually concluded. An awkward pause broke when the shopkeepers remembered to offer coffee to their guests. Ian wondered what the correct response was: 'Paul' had no doubt; he accepted their offer. Fresh coffee came in delicate tiny cups, and the men exchanged careful words about weather, business in general and how much the visitors liked Morocco, without any reference to the camp.

Things improved with each subsequent visit. The three Europeans bargained for some items, then came coffee. Their hosts, it turned out, were brothers. The younger, whom they called the 'fat one' when they spoke of him back at camp, taught at a boy's school part-time. The store was started by their father and had always sold a little bit of everything. The brothers stayed informed about the current state of world affairs. They had opinions about whether Roosevelt would win the election next month and knew that Paderewski, the Polish pianist and former President, was on his way from London to America via Lisbon. They listened politely when the Europeans told the story of how they'd been classmates from Poland who went together to France and volunteered for the Polish Army before France fell, and how they heeded the call to reach England to fight on, but now they were stuck in Vichy Morocco.

An outbreak of something spread through the camp — a few days of fever, vomiting. and diarrhea — which brought down Christophe. Ian made him tea and kept him company. On the second day 'Paul' pulled Ian outside. It might be important, he thought, that they keep their schedule with the brothers so they would not get nervous or suspicious. 'Paul' volunteered to go alone. He was back several hours later with honey, mint, some fresh yoghurt, and other folk remedies for gastrointestinal disorders. Christophe managed to keep some of the nostrums down, signaling to all he would recover.

Before lights out, 'Paul' and Ian shared a cigarette by the fence. "I talked to the brothers," he said. "About a boat."

"Oh, yes?" Ian said. "What did they say?"

"I told them we were just looking to hire someone to take us to British territory. Suggested they perhaps speak to the men they get their fish from. They volunteered nothing; I think they are just being careful. I feel like I will need to go back a few more times."

Which is what happened. After Christophe recovered, he and Ian went every other day for shopping, while 'Paul' went on the alternate days for his business. But nothing changed, not for Ian and his friends or for the men in the camp, and after two weeks, Ian sensed the general level of despair in the camp deepening in parallel with his own. Major Wysoczanski probably recognized it too. He conspicuously went several times a day into the camp headquarters building, and eventually there was a steady increase in the comings and goings of police commissionaires, French Army officers, and important looking civilians. Rumors began to spread like the illness that had laid them up earlier that month. They were going to be moved, or conscripted into the Vichy French Army, or the Foreign Legion. They were going to be sent back to France. Christophe believed each one until the next one came along, while Ian tried to analyze the logic, indications, and odds of each. 'Paul' was the most disturbed. At one of their cigarette meetings by the wire one evening, Ian asked him what the matter was.

"I am tired, Ian. Tired to my bones." 'Paul' finally admitted.

"We all are."

"You are what, nineteen, twenty? And you are very wise for your age. I see this. But wait another two decades and see how ground down you become."

"Your melancholia again?" Ian tried not being offended.

"Maybe. I don't know. I feel like I am sinking down into the sand, like one of those snakes they warn us not to step on. We are stuck, trapped on a patch of dirt in a corner of Africa." He paused, like he often did. "There was another place, far away like this, in my previous life, the one before Hitler and the other madmen launched this war. It was a small village, called Fougerolles, maybe two thousand souls, about a hundred kilometers from where I was born." The older man took the last puff on the cigarette before it burnt his fingers. "I had a life in Fougerolles, of a sort. There were people like you there, friends whom I met for dinner. Mostly I had time to think, which I did much more of then. But I did realize that I could never live in a cave and drown in my own thoughts until I see visions of fighting the Devil, like Saint Anthony of Egypt. Perhaps there are too many devils in real life that deserve attention, or maybe I knew that I cannot win such a fight."

Ian finally asked what he'd wanted to for weeks. "Were you a priest there? Are you a priest?"

'Paul' turned to stare at him, then took in a deep breath. "I was. Not a common thing to be able to say. I taught at a school there, St. Joseph. Then I left. Not only the school and Fougerolles, but the Church." He turned to look out through the wire. Ian wanted to know more. He knew it needed to come unprompted.

"We need to get moving, to get ahead of this avalanche of history. If we stop, we will be buried by it, Ian. The Nazis will take over Vichy, they will make them enforce their vicious ugly laws and you will be rounded up. We need to move. Waiting to see what Wysoczanski has planned for us is not going to ensure our survival. I need to go see the brothers tomorrow and get us a boat."

'Paul', who had been Yves who had been Claude, kept using plural pronouns. Ian put his hand on his friend's arm and offered to share the burden.

"No, you stay here," Paul said. "They are used to dealing with just me about this. I'll be okay. We'll need some money to take as a down payment though."

Being able to give some of what was left of his blood money to help his friend salved Ian's conscience.

Henry — Hempstead, New York, 8 July 1970

I was fourteen when I finally convinced my parents that the polio vaccine made it unnecessary to exile me to camp in the country every summer. Me hanging out at home was not an option for them, and summer school was not one for me, leaving employment as the only choice, and when I could not find anyone willing to hire me for more than an odd job, my uncle suddenly discovered that his architecture practice needed an office boy.

Each day, I rode a train packed with real commuters. My first task on arrival was to head to the office of David, the junior partner, for his breakfast order from the restaurant downstairs. Where most would be happy getting the same coffee and bagel, he wanted to be inspired each day, as if the same order might be a sign of a loss of creativity, followed by middle age and then death. Between phone calls, questions from the draftsmen, meetings with my uncle, and his chronic indecision, the final order often took an hour or more each morning. Sharpening pencils, addressing mailing labels and other busy work still left significant idle time. Then I discovered his shelf full of the Architectural Record. I loved turning the thick pages of the glossy monthly to admire the beautiful photos of the featured projects — small jewels sited on promontories overlooking the ocean, or spectacular museums where the building was as artistic and sculptural as anything contained within.

The practice had a developing niche in the design of new shopping malls. Intricate models for these covered most of the horizontal spaces in David's office, made with layers of corrugated cardboard, paper, and toothpicks, together with plastic people and plastic cars. The contrast between them and what was in the Architectural Record was obvious even to me.

"David," I said one morning.

"Wait," he answered. "I haven't decided yet. Buttered toast or a cheese danish or a bagel and cream cheese?"

"Would any of our buildings ever get into Architectural Record?" I asked anyway.

He stopped what he was doing to reach over and take the magazine from my hand to leaf through it. "See, this one here is like the mall we're designing." He was pointing to a flooring ad, not a feature article. I must have looked disappointed.

He sat next to me. "Look," he said. "It's not easy to run an architectural office, to make it work as a business. You have bills, responsibilities, especially the salaries of everyone working here, people who depend on you. So, you must take what comes through the door and generates income. There are very, very few practices that can do that with this other stuff." He pointed to the magazine. "And those that try pretty quickly fail. I mean, it would be nice, but having a house and food and clothes for your kids — that's nicer, you know."

He read my face. "He could do this. He absolutely could! He is one of the most amazing designers I know. He takes out his pen and produces something not only practical but beautiful. I am a good critic, I can see what works and what doesn't, but he creates, as well as anyone in there," he said, dropping the magazine onto the floor. He decided on the cheese danish and I left to fill his order.

Daniel – Kenada, Khabarovsk Krai, 11–14 October 1940

Daniel liked the camp office better. Originally constructed to house guards and administrators, it not only had a good stove, it still had all its caulking. He could stay in shirtsleeves, as he'd done in Warsaw. When bent over one of the long tables engrossed in work, he sometimes detected the edges of a sense of normalcy he'd not known since the first of September 1939.

Another major contributor to that feeling was that he now had his hair. Each week, inmates presented their heads to the barber's clippers to shave off all but a few millimeters, except for those who achieved a certain level of responsibility within the camp, which included those in the engineering office. They were permitted to grow their hair to a length where they could wash, part, brush, and arrange it. Not a week after he gained the privilege, Daniel traded four cigarettes for a comb. He felt pleased and a little proud that visitors to the office could not differentiate him from one of the 'free.' The 'free' were people with special skills who worked in the Gulag, without being owned by it. A few were volunteers or contractors unable to succeed in civilized locations, but most were former prisoners forbidden from returning to their homes after completing their sentences, who found the only employment available was within the prison camp they'd recently left. These men looked and worked like Daniel, but at the end of the day, they retired to their lodgings, some with wives and even children. The free earned enough money to buy food, including meat sometimes, and packs of cigarettes.

The chief engineer had his own office, with his own stove. and a door behind which he shut himself off from everything. Anyone with sense agreed with the Commandant's unspoken though clear judgment, that the chief engineer was an idiot, and he must be a relative of someone important. As long as the work kept pace with the schedule set by the central authorities, the Commandant left that pantomime alone.

Out in the big room, Daniel and the others did all that was necessary to make the chief appear to be an engineering wizard. Their real leader was a man named

Rybak, formerly a guest of the Gulag, now free but exiled from his native Byelo-russia because he came from a family of well-educated Poles, which was doubly damning for Stalin's plans for Minsk. To the chief engineer, the Commandant, and their flunkies, Rybak was haughtily obsequious, a curious and, for the Gulag, a unique attitude. Among his colleagues, he was pleasant, even funny, like the real professional interactions Daniel had experienced in his previous life.

As a veteran of the Gulag, and a survivor of its turf battles, bureaucratic skir-mishes, and lethal purges, the Commandant knew how to work the system to achieve what his bosses demanded. Rybak was his latest and best acquisition for the whole project. To quickly solve the immediate problem, the blockage from the cave-in, he pulled other strings.

"Regulations limit rail system to mines, not tunnels. So I called our project a coal mine. Approved like that!" The Commandant snapped his fingers. Usually taciturn, he couldn't help himself the morning he appeared in the engineering office to order the chief engineer install his narrow-gauge rail and train. This plus more lamp oil, more shovels and pickaxes, more men, and the arrival of Rybak, made progress noticeable. Rybak was, Daniel realized, a consummate engineer, able to grasp a problem, break it down into its parts, develop options to address each, pick the best ones, and efficiently marshal the resources needed to complete the selected task. Rybak made sure everyone was reasonably happy: the Comman-dant about his schedule, the chief engineer for his job security, and Daniel and his compatriots for generally being left alone. Rybak also managed to eke out minor concessions from the system, like more frequent breaks, cigarette rewards, and the like. Ian, Daniel thought, would have benefited greatly from such a mentor.

Daniel's proposal to drill into the floor of the tunnel to drain the water had worked. The next task, to deal with the streams which had compromised the tun-nel's integrity, was far trickier. Only Rybak's plan to install iron pipes to catch and run the water out and beyond the tunnel entrance made it possible for the moun-tain to again be attacked by hundreds of men intent on boring through its heart.

Daniel's other office was at the entrance to the tunnel. There, he kept his jacket on because there was no stove and the windows, surplused from another camp, did nothing to block the steadily colder air arriving from the North. His sole function there was to brief the brigade leaders about the work assignments. Back in the tunnel, Daniel measured, assessed, and gathered whatever data Rybak needed. Whether his day ended at the tunnel or the camp office, though, he joined all the other prisoners to endure the roll calls that often lasted hours, as the guards couldn't or wouldn't get it right. He ate the same ugly food: black bread that resembled bricks, and the soup, which appeared to be water in which, at some remote time, meat and vegetables briefly swam. Finally, he lay next to three other men, each wearing all their clothes, on a wooden pallet, until sleep arrived. Sometimes he didn't sleep. His hair also marked him here. He was a trusty, therefore not considered a faithful fellow prisoner.

Whispers began to circulate that the quota system was to change. He'd heard about this at the camp engineering office. Quotas would now apply collectively to everyone on a shift. This would align everyone's efforts to the immediate goals. It was more accurately measurable. It fit Marxist orthodoxy, plus under such a system the weak were less likely to spiral down to their deaths. Daniel was not surprised, though, when the rumor brought Lyadov to his bunk after lights out.

"I hear you want to change things, Daniel." He made a show of saying the name. "That would be unwise, unhealthy."

Daniel's attempt to explain was cut off.

"Do not change it. That's all we are going to say, and only this once." Daniel spent the rest of the night preparing the arguments he made the next morning to successfully get the idea, rather than him, killed.

This whipsawing drained him. Midmornings in the camp office on one side, his best circumstance since he'd left Warsaw on that motorcycle, when he opened the engine for a few minutes and foolishly convinced himself he would soon rescue his father. At night, though, not moving on his hard pallet, he felt his density increasing, less a human being and more a stone rolled from place to place, molecules of his fear becoming mass and attaching themselves until, becoming so heavy, he would stop moving and sink into the earth. If not now, then next time. When the tunnel was completed, there would be another project, another camp to punish and kill. More stacked frozen bodies. More burials. The showers that didn't wash anything away. The weekly meetings where commandants instructed them on the beauty and historical inevitability of Marxism and the Soviet system, so they should be grateful to participate in this glorious cause and view their current situation as a necessary step to a future where no one lacked for necessities and the proletariat reigned. Daniel pictured the this proletariat — men, women and children, teachers, dentists, shopkeepers, soldiers, bosses, kulaks — in a painting. The features of the figures in front were distinct. The next ranks were only forms of torsos with limbs, and further back they were pale blobs. But those blobs pressed forward, like an ocean tide inexorably overwhelming and subsuming the human beings in front. Eventually it would become a giant moving wall of flesh, with an arm here, an ear there, rolling slowly forward over history.

Outside, snow fell, ushering in another winter to sap their strength and will. Even worse, the light was going, and soon the daylight would have the same strength as their soup. It was his second winter. If, as it now appeared, it was not to be his last, there would be another, and then another.

This morning, he decided that he needed to focus on the camp office as a sanctuary, where he might forestall sinking again into a personal abyss, so he turned his attention to the calculations required for Rybak's plans outlined on the papers in front of him. He moved his work nearer to the strongest light bulb, the one by the entrance door, and leaned in to decipher the numbers he needed to use. From the other side of the door came sounds of wind and ice pellets. It was good to be inside. That was something positive, he told himself

The door opened and his papers lifted off the table and shot across the room. "What the hell!" Daniel yelled, before he realized that it might be the Commandant. Thankfully, it wasn't anyone in uniform. The newcomer wore a well-padded coat and trousers, and a real pair of boots, not fashioned from pieces of rubber tires and rags like his. A special *pridurki*, a toady trading far more of their pride and dignity than he would ever, no doubt. Or maybe a free person who squeezed extra rubles out of every service, to afford such clothes. Either way, they would have hair like his. When the felt cap with the ear flaps came off, though, out fell long, luxurious hair clearly covering the head of a woman.

She shot him a quick dismissive glance, which went through Daniel's eyes to his brain, before she marched over to Rybak. The two of them huddled together, as everyone else pretended to work, except Daniel, who sat up straight and stared. Korbochevsky, an electrical engineer originally from Moscow, whose secret ambition to be a poet was not a secret to the NKVD, sidled up next to Daniel to whisper in his ear.

"She is Nadhya. She is free. She has a history with Rybak, but I don't know the nature of their relationship. I understand that she found a house in the village, and that she sleeps with a gun and a knife," Korbochevsky said with a chuckle. At that moment, Nadhya looked up and spent a few seconds inspecting Daniel's face, as he was memorizing hers.

Daniel — Kenada, Khabarovsk Krai, 15–29 October 1940

"Bah," Rybak spat onto the ground outside their camp office. "I will never learn to accept this rancid *makhorka*."

Few believed that it contained any actual tobacco. Likely a mixture of sawdust and grass. Its composition had no effect, however, on its value in the camp. Real cigarettes were rare and, therefore, too expensive for almost everyone, leaving the makhorka which, when wrapped in any kind of paper, became the primary currency of the underground camp economy. Daniel did not hate it as much as Rybak, likely because he no longer remembered the taste of a real cigarette. Since everyone, from the Commandant and guards to the free and the imprisoned, smoked — men lying in the infirmary waiting to die smoked the most — a subconscious deference was often extended to someone with a lit cigarette, affording them a very brief time that was their own. This was how he and Rybak began their periodic visits outside, which the chief engineer tolerated. Of course, he may have decided that, since it was Rybak and Daniel, it was in his best interests to concede this small thing.

The two men ignored the flurries and the low, pregnant clouds. Rybak tended to treat silences as wasted opportunities. As a result Daniel knew that the other man was fifty-two, that before his arrest he had been the engineer in charge of a large factory making turbines, that he liked reading westerns by Zane Grey when he could find them on the black market in Minsk, and that, after his arrest, he made his father, mother and two brothers publicly condemn him and his crimes, so they would not suffer by their association with him.

Rybak exhaled a careful dose of smoke and looked over at Daniel. "You are bursting to ask me. I can see it. Go ahead."

"What are you talking about?" Daniel protested.

"Nadhya. You want to know about her. Who is she? How did she come to be here? What is our arrangement? No?" Rybak smiled when he said this.

Daniel's denial of any such thoughts merely fueled an even broader smile.

"You and every other man in there who still breathes. You stop when she enters, your pencils erect in midair. It is so funny to watch when you catch yourself staring and then try to look but not look."

Daniel felt his face color, probably the first time he had been embarrassed since Warsaw. He smiled his confession back to Rybak. But now the other man became more somber.

"She is here, which is a sad story, a tragic story. She is originally from Leningrad, her father spent two years in Siberia after 1905 so she was of acceptable provenance for the Bolsheviks. She came to Moscow to attend the State University, worked for years on her doctorate."

"In what?" Daniel asked.

"Russian literature, unfortunately."

"Why unfortunately?"

"She met a man, you may have heard of him, Arkady Mikhailovich Polevy."

"Sorry, no."

"Doesn't matter. He was a fellow student, reputedly a brilliant speaker and writer. But unlike Nadhya, his father was a priest, and not a poor one, a wrong combination in our country. They had their eyes on Polevy and being young, he could not restrain himself from writing of things without due consideration, until finally, in 1936, he was picked up and, well, he may be somewhere in this," Rybak gestured around the camp. "Our secret society within society. Or he is dead. Nadhya doesn't know. Of course, they picked her up, too, and chose to misinterpret some of her writings to justify sending her to the Gulag. To Kolyma. thankfully for only two years. They released her when the war broke out."

Daniel wondered why she was still here. Was it because of Rybak? An engineer, admittedly twenty or twenty-five years her senior, clearly charismatic, and as successful as a prisoner could hope to be, the acme of prisoners. The Commandant did what he needed to satisfy his commanders, so had no problem including rewards if it served him. Thus, Rybak lived in the village. Perhaps Nadhya was another such carrot.

Rybak spoke. "She is here because she is still exiled. Where she is permitted to live, she does not want to go, where she wants to go, Moscow or Leningrad, that is not permitted. I sometimes think she stays because she hopes that Polevy might appear one day. Whatever the reason, she was living outside the last camp… no, it's two camps ago, they all are starting to blend together, and her job was to provide secretarial support for my little office. It was easy to see that she was no mere secretary, she could organize anything. So, when they moved me to my next camp, she said she wanted to come with me, and, I don't know, they have done it twice now, I cannot fathom why but do not question my good fortune."

"So, you and she…" Daniel did not finish the question.

Rybak laughed, a rare sound among prisoners, or even guards, which devolved into a coughing fit, to which Rybak was becoming more and more prone. He turned his face away and spat a red stain into the snow.

"I really like you, Ciszek. You remind me of myself twenty years ago. You are clearly smart, and you watch and choose your moments."

No one had ever characterized Daniel that way before.

"But there is one big difference," Rybak continued. "It's probably stupid of me to tell you. Probably doesn't matter, considering. But I like you."

Daniel looked confused again.

"I'm not inclined towards women. Not that way." He looked directly into Daniel's face, waiting for the reaction.

"Oh," Daniel said, followed by, "Does she know?"

The other man laughed again, more gently to avoid the cough. "Yes. I guess that means there are now two people here who know. Anyway, let me warn you, I am the source of the rumor about the gun and the knife, but there is truth buried within it. My Nadhya is a very strong individual."

He took a last drag before carefully extinguishing the tip in a small patch of snow on the railing. He checked that it was out and put what remained into his pocket. "She may be watching for Polevy, but she is not entirely waiting for him," he said. "She chooses her lovers carefully; she seems to prefer brains to muscle. When she started to choose me, I had to tell her, and we became colleagues and friends, which is a far better arrangement than lovers to be used and discarded. Be warned, young Ciszek. You are definitely her type. Also, if you hurt her, I will have you transferred to the uranium mines in Chutotka." No one survived working in Chutotka.

Rybak turned to reenter the office, Daniel close behind him, his head swirling with all sorts of unconnected thoughts.

***

Along with the ninety-one metric tons of mountain that formed the blockage, 127 bodies had come out from the tunnel. After that was finished, Daniel worked on electrifying the lighting and, lately, on justifying fans to move dust-laden air out and improve the work environment. Not that they would notice it.

"We need more than the five fans they sent!" he angrily demanded at a planning conference, with the chief engineer and the Commandant's adjutant present. "We showed you. With better air, work can increase by up to fifteen percent!"

Rybak interjected. "We have to make do with what we have, for now. We will use these five, thank you for acquiring them, Comrade Vrosovich." The adjutant's shoulders relaxed, and Rybak shot a look across the table to tell Daniel to calm down, which he did immediately, as much to please Rybak as to avoid angering the adjutant or chief engineer.

Six days a week, whenever the office worked, she came. Sometimes she was there for an hour or more, conferring with Rybak, going over memos and requisitions and all the paperwork that is the lifeblood of the Gulag. She was the conduit between Rybak's team and the administration and outside world. When they needed more wooden ties for the rails, she negotiated with the village woodcutters, and the ties arrived early and for a really good price. Somewhere, a functionary read the progress reports, checked them against the prescribed timeline, and stamped 'Acceptable' before filing them away, not caring that it was due to a small office of engineers (one an architect) and a woman who had once valued words.

Five days after Daniel's eruption about the fans, she entered the office, so routine now that no one looked up from their work. Except Daniel, who still watched her surreptitiously as she shook off her coat while transferring papers from one hand to the other and for the first time, walking over to his workspace. He straightened up and was considering whether to stand and offer his seat, when she dropped the papers on his desk with a thump.

"Here. Twelve more fans. Should be here by the end of the week." She looked directly at him with no emotion on her face and went to her usual spot next to Rybak while Daniel silently chastised himself for not at least thanking her. She had never spoken to any of them before, only Rybak, and that was in whispers and low voices. Her real voice, a direct low alto, was a revelation. Her eyes, Daniel noted, were green, to go with her chestnut hair, streaked with some gray.

If anyone needed confirmation that Daniel was number two in the office, not counting the chief engineer, it came not from the way Rybak assigned him tasks or asked for his input during meetings, but from how, after the fans, Nadhya increasingly interacted with him, to the point where the other men wagered whether she would speak first to him or Rybak. If any of them were jealous, they quashed the feeling. They were in as good a situation within the Gulag as anyone could wish for, and jealousy was a ridiculous reason to risk it.

The office became consumed with a major challenge to solve regarding bracing in the tunnel. Daniel scribbled long calculations on pieces of precious scrap paper, his concentration so intense he failed to notice Nadhya's entrance one morning until she stood by him offering an actual slide rule. By now, she could sometimes even smile, and one now lit her face.

"I saw this on a desk in Sovetskaya Gavan when I was there last week. Thought you could use it more."

Daniel accepted it with thanks. She invited him outside for a cigarette break in response, and they stood on the little porch. This began their daily ritual. It was often almost too cold to speak, but they managed to exchange stories of their families, what they missed most, what they hated most. Each morning Daniel cleared a space for them outside the door. When she had to travel, which she did every week or so, he missed seeing her. That was why he became so upset when Nadhya failed to appear the day after she was supposed to return from one of her scavenging trips. Rybak came outside, as Daniel stood looking out for her. Rybak couldn't smoke anymore, it caused him to cough too much, so he stood rocking from foot to foot in the cold.

"I don't know where she is, my friend. No one has said anything to me," he said.

"Can you send a messenger? Can you go yourself to her place?" Daniel asked.

Rybak knew that such a walk might be beyond his capacity. He had a better idea. "Come inside," he ordered Daniel. There, he put together a bundle of papers and called for one of their guards.

"I need these taken and discussed with Miss Simonova in the village. It can't be by messenger. Ciszek here needs to talk with her. Arrange for an escort, please."

Rybak could do that, get the guards to do some of his bidding. The young fellow conferred with his superior and came back to confirm that he would escort the prisoner. Daniel forced himself to maintain a normal pace to the village and up to Nadhya's cottage, where, to his relief, he saw smoke ascending from the chimney. She didn't open the door at his first insistent knock because she had to hobble over. Ice on the steps of her railroad carriage on the return trip. Only a badly twisted ankle.

Her room was simple, a fireplace where the food was cooked, some sort of brown rug over a wooden floor, two chairs and a table. Against a far wall, there was a bed layered with blankets. They put the chairs together and sat, knee to knee, so Rybak's papers covered their contact point. The guard happily went into the kitchen area to make himself tea and have some of the *sushki* she'd baked earlier. On each of the next three days Rybak ordered Daniel and an escorting guard to Nadhya's, and no one said anything, not the other men in the office, not the guards, not even any camp administrators. Finally, though, when Rybak signaled another trip was necessary, a lieutenant appeared.

"Ciszek." The lieutenant barked.

"Yes, citizen," Daniel replied, as he stood by his desk.

"You will go directly to Miss Simonova's house, you will not stop anywhere else, and you will come directly back. You know that there is nowhere for you to go, but if you try to escape, we will hunt you down and kill you."

And so, Daniel became a *beskonvoinyi*, one of the unguarded. He almost ran to her, standing there panting and grinning when Nadhya opened the door and saw him, alone. She grinned too and pulled him in, and they became the lovers that Rybak clearly hoped they would be.

Ian — Casablanca, 26–27 October 1940

Major Wysoczanski stood on a chair in front of the restive crowd. In Poland, even in France, his rank, rigid posture, and arrow-straight gaze would have been enough to command their complete attention. Now, it took time and effort for the static and hiss of disappointment, fear, and regret to dissipate.

"Men. It has been many weeks since we landed here for what was meant to be no more than a brief stop before joining General Sikorski and our brothers in England, to get back into the fight, defeat our enemies and reclaim our homeland." He paused for the cheers, which were noticeably dampened when compared to Toulouse or Marseille.

He went on. "You should know, first of all, that you are not alone. Together with your compatriots in Rabat, Fez, Oujda, and Marrakesh, you make almost a full Polish division! As senior officer in French North Africa, I have visited each camp, to establish proper organization and ensure the Vichy authorities are doing their duty. Even before the blockade, the authorities here have not always seen to their obligations. A full report will be made once we reach England."

Ian snorted and leaned over to whisper to the other two, "So far, it is only politician-speak," before someone shushed him.

Wysoczanski picked up steam. "The events at Mers-El-Kebir severely damaged relations between Vichy and England, especially here in French North Africa. There are only two reminders of Britain here now, one of which is us. The other is the few personnel at the British embassy and its consulates here and in Marrakesh. I have been informed that after the attack on Dakar, they are being named persona non grata. A ship, the *City of Nagpur*, is arriving in two days to evacuate them."

All the men, including Christophe, 'Paul,' and Ian standing together at the back, wondered how the expulsion of a few British diplomats meant anything.

"The *City of Nagpur* is a fortified passenger ship with room for almost four hundred. The British consul informs me that they will require no more than forty berths, and he has offered us the remaining places. Passage to England on condition that on arrival, each man reports to the Free Polish Army. On your behalf I accepted!"

Amid the cheers, Ian did the arithmetic. After desertions, and an unfortunate handful of deaths, 360 slots meant about a forty percent chance for any man, but only a one in fifteen chance that all three would be selected.

Someone finally asked the question.

"Who, Major? Who goes?"

Wysoczanski looked toward the questioner. "Not me, Bogdan. I am staying, as will Captain Zysnewski and half the other officers, to lead those who remain and to find other means to get them to England. Anyone who wants to volunteer can join us. This will still mean more who want to go to England than there is space for so we will hold a lottery tonight. Those picked will need to get ready, the boat leaves the day after tomorrow."

Right after dinner, tables appeared at one end of the room, where four officers sat to write the names on slips of paper. Four lines of lottery registrants spontaneously formed. Ian put himself into the back of one of them. He hoped this would give him enough time to consider the options, but as always seemed to now be the case, minimal information was available with which to choose a potentially critical path. What would happen in the camp once almost half the men were gone, and what exactly would those who remained be doing? On the other side, the newspapers at the brothers' shop reported almost daily about German U-boats sinking Allied ships. Was there going to be warship escort? And if only his name was chosen, could he leave Christophe again, and what about 'Paul,' who had his own need to avoid the threat of discovery? But the tide of men moved him steadily forward until he stood in front of the table and saw Christophe and 'Paul' near the front of the other lines. He gave his name and returned to the back of the room to await whatever came next, confused at his confusion.

They put all the names into the pot used to make the fish head stew they ate on Fridays and the process of pulling out a strip of paper and reading it out loud began. An officer recorded each name in a book, the cast list for the next act of their lives. Each of the first few dozen sparked applause or happy shouts and congratulations. One of these was Christophe's, and Ian and 'Paul' celebrated with him, but as the number of names called approached and passed the halfway point, the room quieted, everyone straining to be sure they did not miss their own name, so 'Ian Ciszek' came clear as a bell.

At the end, the Major stood on a chair again. "Those of you selected, one small bag only and be ready to move at eighteen hundred hours tomorrow. You'll go to a staging area near the harbor and board the City boat later in the evening. God willing, you will be in England and joining your units within the fortnight. For those who volunteered to stay or whose names were not selected, do not be disheartened. We will find ways to fight from here, and we'll look for other opportunities to repatriate you to England."

There was no singing this time, only a segregation of winners to their barracks and bunks, and losers to quieter, darker spaces that reflected their moods. Christophe strode ahead, while Ian hung back to walk next to 'Paul' in the warm night. Ian could not find words that fit.

'Paul' did. "Fate seems to have been kind to you, for a change. Your guardian angel is clearly far more effective than mine." The tone was rueful.

"What about the boat? That might be a better option, for you and me. Then I could give my spot to someone else," Ian suggested.

'Paul' stopped walking. He put his large hand on Ian's thin arm, to turn him so they faced each other, and with the weak light from the lamppost by the front gate, looked into his face.

"We were put together by happenstance, and through our travels I have discovered that you are a good man, Ian. That may not only be an anomaly in these times, it may be dangerous. I worry you will be far more deeply hurt by this world than one who is either too naïve," he said, jerking his head toward Christophe's back, "or too cynical, like me." He smiled, then continued. "But it was happenstance, and it appears that happenstance leads us to part. Our time together should have taught you one thing, my young engineer, that in the current state, we are given little control in how our lives play out. Maybe we never really have control, maybe it is more accurate to say that the illusion of control is erased now. Whatever the case, you must take the opportunity that is being offered to you, the chance that one day you will see your family again. You and I only owe what we freely choose to bestow on each other. When we met in Zemmour's yard, the best we could hope is that we would not hinder our individual journeys. Instead, I have been a grateful recipient of your multiple kindnesses, Ian." He started to walk again. "Now, it is time for you to look out for our young friend here, and for me to go on my own path."

'Paul' was gone when Ian awoke in the morning, probably still trying to find a way out of Casablanca. There was no reason for Christophe and Ian to go to the *souk*. They spent the morning selecting what to pack, then repacking. It happened to be a mail day. Ian wrote one last letter that might get through.

Dear Father,

Since I last wrote, only one thing has changed. We are leaving Casablanca, hoping to reach England. If I were home, you might ask me to calculate the shortest distance, curved or straight-line, and I promise I would not complain. I understand now that this was your language, your vocabulary. This I have written to Daniel, and I hope he gets my letter and he sees this too, so that you and he can speak again. He loves you and I know you love him.

To be truthful, two things have changed. That other thing is me. How anyone could not be changed by the loss of the map their mind uses to navigate their life is beyond my comprehension. Or from seeing horrible things or being terrified.

I mentioned in a previous letter that Christophe is here with me, and I am sure you wouldn't even recognize him. He is still not a genius, but he isn't Paul's pet dog, or, since Paul was killed, mine.

There is one other person I should mention. Since leaving Paris, so long ago now, I have traveled with an Alsatian, an older man. I will tell you all about him when we are together again. For now, I am not sure I would be here, able to write to you, if it were not for him. You and Daniel will be relieved to know that I no longer hero worship anyone, like you used to worry about. He is complicated, and there are parts he does not reveal, so I see him as a normal three-dimensional man.

The sea voyages in the books I read, Robinson Crusoe, Robert Louis Stevenson, Conrad, even Tarzan of the Apes, often did not end well, but it appears that there are no choices anymore. I am off to sea and whatever happens.

What keeps me moving, however frightened or confused I might be, is the overwhelming desire to see you once more.

All my love,

Ian

He presented the envelope and stamp money to the postman. That left only one more task. In the midafternoon heat, when foot traffic was at its lowest, he and Christophe headed out to the stone wall to retrieve Christophe's money, only to find it gone.

Ian sat in the meager shade of the wall as Christophe kicked stones, walking in tight circles, and cursing. "Over ten thousand francs! God damn it. It was your friend, it had to be. What's his name? It's not Paul! Claude? He's the only one who knew it was there besides you and me!"

"It might be someone else, some local," Ian ventured, even if he did not believe it. "Maybe he needed it to get the boat."

"Sorry, that doesn't work. The only way that it was for a boat was if it was for the three of us, and you and I don't need it now. So that makes him a thief, a goddamn thief of my money."

"Who's a thief?" The accused was suddenly there, smiling from one to the other, holding a fat roll of francs in his hand. "I am sorry, I thought I could put it back before you came for it. As you can see, I am not a thief." He peeled off bills and offered them to Christophe. The young man grunted his acceptance, and Ian felt relief that his last impression of the man would not be tainted.

"Did you get a boat?" he asked 'Paul' as they walked back to camp.

"No, but I'll meet you in a half hour with what I hope is good news," his companion answered. No more information could be pried from him.

Almost thirty minutes later, 'Paul' walked into their barracks and sat down on the cot next to Ian. "I am going with you," he announced, quietly.

"What? How?" Ian asked.

"A small confession. I used Christophe's money at a gaming room the brothers told me about, near their shop. Had some luck, too. After I gave Christophe his money back, I had almost forty thousand francs, and with that I have purchased passage from one of the other men. I am now Jerzy Dubinski, my fourth identity, but I will only need it until we get to England. The British will not mind if I join de Gaulle instead of Sikorski."

Ian was pleased. "We continue on our journey together!"

"So it seems. Today we are in this camp, tomorrow we are to be on a ship, and after that, who knows?"

Ian — Casablanca, South Atlantic, 28 October–10 November 1940

Up the forward gangplank of the *City of Nagpur* went the British evacuees — diplomats and clerks with their wives and children — while the Poles marched smartly up the aft one and into cramped cabins and berths. The impatience of the French authorities standing on the dock was as palpable as the morning heat.

With just half a hundred left, including Ian, Christophe, and 'Paul,' who was now 'Jerzy,' the line suddenly halted. Word came back that there had been a miscalculation, that there was no more space. A ship's officer tried to order them, in English, to turn around and disembark, but all refused to budge. The appearance of additional sailors only increased the tension, until Major Wysoczanski squeezed past and after a few minutes parley with the officer, he ordered the men to proceed through a different set of stairs and into a hold that normally housed luggage or cargo, right next to the engine room, based on the constant thrumming. Four silent Indian ordinary seamen dumped mattresses, blankets, and tarps at the entrance, which the men turned into walls, beds, berths. An area near the door provided common space. The bathroom was up a level, to be used at will. Going outside was forbidden for now.

"How soon will we get the convoy escort?" Christophe asked, after the three claimed their space against a wall opposite the entrance and common area.

"Not long, I imagine," 'Jerzy' answered. "Hours, at most a day."

The others arranged themselves around the hold. A few, perhaps with shipboard experience, had brought playing cards or dice. Well-read books occupied others. Most lay and dozed. Within the metal walls, it was impossible to sense the rhythm of the day, except by assuming food delivery coincided with mealtimes.

"Shouldn't we be allowed on deck by now?" Christophe complained intermittently.

Soon after the fifth meal, a uniformed Brit appeared, with one of Wysoczanski's officers.

"We have received a change of orders." The translation elicited a groan.

"We are directed south to pick up diplomats and civilians from The Gambia and Sierra Leone. Bathurst and Freetown. We will have no escort but there are no reports of German Navy activity in the area." Translation, followed by, "We will need to spend a few days in Freetown, to await some personnel and to load fuel and supplies. In the meantime, you may go up on deck for short periods, only at night. No lights, cup your cigarettes!"

Christophe was the only man in the hold not disappointed. "Isn't Sierra Leone where Tarzan was born?" he asked Ian, to whom he deferred for anything Tarzan. It did not matter that Ian said Burroughs never specified the exact location of the birthplace, that it could have been Sierra Leone was enough for Christophe. Ian's concern was whether new British passengers meant moving to worse quarters, or even leaving the ship.

'Jerzy's' reaction was "Fools!" He didn't care what the officer said. Longer exposure to U-boats and Kriegsmarine surface ships on a barely armed passenger boat merely to pick up a few inconvenienced Brits made no sense to him. As Ian grew alarmed at this analysis, though, the older man's face recomposed, and he lay back on his mattress, eyes closed, his lips still moving occasionally. He stayed like that when Ian and Christophe went up for an hour to partake in some fresh air. The lack of moon or stars made it too dark to see any beaches bordered by thick jungle, let alone the remains of a cabin. Ian didn't tell Christophe that they might be miles off the coast.

They were not permitted to step off onto The Gambia after docking in Bathurst five long days later. Asserting his naval experience, 'Jerzy' claimed it was because of the brief nature of the stop. Instead, Ian and Christophe spent the hours leaning on the rail inspecting Bathurst. A customs office and some other government-looking buildings fronted the harbor, the few gun placements pointed out to sea or up to the sky. Several church spires and two minarets rose above the town beyond. No signs of jungle. The only novel sight were all the black faces looking up at them. They'd only seen Negroes before this in movies like *Showboat* and *Tarzan*, singing or ineffectually throwing spears.

The next morning, steaming south and twelve hours out of Bathurst, a crew-member let Christophe look through his binoculars to what he said was Senegal. The young Pole swore he saw deep green trees and a white beach, and no one even attempted to convince him that it wasn't where Tarzan was born. Something about Christophe's joyful obsession and its disconnection from their reality appealed to the men.

It took two more days before they felt the engine noises deepen, sparking hope that Freetown was near. When Ian could finally take Christophe up on deck to look for more jungles, they found the *City of Nagpur*, surrounded by British Navy ships, easing into a berth like a young child nestling into their mother's breasts, weightless and buoyed and impervious to harm.

All of the men from what was now a dank and smelly space accepted the opportunity to leave the boat, even if it was too hot to do more than look for shade, except for 'Jerzy.'

"I am not feeling well enough. Probably from the sea voyage. I will just slow you down," he said.

Ian told Christophe to meet him by the gangplank, and when they were alone, he said to 'Jerzy,' "I have been thinking about the money you won with Christophe's stake,"

"What about it?"

"Was there anything left after you paid for your passage? I mean, one could argue that it belongs to Christophe," Ian said

"Interesting question. Who profits if there are winnings, the gambler for his skill, or the investor who put up the stake?" 'Jerzy' said.

"That presumes the gambler wins solely by skill and never by luck," Ian replied. He chose not to point out that there was no true investor here. "But if there is anything left, Christophe could use it to buy something to remember his jungle," Ian said.

"I wish there were, I would gladly return it. Sorry. Look, I am not proud of what I did, but what choice did I have? Remaining in the camp, maybe being sent back to France, you had the same fears. You might have taken the money if it had been you who'd lost the lottery." He stopped, sensing he might have gone too far. "Ian. It is our circumstances. It is always our circumstances."

Ian and Christophe delighted in walking on ground that did not pitch and roll. Their empty pockets simplified their choices and they quickly passed through the busy commercial center behind the harbor. A few streets away, nice homes sat behind lawns being carefully tended by black men, notwithstanding that the owners of many were either already gone, or due to depart on the *City of Nagpur*. On the other side of a wide boulevard came a neighborhood of bars and dance halls, open at this hour mainly to clean up and air out from the night before, then one filled with houses and shacks obviously meant for the workers and their families, populated by old black men, half-naked children, and wives peeking out from darkened doorways. Finally, Ian and Christophe crossed over a small river along which women were doing laundry and on the other side, they entered into a green tunnel. Ian slowed his pace to allow Christophe to move a few meters ahead on his own. Suddenly, Christophe made a ninety-degree turn and was swallowed up by ferns and bushes, vines, and tree trunks from which spouted an umbrella of leaves, by insects and bird calls, by the smell of verdancy and of decay. Christophe stopped, his eyes closed, his arms stretched out, as if he knew this would be his only time, and by maximizing the surface area through which he could absorb it all, he would remember more. Ian stood off near the road, his senses screaming alarms in this alien environment. He waited until he guessed Christophe was full. With regret, he finally tapped Christophe on the shoulder to tell him it was time to leave the jungle and the ghost of Tarzan, to go back to the ship.

'Jerzy' must have recovered and gone somewhere himself because he appeared, breathless, just in time for the curfew, and went straight to the meal line, avoiding Ian's questions about his health and Christophe's excited reportage about all he had seen. Everyone was excited; there were fresh vegetables and fruit, and cake for dessert.

The first two days in port saw new supplies come on board, along with a few first-class passengers, and then there was nothing. The Polish officers ordered calisthenics and clean-ups, but each afternoon, the men could go ashore, and Christophe led Ian to his jungle. 'Jerzy' stayed on board, saying too much green made him ill. Rumors bubbled up and faded like the tides. They were waiting for a waxing moon, they were waiting for a convoy to form, or for escort ships. On the fifth morning, the three were up on deck when a small convoy of large cars pulled up to the forward gangplank and disgorged a distinguished, clearly senior, British officer along with his young wife and their child. Black men carrying luggage followed them up to the ship.

"Now we will be underway," 'Jerzy' guessed, and he was right. The ship's horn sounded several times and a couple of hours later, after confirming all were aboard, the *City of Nagpur* pulled away from Freetown and into the Atlantic, out of sight of the coastline, and before nightfall, turned to starboard to begin picking its way across the five thousand kilometers to England.

Time on deck was no longer permitted during daylight, which meant it was back to living in a steel-enclosed airless hot space. The men reversed their day-night cycle, trying to sleep as best they could during the hottest part of the day, then spending as much time as possible out in the sea air after dark. Inside, they configured themselves to create as much distance between heated bodies as possible. At night, the deep darkness made each man feel like an island, if he chose to be alone and think about what they had left behind in Poland: mothers and fathers, sisters, brothers, wives and lovers, children, and friends. Others thought of the future, of fighting again. Underlying all was the constant fact of water. They saw it only in the phosphorescent waves thrown off by the ship and yet it was the overwhelming presence. They felt surrounded by it, on it but also under it, floating within it and sensing its salinity and tides and currents and buoyancy and, most especially, its slow gravity pulling them languorously downward no matter whether they struggled or not. They were several hundred comrades on a ship and yet those first nights, they could not help feeling alone on and in the liquid vastness.

On the third night, one man broke the silence. "Hey, how come we can't see any other ships?"

"Maybe they are not supposed to have any lights on, like we aren't allowed to smoke out in the open," another answered.

"But we have a few lights," pointed out a third, referring to the small blue bulbs on the mast and elsewhere. Fear levels rose several notches.

Those who'd heard the rumors in Freetown now shared the information that, in the last four months, a half dozen ships running for England from West Africa had been lost, sunk by U-boats, some in convoys, some not. It made them feel even more vulnerable.

"What does it mean, that we are not in a convoy?" Christophe asked Ian.

"Probably nothing," Ian answered. "You remember the maps of the world that hung on the walls of Mr. Wadislawa's classroom, how much was blue? Well, think about it, our ship would not even be a speck of fly shit on that map, we are so tiny. The chance a U-boat finds us is as low as the chance that I ever got kissed by Renata Dobrowski." Christophe laughed at the idea that the prettiest girl in their school ever even noticed Ian. They stayed at the starboard rail, watching in the dark for ships, periscopes, porpoises, mermaids, or the edge of the jungle on the horizon, until an English officer shooed them down to their hold.

"Anything new?" 'Jerzy' asked them when they got to their little encampment.

Christophe said. "Still nothing but water." The other two laughed.

"What have you been doing?" Ian asked 'Jerzy.' He rarely went out with them. In his little kit bag, he kept a Bible, and he spent hours silently reading it now. Conversations were rare. Ian was content to give him room, assuming that after running, hiding, changing identities and God knows what else, he now had time to rest, recuperate, and to seek solace from that book, it was not all random, that between that and whatever one chose to do did have impact on what happened next. Ian was trying to do the same and failing. He wished he'd not grown up so fiercely secular, so he could find the answers he sought in 'Jerzy's' book. Or be like Christophe, asking no questions. Either one would definitely make it easier.

Ian — South Atlantic, 11 November 1940

By the fourth night, even 'Jerzy' required some time out of the hold. Ian found him near the stern on the port side, looking out into the darkness where the interface between Earth and sky was supposed to be. 'Jerzy' turned around, and they sat down on the deck. Ian accepted a cigarette from his friend.

'Jerzy' sighed. "My body is so confused; when is it day, when is it time to sleep? Naps reduce the fatigue and pass the time, but I think they add to the confusion. I worry that I will not know to answer to Jerzy."

They were each aware of the boat under them, the railing at their back, and the infinite vastness all around them. Perhaps in response, 'Jerzy' moved his kit bag to the other side and inched close enough to Ian to reinforce that they were not alone, and they sat and listened to the rumble of the screws propelling the *City of Nagpur* through the moonless night.

"Never liked sea voyages. Brings back too many bad memories," 'Jerzy' said. Ian waited, sensing there was more.

"I never really met a Jew before, you know," unexpectedly came next, to which Ian reflexively tensed. "The brothers who taught me as a boy, and the priests in the seminary, they made that a good thing. Never meeting a Christ killer, a usurer, a parasite, I mean."

"So, what do you think now?" Ian ventured, carefully.

"Oh Ian, even at that age I knew they were fools. They believed the poisoned thoughts they were taught. Unlike you, I am not an empiricist. That's incompatible with the priesthood, for sure. But things must make sense. What they said made none. Plus, the Jesus I fell in love with was the inclusive Jesus, the one who welcomed everyone, leper and beggar first, not the one claimed by one group in order to exclude others. And you, my young friend, have provided the definitive proof that my instincts were correct. Thank you." 'Jerzy' inclined his head in Ian's direction.

"I am not the best example by which you should define a Jew. My father says there are four kinds of Jews in Poland. The traditional religious ones, mostly in the *shtetls*, the Communists, the Zionists, and the super Poles who assimilate. We were assimilators," Ian explained. Silence ensued again.

"Can I ask you something," Ian said.

"Sure."

"You've been reading your Bible a lot since we left Casablanca, and… Well, why did you want to become a priest?" He silently berated himself for his childish impertinence. "Not that it matters. I mean, it's your business."

"My mother so much wanted me to become one. My teachers believed that I should go to seminary."

"What happened?"

"Would that it was so simple — a tale of horrors witnessed in the trenches prompting me to question everything — except I never saw a trench, or even a significant battle. When I joined the Kaiserliche Marine, my faith was strong, including a belief that whatever I did not yet understand would be cured by more study, more faith, and that one day, His blueprints would reveal themselves to me."

"What happened?" Ian asked again.

"Nothing, not right away. Kiel was a bomb but with a very delayed fuse. Kiel was a few officers almost sacrificing thousands of men for the vanity of their supposed honor, but the question — how could God endorse that? — it didn't crystallize for me until much later. When I was demobilized, I went back home, my mother hugged me. The old priests, after they made sure I was uncontaminated by Communist thought, began to plan my life again. I let them, had no reason not to at the time. But I couldn't help wondering how, and then why, God adjusts the trajectory of the shell fired from a battleship so that one passes overhead, and another blows a thousand men into pieces. Or, in my case, how hundreds of bullets fired into a mob, one finds my neighbor, and not me." He paused, seeming exhausted.

"What did you conclude?" Ian asked.

"I am still searching for the answer. Hence," he pulled the Bible from the kit bag next to him and held it, with respect if not reverence. "I wish I were you, Ian, with twenty more years to figure it out. I think you are far more likely to get to your answer, where I will never have anything except questions. A disappointment to many."

"No!" objected Ian.

'Jerzy' smiled in response. "Maybe we can continue this discussion later. Here, I saved two cigarettes. Take one. Let's try and meet up on the deck tomorrow night for a smoke." He put his Bible back and walked off toward their sleeping quarters. After a few minutes, Ian followed.

Time passed like water from a slightly leaky faucet. Each minute was a drop that formed and hung there, growing large and heavy until it couldn't bear it anymore and fell, followed by an identical drop and another. Men got up or lay back down. They reread the last letters received from a home that was a couple of oceans and a continent away, from a country that existed only in belief. A foursome played cards at the edge of the common area using nails as counters. Even the evening meal was insufficient to break the mood.

"How long before we reach England?" Christophe asked again and accepted the same answer. "It'll be good. We weren't in the Army for very long, Paul and me," he continued. "But it was good, it made sense, you know…"

He stopped mid-sentence. A junior British officer was at the door, saying something in a strangled voice, full of urgency but not volume.

"Stop! We must be quiet. No one move!" The Polish translation came, clear and equally urgent.

"The engines!" Christophe said.

"Shhh," Ian hissed at him, but he noticed too. The engines had stopped.

A whisper began at the door and spread like the ripple from a pebble tossed into a pond. A burly man next to Ian leaned over and with his unwashed breath, softly said, "They think they see a periscope. Not sure if it's one of ours or theirs, or even French."

The drop now hung there, fat and full and refusing to fall, because it would make a loud 'plop!' when it did. It hung, growing bigger and bigger, as the men waited for an order, for an action, for an explosion, and the tension from fear was replaced by the tension of waiting. It only broke when the engines restarted, and a seaman announced that it was likely nothing, that they would rendezvous with their convoy in twenty hours.

"What do you think it was?" asked Christophe.

"You know as much as I do," replied Ian. "Someone thought they saw a submarine. They weren't sure, though, and if there was one, which Navy did it belong to?"

"Could it be British?"

"Probably was, since we weren't blown up. If there even was one."

Deck access was pushed back to after 2100 hours, so Ian and 'Jerzy' stayed on their mattresses, and Christophe went to observe a card game. As in probably all the other conversations around the hold, Ian reviewed the few facts with 'Jerzy,' and the speculation, concluding with, "It doesn't sound like much except the fear we all have being here, alone and, for all intents and purposes, defenseless."

"When did they say we would join the convoy?" 'Jerzy' asked.

"They said twenty hours."

'Jerzy' grunted and turned on his side, spooning his Bible bag, and falling asleep — an indication of how little he thought about the whole thing.

Ian woke later, unsure how long he'd slept. Christophe was snoring gently on one side, but 'Jerzy' was not there. Ian found his cigarette and carefully made his way through the other sleepers to the stairs and up to the deck. Moonlight diffusing through low clouds was still insufficient for Ian to see 'Jerzy' until he almost ran into him at their usual spot.

"Ian! I am glad you woke up and came to join me!"

They sat together and smoked their cigarettes.

Ian spoke. "You know, they expect us to join the army when we arrive?"

"Do you worry about that?" 'Jerzy' asked. "It's normal, to wonder how you will act under fire. That is what training is for, to prepare you. I mean, Christophe was a good soldier after barely a week or two."

"Not to insult Christophe but does that mean that you put your brain in a jar for the duration and retrieve it if you are lucky to survive?" said Ian.

"Some do. Maybe most," 'Jerzy' explained.

"But you... it changed you, eventually."

'Jerzy' spoke deliberately, directing his speech more to the night than to Ian.

"I tried. I entered seminary in Metz prepared to give my thoughts and love to God in all of His magnificence, as I told my teachers and my mother. It gave her such pride, in our little town, her son becoming a priest. My name, by the way, was Hermann Bloch at that time, the name I was born with. But I left after four years, and the shame of it meant I couldn't go home and face her disappointment. Instead, I spent some time traveling around France, eastern Germany and Switzerland, tutoring and guiding tourists. Finally, I found a position as a teacher at a school in Fougerolles. It was far from where anyone knew me, with hills and forests through which to walk and ponder. It was a good life, teaching the boys philosophy, religion, sometimes even mathematics and science when there was a need. My mother still believes I am a priest on a mission in Africa. Every few months I sent her a letter that appeared as if it is passed on by my superiors in France."

Ian recognized when his friend needed a few seconds to collect his thoughts, but the prolonged silence made him wonder if the story was over. Finally, right before Ian prepared, out of kindness, to change the subject, 'Jerzy' began again.

"Even little Fougerolles could not hide from the world as this war began. The older boys wanted to go off and fight, but the little ones were scared and sometimes, at night, their fears and nightmares became unbearable and the whole dormitory was crying. I moved my bed into the junior room to show them by my presence that it was still safe."

Another inordinate pause, as if 'Jerzy' needed to chew a hundred times whatever he was trying to swallow.

"A few of the boys would still get nightmares, and the first time I let one, a little fellow named Maurice, into my bed, I only comforted him." He searched for the right words, then said, simply, "But it didn't stop there."

The rest came in a rush. "One of the boys told the headmaster. I was arrested, taken to jail, and if I'd had the courage, I'd have killed myself, one mortal sin to pay for another. Instead, I have to live with myself, with what I did and what I could not do. They gave me a one-way ticket to Paris in exchange for a promise to never teach boys again, which I had already resolved. The school, the order, they did not want the publicity. But once the Germans captured Fougerolles, I feared that they would review the local records, as they do, then go searching for me. I knew that Zemmour sold new identities and I purchased Yves Lachance, which is where I met you."

Ian did not know what to say. They sat for a while.

"Do you know what I wish?" 'Jerzy' asked. "I wish I could put myself over the railing and into the fate I deserve. You worry about how you will behave in the army. I already know."

"You can't be sure," Ian argued. "You... doesn't your Jesus preach forgiveness? What about redemption?"

"How? I cannot smartly march home in uniform to my mother one day. To her I have been a priest all these years. Her disappointment in me would only deepen. I can picture the shame in her face; it tortures me every day."

Ian heard soft sobs and reached over to put his arm around 'Jerzy,' acutely aware of how much he owed the older man for Tours, Bordeaux, Marseille and Casablanca, which at this moment outweighed what he'd just confessed to.

"Thank you, Ian." 'Jerzy' recomposed himself. "I had to tell someone, or I had to tell everyone, you know what I mean? And I needed to have you see the real me, a very flawed human being."

"I am learning that everyone is, to one degree or other," said Ian. Was this the time to tell about the truck driver? No, he decided. Not yet.

"But this is monstrous. This makes me a Hitler."

"Not even close," Ian said. "It does explain why you have been so distant recently. I was beginning to worry that it was something I said or did." He stood up to guide his friend back to where they would try and sleep.

Daniel — Kenada, Khabarovsk Krai, 12–13 November 1940

The pleasures of spending every night in the village came with only one caveat: he had to be at the camp in time for roll call. During one of the blinding snowstorms whistling through from the North with depressing frequency, he could easily lose his way as the road became obliterated and the trees lining each side invisible. It had happened to others. He left Nadhya's bed earlier on these mornings, before the sun came up, because while daylight would not help, extra time to carefully navigate his way might. It saved him the one morning he overshot the camp by a hundred meters or so.

But for this one inconvenience, he reminded himself, he looked and lived as close to a free man in Siberia as a prisoner could hope to. He also admitted that a portion of his stature within the camp came from the shadow that Nadhya cast, from the recognition of how important she was to the success of the tunnel project. Over the months working for Rybak, she had acquired the skills needed to find and corral any necessary equipment and tools, using her persuasive abilities to remind bureaucrats that Rybak's goals were those of the Gulag and that if they aligned themselves with her requests, everyone, up to and including Moscow, would be pleased. And if that didn't work, she was excellent at horse-trading.

More personally, years living as a poor student, a prisoner, and an exile in the remotest parts of the Soviet state had taught her how to sew, patch, and scavenge, which meant a warmer coat for Daniel thanks to added quilting from the remains of an old dress she claimed she never wore, and boots with an extra layer of padding between the snow and his newly darned socks. She exploited the capitalist system in the village as if she lived for years in the West. Nothing was given in this remote pimple of a settlement, everything, from a roof to a potato, had a price. No money meant death. A few of the exiled women made theirs on what the guards were willing to pay for companionship or relief. If any of them, in the weak light of a frigid February morning when it felt like winter was permanent, weighed their current sin against the one that clung to your soul if you chose to end it all, trying to decide which would be more likely to consign you to hell, no one knew and no one judged. Nadhya had no need for such thoughts. Rybak had demanded that his assistant receive a salary. It was not enough, of course, but she made it work, finding a way to get a cabbage here, a turnip there, stretching one hundred grams of some kind of meat — it was best not to ask — for days. She traded for salt, pepper, dill, and dried garlic, and to his relief, Daniel found both his ability to taste, and his memory of taste had not atrophied. In the time between when dinner finished and they went to bed, they sat near the fire and read from her valued collection of books. Daniel's ability to read Russian wasn't up to his skill in speaking or swearing, but he understood and appreciated Gogol, for example: "There are occasions when a woman, no matter how weak and impotent in character she may be in comparison with a man, will yet suddenly become not only harder than any man, but even harder than anything and everything in the world."

That first time he and Nadhya made love, he only felt it in his lizard brain, the only part remaining fully operational to address the basic life functions of fight or flight, hunger, fear, breathing. As he watched her undressing, the urge to throw her down onto the bed and mount her from behind overwhelmed him. Afterward, he repeatedly, tearfully, apologized.

"I understand," she said, holding and soothing him. "Sometimes I feel the frustration too, double frustration with having nowhere to express it." When he calmed, she told him, "It can't be the only way we use each other."

There were times where she pushed him onto his back and lowered herself onto him, to use what she needed at that moment, and others where he went from a warm embrace to a rampant bull. With time, though, it was like a dance, of where to put hands or lips or fingers, slow and gentle until, briefly, it was not. Like lights coming on in rooms when someone returns to their long-shuttered home, it became less limbic for him and more complex and cortical. Her warmth enveloped him, spreading from his groin to his belly, down his legs and up to his chest and face, like he was lowering himself into a bath.

On this very snowy morning, the guards also had little desire to stay out in a blizzard and they completed roll call in one pass, giving everyone in the camp office a first reason to smile. Daniel looked at the papers splayed around him on the table representing the problems requiring solutions in order to accomplish the next steps of their tunnel, solvable by logic, math and time. Their direct relation to what he'd studied at university was tenuous and they were so far from what he and Joseph obsessed over and argued about in his previous life as to almost be from another planet, but they gave him something tangible and valuable: a license to his current privileged position. Sometimes, like this morning, it was even more than that. Working with Rybak provided opportunities to feel the satisfaction that comes from completing a task, something men in the brigades cutting down another tree or chipping away another bit of stone could never feel. He was no longer always cold. He was not especially hungry. He felt a human connection to Rybak, and to Nadhya. As he listed, inspected, and turned these over in his mind, he had to remember there were still guards outside the door. This space protecting them from the blizzard had been constructed by slave labor. When they solved the current engineering problem, and then the next one, when all the problems were solved and trains moved through the tunnel, there would be another camp, and he would still be a prisoner thousands of kilometers from where he was meant to be. The reason it didn't matter as much today, he acknowledged, was that there was someone he could share this with, proving that what had been slowly destroying him was the paradox of being alone amongst thousands.

Embers from these thoughts lingered as he and Nadhya sat together in the evening, Nadhya mending something with quick, economical movements, Daniel concentrated on a slim volume he'd picked from her shelf called The Fate of Russia by Nikolai Alexandrovich Berdyaev. He read and reread a passage before sharing it aloud with Nadhya, "The Russian soul is stifled by the boundless fields and the boundless Russian snow, it sinks and dissolves in this boundlessness."

"Do you think that's true?" he asked her.

"I don't know. Maybe, but I think not. We are here, in the quintessential Russian vastness, and I still write. One day, I believe, you will draw again," she answered.

Daniel put the book down. "Doesn't it bother you that whatever you write will likely never be published, or maybe even read?" He pointed to the twenty or more notebooks on the shelf above her table. "I have not thought seriously about Functional Humanism since… since I don't remember. I would be angry that I will never complete my manifesto, if I remembered more of it."

Her green eyes looked directly into his blue ones. "Art cannot ignore that there is a war on in the west. We have both been in far worse circumstances, and that might happen again, and what's more, we are powerless to change where we are. But I would like to think that, in our small way, we have done something miraculous here. We have created something, which is also art, and in a place where it is virtually impossible, even criminal. I know you heard the stories about me. In previous camps I had others, I am not proud of that, not ashamed either, but they were utilitarian. This is different, Daniel. For me, at least." Her look challenged him.

She was right, and he did not hesitate to tell her. Misery was no longer his only state of being. He was grateful for sharing her bed, for her companionship, for someone to care about, for someone who cared. The Gulag was still there, but not as overwhelmingly. They kissed with that care, then more passionately, and then made love. Nadhya fell asleep, as did Daniel, after repeatedly reminding himself that his future was beyond his vision or control, and he had to accept it.

Kenada, 13 November 1940

Dear Ian,

I write often to Father but haven't received anything back. I fear the worst, he was not the most practical man, and in a world reduced to the most basic functions, the skills of a mathematics teacher may not have been enough. You must find it funny that I worry about him so. It surprises me too.

You were younger, and in the West, when the crack to Hell opened, so my hopes that you are somewhere safe are stronger. Given the current situation, the chance that this letter gets to France, let alone finds you there, are as remote as anything these days. That I am not just sending this letter out the door to be picked up by the wind howling outside shows that I haven't given up on civilization either, I suppose. Or that I am crazy!

My health is better now, and my work for the State is rewarding. (Hello censors!) Tomorrow, it is likely to snow again, and over the next few months there will be days colder than we ever experienced at home. But there is a tomorrow, and maybe with enough of them, we will see each other again. That is a thought that comes to me and comforts me every day.

Stay alive, please, so I can keep dreaming of something better.

Love,

Your brother, Daniel

Ian — South Atlantic, 14–15 November 1940

BLAAAH-BLAAAH-BLAAAH!

The klaxon jolted them all awake. Everyone tried to source the origin, then go the other way to safety, except the metal walls reflected the sound all around the hold. An alarm this dramatic must signal a serious threat. Christophe put his hands over his ears. Engine noise ratcheted up as they felt the floor tilt, indicating a hard turn. Sound and proprioception as their only data sources only added to their anxiety.

Unaware they were holding their breath, the men in the hold surprised themselves when they collectively exhaled as the door opened, but it was only 'Jerzy,' embarrassed that everyone saw him returning from the bathroom and murmuring his apologies as he weaved his way toward the back. But as he passed a burly artillery mechanic, the man turned, and his arm sent the kit bag skittering onto the floor. Friction slowed the progress of the canvas bag, as momentum propelled the Bible out a good two meters, followed by what many recognized as a crystal radio set. No one moved.

"Submarine!" came a shout from someone at the door.

The word triggered two men to dive down and retrieve the radio. The big mechanic's hands gripping his shoulders pulled 'Jerzy' back into a suffocating hug. The commotion brought two officers over to find out what was more important than a submarine finding their ship in the middle of the immeasurable sea.

Men brought Ian and Christophe to where others held 'Jerzy' and presented them, together with the bag, Bible, and the radio to the officers. Above the klaxon bray, one yelled, "He must have signaled the submarine!" followed by cries of, "He is a spy!" and "They are spies!" and, eventually, "Kill them!" because that is what happens when fear infects a crowd.

"Stop! Bring them with me!" the senior man shouted and marched to the common space near the door, confident that what he commanded would happen. Mortal danger from a U-boat, or from a pack of them, had no effect on the murderous stares aimed at Ian, Christophe, and 'Jerzy.'

Now four officers scrummed off to one side, as the floor tilted in the other direction, then back again a few minutes later, like the ship was a porch swing swaying in the breeze and not a seal trying to escape a killer whale. Someone produced rope, and the three bound men were dropped into sitting positions in the center of the common area. Ian wondered if a torpedo would solve this problem that he could not understand. What was 'Jerzy' doing with a radio and where did it come from? Meanwhile, 'Jerzy' sat with his eyes down, and his skin was as pale as possible for a person whose heart was still pumping blood.

The klaxon stopped, even as the ringing in their ears continued, but it was another half an hour or so before Major Wysoczanski appeared.

"A U-boat, it fired two torpedoes, which missed, and we have somehow broken contact with it. That is all we know. But the Captain has decided to make for the convoy much faster. We should be at the rendezvous point in six hours."

It still meant hours of lethal vulnerability. No one seemed relieved. The focus returned to the three accused spies.

Christophe looked around, not understanding why he was tied up. 'Jerzy' now appeared to be praying. The junior officers stepped forward to explain the facts, without speculation or accusation. They handed over the radio.

The Major stood in front of Christophe first, holding the papers taken from the young man's pockets while focusing on his face. Christophe looked back, blinking. After a while, the officer moved to Ian for a shorter stare, and then to 'Jerzy,' who still would not look up.

"Jerzy Dubinski, from Lodz, 4th Division?" Wysoczanski asked him.

The prisoner did not respond. The Major repeated the name louder, when someone shouted, "That's not Jerzy Dubinski!"

"Who are you?" The Major demanded. 'Jerzy' stared back at him. The question was repeated, first in English, then in French. "*Etes-vous* Jerzy Dubinski?"

"Ah, yes, Jerzy," the man finally spoke. "That's my last name."

"Your last name? What is your first?"

"No, Major, I mean that has been the most recent name I used. It was not the one I was given at my baptism."

"And what was that?"

Jerzy/not Jerzy looked over at Ian, blankly. "It was Hermann Bloch. Then, for a while it was Markus Frederic, then back to Hermann Bloch, followed by Claude Avigot, then recently it was Yves Lachance, then Paul Sebak and now it is this Jerzy Dubinski."

The Major picked up the radio and put it in front of the man Ian thought he knew. "What is the meaning of this?"

'Jerzy' took a deep sigh. "First, Major, and this is a truth I swear before Jesus, Mary, and Almighty God. I alone am responsible for this. Neither of these two knew anything about it. They are completely and utterly blameless." He paused to look directly at the Major.

"That I am someone who deserves whatever fate you consign me to, this became clear well before now. I won't burden you with the details, but the presence of this radio stems from something I did elsewhere several years ago, and had I your courage, Major, I should have ended the matter right then. Except I didn't. I escaped, both the consequences and myself. But after the invasion of France in May, exposure and worse became a possibility. I ended up buying a new identity, Yves Lachance, which is where I met Ian here. He knew nothing about me except I was a fellow runaway before the Germans arrived to Paris. When we got to Toulouse, I took over the papers of their friend, Paul Sebak, who'd died a few weeks before, thanks to the unknowing kindness of this other young man." He pointed to Christophe.

The Major appeared skeptical. The prisoner hurried on.

"The radio came to me in Freetown. The agent, he called himself Frank, he told me that they needed to locate the convoy we would be joining because there was someone important on another ship. He gave me the radio, instructed me to send a signal each night, and a code for when we joined the convoy."

"Were you contemplating suicide?" asked the Major. "Why did they torpedo this ship?"

"I have proven incapable of taking my own life, no matter how much I deserve it. No, Frank told me that they were looking for another ship, that they only needed to follow us to locate the convoy."

The Major considered this and went on. "And you sent those signals?"

Hesitation, then confession. "Yes, each night. I did what I was told. They did not attack, so I believed them."

The ones in front who could translated for the ones behind, and as the words rolled outward, a growing wave of anger at the betrayal and at the prospect of being violently cast down into the deep ocean rolled back. Its growth was exponential, pressing the Major toward the trio.

"Traitor!"

"Throw him overboard!"

"Kill him!"

"Major!" Ian shouted as loudly as he could, and miraculously, it worked. Everyone stopped to look at him as he struggled to stand next to the stranger he'd come aboard with.

"What?" the Major demanded.

"We are not on a Polish ship. We are on a British ship, by their good graces. If we do this, on our own, how will they respond? Could they possibly refuse to take us to England?" Ian demanded.

The Major thought about this. "What do you propose?"

"He didn't only put us in danger, he risked the whole ship. Turn him over to the English. They will deal with him by their laws and credit us for respecting their authority."

"He lived among us, wore our uniform," came from another voice.

The Major looked serious. "We can't form a court-martial; he is not a Polish soldier. I agree, we need to give him to the British."

Angry words and shouts followed this decision. Fear appeared to be ready to trample discipline. The Major unbound Ian and Christophe.

"Here, take the radio, go!" he urgently ordered Ian. "Get him out of here, take him to the bridge and report to the English officers what happened."

Ian pushed his former friend, now prisoner, toward the door. Behind them, the Major snapped out orders to regain control. It might have worked except, at that moment the klaxon began again, swallowing his words and adding panic to anger. As soon as they were through the door, the Major shoved it closed, and saved them from the mob.

"Thank you," the multi-named man spoke.

"Shut your fucking mouth! You do not have the right to say anything anymore," Ian snapped.

"You have every reason to be angry."

"Don't be so fucking condescending. Nothing about you is genuine."

"Not true. I never lied to you, Ian."

"I don't believe that." Sailors rushed past them on their way to duty stations, as the two began their journey to the bridge. Ian hoped someone there spoke Polish or French.

"You will be surprised at how our conscience works to preserve our self-delusions. You are still young…"

"You should be grateful that I am not old and jaded, not bothered by what a mob could do to you."

"It's better that the British hang me instead?"

"If that's what their justice decides, yes."

The older man stopped, forcing Ian to do the same, forcing them to face each other across the narrow passageway. "What explains how a policeman from Fougerolles ends up as one in Casablanca? I don't know. Is it fate? Could it be God, finally? He recognized me, of course, and one morning he pulled me in. But he let me go on condition that I come to his office every time I left camp. A few days before we left Casablanca, there was another man there, a German who had with him the records from Fougerolles. The Gestapo man… he told me that my mother was alive. Not only would he make sure that my story would be printed in all the newspapers in Alsace, but they would also arrest her. I think she would die first from finding out that I was never a priest, not even worthy of being a priest, before the Nazis could even take her in, but, God forgive me, she is almost eighty and she is the only human being who ever believed that my soul is redeemable." He looked down at his feet as he went on. "They did not ask me to do anything, only contact a man when we got to Freetown. It all seemed so simple, just keep in touch with them, and we would soon be in England, and I would be free."

"You believed them? Even that they only needed you to find the convoy?" Ian demanded.

"What else could I do? What would you have done?" asked Bloch.

Ian refused to answer and give the man any solace.

Bloch looked back up. "Why did you pull me out, Ian?"

Ian didn't owe any explanation, except to himself. "Gravity. It's a rule, without it everything flies apart. There are rules for our behavior, and we see what happens when they are violated." Was he referring to this moment on the *City of Nagpur*, or to the wider world?

"My hope, Ian, maybe the only thing that I can offer from what remains of my soul, is that we met when you were young enough that the lessons of my life might help you learn how to avoid the traps and temptations that ruin so many of us. You are a *rara avis*, an innocent, but not a fool."

Ian's fury felt uncontainable. "Damn you and your fucking condescension. I am sorry we ever spent a minute together, that I was there for you to feel superior to because you thought you were some sort of fallen angel." He pressed on. "You are not a fallen angel, just another corrupt… man. And for your information, that money you used, Christophe's and mine. We robbed a truck to get it, and we killed the driver. No one is innocent, you bastard!"

Ian grabbed Bloch's shoulder and turned him towards the stairway, adding a shove to end the talk and get him moving up the passageway. At that moment, Christophe stepped from a connecting hallway to block them. Ian saw only his face, Bloch's body hiding the knife Christophe held, and the thrust that went deep into Bloch's upper abdomen. He only saw Bloch straighten up abruptly, before collapsing to the deck with the knife handle centered on a rapidly growing pool of blood. Christophe stood, his feet a little apart, like a prize-fighter over the opponent he'd knocked out.

Ian looked from Bloch to Christophe. "Why?" he asked.

"He tried to get us killed. He was working for the enemy."

That was all Christophe would say. Ian bent down to attend to Bloch, but it was too late. He was dead.

Daniel — Kenada, Khabarovsk Krai,
29 September–22 November 1941

His little Pallas's leaf warblers were gone. Ian knew their name because one of the men in the office, Kharnovsky, had not only been a municipal sanitation engineer in his previous life, he'd also been a passionate, albeit amateur, ornithologist. This was what could happen when one worked in the Gulag with men who did not have to guard everything, from a husk of bread to their hopes and fears, or their trust. Each of the men in the camp office were now individuals, with a name and a story, exposed layer by layer over the year. It bore a resemblance to what he remembered of the manifesto he and Joseph had been creating; too many people or too small a space meant competition, with its consequent ugliness, while on the other end of the spectrum, alienation and isolation grew when one felt over-whelmed by spaces like the endless forests of Siberia. A long rectangular office, outfitted with lights, windows and a good stove permitted Kharnovsky to reveal his love of birds, and permitted Daniel, after he arrived early one summer morn-ing, to ask him, "Do you know what bird I see every day? It is not very large, maybe ten centimeters, and it has a yellow strip above its eye and two short yellow slashes on each wing. A pair set up a nest in a pine tree by the road and I think the chicks have hatched because I see the mama and papa bringing grubs and such…"

Kharnovsky rubbed his chin animatedly, not unlike an old professor consider-ing his best response. "It must be a Pallas's leaf warbler. Those wing stripes, it can't be a yellow-browed." He whistled a fast series of melodic notes, which Daniel as-sumed was the appropriate bird call.

So routine was the walk from Nadhya's bed that those warblers could have given directions to their four offspring and left for their winter quarters yesterday or two weeks ago — signs that summer was gone accumulated whether he noticed them or not. When one day varied little from another, perception of one's envi-ronment faded, like a turtle withdrawing its head into its shell. In a new environ-ment, the senses are hyper-alert, but in the same room or on the same path every day, when nothing happens, the senses deaden. That's what he should call himself, he told Nadhya in the evening, after he'd walked back to their cottage in the late dusk, the Gulag Tortoise.

She still had fresh vegetables to serve with the evening meal, with two mouthfuls of meat for him, and one for her. When the sunlight left, they sat under two oil lamps — no one noticed them missing from the tunnel — and read from her copies of Pushkin, Gogol, Turgenev, a Shakespeare translation, and a single loosely bound book by Polevy. Nadhya laughed at his Tortoise idea, a sound he wished he knew better. She reached for the slim notebook she kept next to her bed and wrote something down. He asked, as he regularly did, if she would read some of her work aloud and watched her face, weathered by things she would not share with him, as she reached a decision.

"Within white-washed walls

Splashed with a gift. The flash of a Redwing

Who could not leave with her lover

Sitting on next year's fire, or roof.

Our room, within the white world.

Your pink body next to mine is warm."

The next evening, Nadhya gave him a half smile as she announced she had something for him. Out of the pocket of her apron came a little package tied up with string.

"What is it?" Daniel asked.

"Open it," she answered.

He saved the string and removed the paper to find two new Faber-Castell Polychromos pencils, both blue. He stared at them long enough to make her worry.

"Sorry it's not more."

He didn't understand whether she meant the colors or the number, neither of which mattered. "They are... wonderful."

Their evening routine now evolved. After dinner, he used paper salvaged from the waste bin at the office, along with Nadhya's gift, to draw, while she hunched over her notebook, wrestling with the Russian language to find the exact word her poem demanded. He drew trees, their trunks and branches like sentinels, dense and neutral. With the addition of a little blue shadow, some of them began to appear as individual, unique members of the forest. Secretly, he also sketched her. Later, she read to him, and he showed her his sketches, except the one of her until he was satisfied that it was ready.

They had to change their arrangements when they moved Rybak into their cottage. Through the summer, his cough worsened, his cheeks hollowed, and his skin began to slip from its subdermal attachments. The camp hospital was no choice — everyone knew it was a death house, not a place of healing. After Nadhya pestered and demanded for weeks, the Commandant permitted her to take him to a doctor in Komsomolsk-on-Amur, a ten-hour train journey, where she spent a month's salary to hear that rest and better nutrition might help and they endured a sixteen-hour return after rain washed out a section of track.

The Commandant came to the office more frequently to monitor Rybak's health. He sent over meals from the officer's mess for Rybak, but nothing could change the trajectory. Snow fell, and when Rybak no longer had the strength to walk to the office, he came to live with them. Daniel shuttled back and forth to report and receive instructions, while Nadhya tried to get the old engineer to take some soup or to sit in the weakening sunlight, wrapped in blankets and quilts, as she read to him from her collection.

He passed away in his sleep as a blizzard blasted out its last centimeters of snow. The men in the office refused to allow his body to be added to the cord of corpses, and instead took a pickaxe to the frozen ground to make a proper grave. Daniel was about to take his turn when the chief engineer and the Commandant summoned him back into the office to inform him that he would be taking Rybak's place as the Assistant to the Chief Engineer.

"This will have no effect on the completion of this project. It is far more important than any one man," said the Commandant, addressing the men at the gravesite. After those two left, Daniel attacked the permafrost until his hands bled.

He only walked from cottage to camp and back once each day now. In the morning, he thought of the problems left over from the day before and how they might be addressed, or what reports were due. In the evening dark, exhausted from running to solve crises at the tunnel face, assigning work to the other engineers, refereeing disputes between them, filling out paperwork to satisfy the masters or to requisition essential supplies, and from constantly worrying that he didn't know what he was doing, he only walked. He remembered nothing about that trip.

Before sleep came, Daniel thought about the way the other men looked at him in his new role. They had trusted Rybak completely, but now it was his responsibility to give no one, from the camp administration all the way up to Moscow, any reason to come for an inspection, or to decide it was better for the men in the office to work in the tunnel, or to transfer them to the mines in Kolyma. If that were to happen, he would make sure he was the first to go. None of them, he was certain, questioned his loyalties. He was not a Party man, before or now. What he did was for survival, his and theirs. If he was compromised, they all were. The tunnel was for the war effort, not to support Stalin and his regime, he always told himself. He shook worry along with the snow from his head before he entered the cottage each evening.

Nights were now long, and despite being surrounded by millions of trees, wood was expensive. They cleaned up after dinner and got under the blankets and quilts in the dark. He lay still in the hope she would think him asleep. His mind raced. How many meters left? When might they break through? At their current rate, it could be within the month. And after breakthrough? Railroad engineers might replace the tunnel office men. No matter what, the tunnel would be complete by spring. Then what? The best would be that he became a new Rybak with a softer existence in the Gulag as he transferred from project to project. Next winter, building a bridge across a frozen river. The next winter, sinking a mine to bring in whatever the Soviet state wanted for itself. The next winter something else, the next winter, the next winter. Ten years, that's what the paper said about his sentence, and after that, more winters as one of the 'free' exiles in Siberia, like Nadhya.

He felt her presence under the covers, her breathing regular and deep, sleeping quickly and easily. He knew her worries after five years focused on the price of potatoes. Or whether she could earn extra income by doing secretarial work for the village leader. Did the right people know how indispensable she was to the success of their tunnel?

***

Nadhya lay awake, but she did not worry. Lermentov, Gogol, Dostoevsky, even Tolstoy, all told her that melancholia was a unique feature of the Russian soul, but she knew they were wrong. Koreans, Ukrainians, Germans, Finns, Tatars, Armenians, Poles like the man pretending to sleep next to her, all succumbed to it. Russia was the source, not Russians, as long dark nights robbed memory of lighter days and the clear evidence in front of them that there would only ever be darkness. She knew that it was a matter of finding something, even the weakest candle, with which to survive until spring. She hoped Daniel had one, that maybe she was one. She reminded herself that she needed to be at the station in the morning, to search the faces of the new prisoner arrivals, as she did with each train.

Daniel — Kenada, Khabarovsk Krai,
28 December 1941–19 January 1942

Its leaders required the Gulag operate by standard procedures, ostensibly because it was so vast. The real reason was that it was safer for its thousands of apparatchiks to follow the rules. Thinking for oneself risked error, or worse, like challenging or embarrassing someone higher up, someone who could have the thinker arrested, along with the thinker's wife, parents, siblings, neighbors, even children. One such standard procedure was inspection, wherein officials from the central office arrived at camp to document that a selection of the byzantine regulations under which the camp was expected to operate were being followed religiously, if that wasn't too ironic. That there were consequences was easily inferred from the seriousness with which the Commandant and his staff took the inspections.

Among the many topics of inspection was lice. Not how many millions there were in the camp — rather, how many men were infested with them. An extra shower involving warmer water and a new sliver of soap, together with an extra heating cycle for their rags, told the prisoners that a 'surprise' inspection was imminent. It also meant that it was time for some of them to get a 'road' in their hair. This was when the Commandant, along with the camp doctor and the camp barber, attended morning roll call. The doctor's job was to inspect the head of every man standing at attention. To give the doctor the best view, the barber clipped all the hair but for the last millimeter in one strip down the middle of the head of the privileged, who, like Daniel, enjoyed longer hair. Rybak had helped Daniel avoid the last two lice reviews by claiming an office emergency. With Rybak gone, and little left to do in the office, there was no way to avoid roll call this time. The barber's clippers completed Daniel's 'road,' and the doctor promptly pronounced him lice free, ignoring Daniel's malevolent stare and moving on to the next man.

Not only did the camp have a barber, but he had a real leather barber's chair. Mornings, the man shaved the heads of the *dezhurnaya*, those who were left behind, while he did the working prisoners in the evenings and Mondays. The afternoons were his to earn a few kopecks from guards, free men, and others.

Daniel was first in line when the barbershop opened that afternoon. He gave his instructions as he planted himself into the chair.

"Shave it off. All of it."

Everyone else who received a 'road' had the remainder clipped to the same one-millimeter length, the barber told him.

"Shave it all off," Daniel ordered again.

Like leaves falling from the copper beech tree that grew in front of his home in Poland, his dark, dearly cultivated locks fell off. The barber lathered the left half of his scalp and razored anything that remained. Daniel kept his eyes closed — there were no mirrors — as he felt the barber's hands prepare the right half, so he only heard a breathless young man crash through the door. One of the Commandant's messenger boys.

"Are you Ciszek?" he asked.

Daniel opened his eyes and admitted as much.

"Thank goodness. I looked everywhere. The boss, the Commandant wants to see you," the boy said, and stood, expecting Daniel to leap up and follow him. Daniel did no such thing.

"Finish the job, comrade," Daniel said. "Don't rush on my account, I don't want to bleed on the Commandant's floor."

The barber quickly concluded that he would not suffer if Ciszek chose to delay, and did his professional best to complete the shave with no nicks. Daniel felt wind where he'd never felt any before. He handed over the few coins he had in his pocket and followed the fidgety and worried messenger down the path to the main administrative building.

One was called to face the Boss either because they'd egregiously violated one of those regulations, or someone had spilled something about them. The summoned were always made to stand and wait, to give them time to imagine what fate they might be facing and to encourage confessions of real or imagined transgressions to shorten the process for all. Daniel only felt a bubbling anger growing for losing his hair over nothing more important than this man's desire to avoid a black mark on his inspection record. He had nothing to confess.

The Commandant sat behind a desk, writing something onto a document, his boots on the floor beside him.

"You are Polish, no?" the Commandant finally asked, a fact Daniel knew was well documented. He confirmed it anyway.

"Comrade Stalin has declared that the Poles are now our allies and friends. You will be discharged from the camp in the next few days," the Commandant announced, in the same voice with which he told the prisoners that the work quota was being raised. He handed Daniel an official piece of paper.

"That is all. You may go," the Commandant dismissed him.

Daniel tried to move his feet. He tried to breathe. He tried to think. Finally, he asked for the information again.

"We are on the same side now. Germany turned around and invaded the motherland. We are fighting now, valiantly, in many sectors. You will be proud to know that the tunnel you helped build will be critical for moving supplies to where our heroic armies are in battle."

Daniel failed to imagine the set of linkages connecting what was happening to huge armies from massive empires to him, a lone individual on the other side of Russia.

"Thank you, Citizen Commandant," he finally managed to say.

"He kept that information until his precious tunnel was finished!" Nadhya declared when he told her that afternoon. She was angrier than Daniel. "They are monsters, every last one of them!"

The order bore the date of August first. It was now almost January. It was true that things reached Kenada and this camp late, but rarely this late. She was right, they'd withheld this because they needed him. He should be angry and disgusted; that he was not confused him. Five months of freedom had been stolen from him, during which he continued to suffer the indignities of being a prisoner of the Gulag, culminating in today's 'road.' But Rybak would still have died if Daniel had been freed. Would the office have operated well enough to keep Kharnovsky and the others from becoming tunnel rats? And perhaps it was true, the hated tunnel was vital to what would eventually defeat Hitler. Plus, there was this woman sitting across their little dining table holding the paper, hand shaking with her anger. In another time and in any other place, their liaison would likely never have happened. Yet, he could not dismiss it as if its value depended only on his status, on his relative freedom.

They did not make love that night. Daniel felt Nadhya next to him seething at another injustice perpetrated by the authorities. Daniel lay in the dark, his own mind churning under his smooth scalp. He tried to remember the faces of the men with whom he'd crossed Russia in that cattle car, or their names, and wondered if any were still alive. He tried to remember what his apartment in Warsaw looked like, and how Joseph and Sylvia looked the last time he saw them, holding onto each other as he left their café. He tried to remember what Ian looked like as he boarded his train to France. There was no order to it; semi-random pictures pulled from his memory library, mostly the brightest and largest recent pictures. There were also the frightening ones from the battle near the bridge, and the basement near Bialystok, Yakimchuk's death, and the water rushing past the wall of rocks blocking the tunnel. He fell asleep when his memory picture show came to rest on snapshots of lamp-lit evenings with Nadhya in their little cottage.

They argued first thing in the morning. Nadhya insisted that he did not have to get back to camp in time for roll call as he was free. Daniel knew how the bureaucracy functioned; until he had a piece of paper in his hand covered with the necessary signatures and stamps, he could be in trouble. He stayed in the camp office until evening roll call before he returned to the village, to Nadhya. She met him at the door, burying her face into his chest. They held each other for a long, long time. He gently pushed her away. He picked up the Commandant's papers and pulled out the second page.

"They are forming a Polish Army. It says it's in Chkalov Oblast," he said. "I asked around; that is near Kuybyshev. Used to be called Samara. South, probably a thousand kilometers from Moscow." And ten thousand kilometers from here. He knew that she had read it too, probably more than once. "I don't have to go."

"Why would you stay in this God-forsaken place?" she sniffled.

"You know why. I hope you do," Daniel said. "Besides, we are both free now. We are valuable to them. There will be more tunnels, or bridges. We could easily make it."

She looked up at him, her tears gone, her gaze direct. "We can't stay here, for maybe years! We might live, but I guarantee that eventually we will wither and come to hate ourselves, and each other. You need to go back to civilization, you need a hundred colors, not just one."

They sat near each other, without speaking.

"Could you not come with me?" He was pleased and relieved with his idea. "You could apply to move to Kuybyshev, and if we married, I could probably, I could get you out as a Pole. We could wait to leave until your papers came through." Going together was so logical and good, he didn't know why he hadn't thought of it immediately.

The gratitude in her hug flowed into him. This was the solution, the one that satisfied their needs and not what the Soviet state demanded. He thought about how pleased Rybak would have been, that his two young acolytes had found happiness and each other, even in a frozen hell.

"You were a wraith when I first saw you, and yet there was something like a dim light in your posture. I am not saying it correctly. What kind of writer am I?" Nadhya said, and Daniel bent to kiss the top of her head. "I will admit that I chose you first as a trial. I am sorry. I have been in the camps long enough to know that transfers, accidents, starvation, jealousy… there are so many things that can happen. In the beginning, I believed that I caught you early, that you hadn't had everything human squeezed out of you and that whatever was left hadn't been permanently immured. It was so refreshing to have someone like that. But I have to tell you something."

She stopped, and so did Daniel's feeling of triumph.

"I have been happy these last months. Happier than I ever imagined that I could be out here. But even with that, I have kept writing to anyone I can to try and find him. My Polevy. To find out if he is still alive. I have gone to meet almost every train which brought a new *etap* of fresh prisoners, in case he was there. I… am ashamed, Daniel." She cried again. When she regained control, she said, "He is dead, I am sure. I promise. It stops. You and I deserve better." He kissed the top of her head again to reassure her. Behaviors that might be unacceptable in a peaceful Warsaw or Moscow looked very different in a Gulag camp in Kenada, he told himself.

He went first to the Commandant. With the tunnel essentially done, the Commandant did not need Nadhya's services, but he did not have official jurisdiction over her and saw no percentage in trying to do anything to help. "Make the request to the authorities in Khabarovosk," he said. "I'll make sure it goes out with tomorrow's reports," was all he would offer.

Their reply was an emphatic no. Several years of internal exile remained on Nadhya's sentence and there was no one at that level who felt safe to make any changes. Only Moscow could.

Daniel drafted a stronger appeal that emphasized how they planned to leave the Soviet Union. Wouldn't that be an even harsher sentence than staying in exile? He hoped that this argument would sway anyone in Moscow who blindly loved Mother Russia, and who could never imagine themselves severed from her.

The office closed the first week in January. The men were reassigned, half back to a regular work brigade, the others put on a train to somewhere else. Soon after, Nadhya received what she was told was her last pay packet. At the same time, Daniel got the permits and papers he needed, and had his name stricken from the roll of prisoners. They celebrated, frugally. The snows deepened, as did the cold, and for several days they had to stay inside the cottage and use a significant portion of their firewood. As soon as the *buran* blew away, Daniel went to forage for more wood, which angered the local woodcutter. The man saw Daniel as an unwelcome competitor for his livelihood and put away his axe only when Daniel convinced him that he was only looking for wood for himself.

Nadhya received a message that there was a day's worth of office work in Komsomolsk. It meant money to survive until they got the permissions they needed from Moscow. She left before sun-up, while he slept. There was a note, telling him that she loved him, that she would be back in three days and that there was some potato soup in the pot by the hearth. He was reading it when the Commandant's messenger knocked on his door. This time there was no reason to delay and this time they let him into the Boss's office right away.

"Ciszek. I have new orders. All the Poles, people like you, have to leave. Someone is complaining about delays, so they have issued orders that you need to be moving to your army. Here. You have one day."

He shoved a new paper into Daniel's hand. Daniel read Russian well now, and it said exactly what the Commandant said it did.

"What if I do not?" he dared ask.

"Then you will be arrested and become our guest again, probably indefinitely."

Irkutsk, Irkutsk Oblast, 12 February 1942

Dear Ian,

Happy Birthday! You are 22 and no one can ever think of you as a boy again. How I wish we could celebrate properly. How I wish I had said a number of things I should have when we were together in Warsaw. And how I wish I had listened better.

A letter is no way to listen, of course. I will just pretend that you are sitting here in this hut and we are talking, although I hope with all my heart that your circumstances are far better than mine.

I am in Irkutsk, which you can find in an atlas. While you are there, see if you can locate the Tartary Strait. It's a branch of the Pacific. My last camp was less than seventy-five kilometers from there. It doesn't mean much, it's just remarkable to think I went to almost the opposite side of the earth. It's even more remarkable that I have survived, except that it is complicated. By some miracle, which is just a phrase meaning that it defies logic, I met someone. A remarkable woman. If only it had been in another time and place. I cannot stop thinking about her and how I was forced to leave. The letter I left will never be enough. My hope is that I never meet her again because I don't think I would survive the shame.

After I left the camp, I met a Polish government representative in Komsomolsk-on-Amur. He, at least, appeared to care. Who knows, maybe he was new. He was processing all the Poles, men, women, and even children emerging from the woods, securing tents and stoves and a kitchen that served hot, real food. He had two helpers, and after only a week, I had a new passport and a train ticket west. West, towards home. Unfortunately, it took me only as far as Khabarovsk. There was supposed to be someone there to relay us along except we never found him.

There is an abandoned warehouse in Khabarovsk that I claim as sort of my own since I urinated in all of its corners. You could have taken a class in shoddy Soviet construction methods there, especially when the snow collapsed the roof and exposed all the structural elements. I am not sure how many days I stayed there, becoming reacquainted with cold and hunger I'd not experienced since the camp at Bira. Remember how long the icicles that hung down from the eaves of our building in the early spring grew? That's what I turned into.

We had to leave when the police started making noises about violations of labor laws and parasites. We had no money, our clothing was ill-suited for the climate and with no transit permits or tickets, we had to walk along the tracks until we came to a spot where the trains slowed enough to jump into an empty coal car. There was no roof, but we managed to make a fire from the coal nuggets we found in the crevices and corners. One fellow died on our second night. I didn't know him well. We put him in a corner facing the wall so he wouldn't judge us.

Svobodny must be the most ironic town in Russia. The name means free but it's a major center for the Gulag. Railroad guards found us, and I came close to being sent back to the camps. Luckily, there were officials from the Polish Government, so I got a bed in their dormitory and a new coat instead. Ian, I bow to your passion for good design. This dormitory was perhaps the ugliest building I ever saw but it had solid walls with no chinks for the cold to invade, and there were efficient stoves connected to chimneys that drew out all the smoke! The meals would not be acceptable at Maxims (did you ever make it to Paris?), just good bread, and stews with real pieces of meat or fish, and kasha. I wanted to stay there.

Not really. Whenever I hate myself for my betrayal, the prospect of returning home, seeing you, starting again in Warsaw, these provide a floor below which I cannot sink. If I abandon that quest, my soul will be forever lost. Plus, the stream of released Poles coming from all over the Gulag meant they needed the space. We were sent on to meet General Anders and his new Polish Army. That is the tariff for leaving the Gulag. If I am killed in battle, it proves that I deserved it.

Among the rivulets of refugees flowing toward Anders from all over Siberia are some who did not leave behind the behaviors that come from our deeper and uglier natures. On our train, speeding through empty steppes and even emptier forests, they preyed, first on the weak, and then on anyone they chose. They only had to throw one man from the rear platform to make their point. That's how I lost my train ticket for Tashkent, along with my new coat. Only to you can I admit my shame at what I had to do to acquire a new ticket for Irkutsk and another coat

It is okay now. The Polish authorities have arranged for beds and meals. Not as good as Svobodny. Unsurprisingly, those authorities sleep and eat in far better circumstances, like the city leaders did back home. Some things don't change, I guess.

I should stop before you think I am only negative. The hope, however illogical and preposterous, that I will follow this letter and both it and I will be with you one day sweetens my thoughts. Take care of yourself.

All my love,

Daniel

Daniel — Dzambul, Kazakh Soviet Socialist Republic, 1–7 March 1942

"Daniel?"

Someone was calling his name. He turned to see three people walking towards him and, wondrously, they were three boys from his high school. Not boys from half a continent and ten years away. Men! Finding each other this way prompted a celebration of hugs, handshakes, and shoulder claps. Despite a hat, scarf, and high collared coat, they recognized him as Daniel, and that meant everything. In the mess hall, they toasted their reunion with tea served by the officers' wives to whom they repeatedly recounted the miracle of their discovery.

Vitek, never at a loss for words when they were teenagers, started right in.

"I almost passed you by. By the Blessed Virgin, something made me look closer."

His two friends nodded, as did Daniel, to acknowledge the role of chance. In the presence of people from his faraway home, the warmth from the hot drink and the two stoves penetrated deeply into places long frozen in his memory.

Eventually, they had enough celebration and there was no one else to tell. Vitek took the lead again, asking, as gently as he was capable, how Daniel came to this Polish Army camp, perched on a snowy plain beside the rail lines just beyond the edge of the town.

"After joining the army…" Daniel began.

"What was your unit?" Marian asked.

"It was very disorganized by then," Daniel said. Marian looked disappointed, like he'd expected a star pupil such as Daniel to be in one of the elite cavalry brigades. Daniel went on: capture, exchange, the two Gulag camps, working in a forest and in a tunnel, and then the sudden release and the struggle since Kenada, especially the last leg from Irkutsk to here. Five minutes to summarize two and half years.

"What about you?" he asked the three.

Vitek told their story, how, in November 1940, they left home to look for work, and after spending the winter in Lublin they heard about construction jobs to the east, but they got lost and were picked up by Russians somewhere past the frontier between them and the Germans.

"They wanted to shoot us as spies," Marian interrupted.

Vitek went on, "In any event, we ended up in a camp somewhere north. But we looked out for each other and then, in August, they let us go, and here we are."

They all sat and drank their tea.

"Did any of you… do you know what happened to my father?" Daniel finally asked. His question was like a potion that turned his three friends into stone.

Stacsek finally spoke, though the silence had told Daniel everything. "They killed him. Took him and the other Jew at the school you know, Zylberberg, and shot them."

Vitek added, "Sorry, Danik."

They didn't linger after that, but they promised to meet in the mess hall for dinner.

Daniel drew his coat on slowly, giving it a few more seconds to absorb some additional precious joules of heat. He walked out alone to take his emotional temperature. He was not devastated or even saddened. Certainly, it was not a surprise. He'd always told himself, and Nadhya when he spoke of it, that he expected no one to have survived. Beyond that, and overwhelming everything, he was still in Siberia, fighting for his own life, by necessity keeping many parts of himself buried, or bunkered, or forgotten. If he ever were to mourn, it would have to be in another place and circumstance. He forgave himself, temporarily.

It was a large camp. There were three other mess halls, with hundreds of canvas tents between and beyond them, all sprouting small metal chimneys. Each tent accommodated six, men like himself and his friends, but also families with wives and children. Daniel watched a grandmother scoop up one child out of a group of a half dozen playing with a ball made from rags. Was this the right grandmother, or an informal community network of grandmothers shepherding flocks of children? Or was it the child's mother, prematurely aged by the Gulag?

At the evening meal, he sat with Marian and Vitek. Stacsek was busy some-where else, he would try to join them later. It felt strange. All around him, he heard the phonemes and words in the language he knew, but from a long time ago. Here were people with whom he shared a history, through whom he could begin to reconstruct himself. Their conversation was easy, comfortable, and comforting. The kitchen workers had to kick them out at closing time.

That same mess hall was transformed the next morning. It was time to process the men and enlist them into the 8th Division of Anders' Army. Daniel looked for but could not locate his friends among so many men milling around. The officers organized everyone into lines which trailed outside and around the men's latrine and bath house. In these lines, everyone appeared calm, even happy. This is what they'd come for, to reassert that they still existed, that they mattered. That is how Daniel felt. The camps had stripped that from him. This act of signing his name to become a soldier, to fight with Vitek, Marian, and Stacsek, and the thousands of others, to reclaim who they were, was the necessary crucial first step.

He still couldn't see Vitek or Marian, but Stacsek was there, standing by the end of the table. He seemed to be scanning the crowd, looking for someone. Daniel made to wave, but as Stacsek leaned over to whisper in the ear of the officer who sat in front of Daniel's line, he put his hand down. Only when Daniel got close did they manage to make eye contact.

"Name?" the officer asked when Daniel finally made it to the front.

"Ciszek. Daniel Ciszek."

"Where were you born?"

Daniel named their hometown. To his right, a commotion started: raised voices, tones of protest, a hand slapped down hard on the table. Everyone turned to see an older man, maybe forty or forty-five, protesting loudly as two large young men hustled him out by his elbows.

"I want to fight! I want to fight!" the man yelled. "I want to fight for Poland!"

Daniel turned back to his officer.

"Age?"

Daniel had to think about that for a moment. "Thirty," he finally calculated.

"Any military experience?"

He made his brief time in the chaos of 1939 into as much of a military history as he could without lying. His interrogator appeared unimpressed. Daniel prepared to outline his university degree, plus his building, and now tunneling, skills to prove how useful he would be in this new army, but before he could mention those, came another question.

"Religion?"

"I beg your pardon?"

"Straightforward question. Religion? Are you Catholic?"

"No. I am nothing."

"That is not an answer. What religion were you born with?" The officer had a luxuriant, well-trimmed mustache. He kept his eyes down to where he recorded Daniel's answers on his official form, his pen poised over the spot where the religion answer went.

Daniel wanted this to stop so he could think of the right answer, but he was acutely aware of the long line of men behind him. He looked over to Stacsek, a few feet away, for some sort of help and received nothing back.

"Jewish," Daniel finally answered.

The officer reached over for one of the stamps, inked it on the pad and boomed a red circle onto the paper. Daniel could read it from where he stood.

"Denied? What? Why?" he asked.

"You are unfit for military service."

"What do you mean? I am young, I have a degree from Warsaw Technical University, I can help. I can work with construction, planning, building." Daniel's voice began to rise above the background hubbub.

"Please leave. You are not acceptable. Next!" The officer dismissed him with a look that said that he was about to summon those two big brutes to escort Daniel out, roughly and humiliatingly.

Stacsek was now next to him, whispering in his ear. "Everyone knows. Jews can't fight. We do not want you." Stacsek returned to his post, to finger further undesirables. Daniel found himself back outside in the late afternoon gloom, smoke, and fog, seething and unsure where to go and what to do.

Ian — Kelso, Scotland, 24 December 1943

"You have the duty tonight, Lieutenant?"

Mrs. Goudie spoke Ian's rank as often as she could. "I helped him with his English," she told her neighbors, especially when speaking with those who billeted privates and non-coms. Ian knew that his ability to converse with their British Army hosts and masters was the major reason for his promotion over those who'd fought in Poland, escaped to France, and fought again.

"You're going to miss the fete, you poor dear," she said. "I'll save you some of the clootie dumpling I made, thanks to your sugar ration."

"I thank you," Ian said to Mrs. Goudie and her husband, Hugh, before changing it to, "Thank you" after she corrected him. Talking with them at tea or describing the films he saw up to five nights a week at the Community Center had indeed helped his English, but he gave most credit to the many evenings he spent with Rita Hayworth, Betty Grable, Ingrid Bergman, and Vivien Leigh, watching their lips and mouths make the sounds that he finally could interpret as words.

He didn't mind missing a celebration for a holiday he did not observe, plus it avoided calling attention to himself. Unlike snowbound Christmas Eves at home, the ground here was bare. He could see his breath, but without any appreciable wind coming off the North Sea it was a pleasant evening. He knew his duty circuit by heart: two posts along the river, up to the train station, over to the north road, a shortcut through the fields to the most remote and exposed post, back to ones on the western train line and the road from Stirling, and, finally, a check on the men guarding Wojtek.

Wojtek the Bear. Two years ago, men from the 1st Armoured Regiment bought a cub from a traveling circus set up in a field adjacent to their training ground, near Blairgowrie. Curfews, call-ups, rations, and the general mood made it a bad time to own a traveling circus, so the soldiers pooled their English coins and bills, and Wojtek joined the Free Polish Army. He grew bigger on milk and army food, though now he preferred drinking beer from bottles he dexterously opened himself. During the day, he accompanied a supply platoon and loved to carry ammunition boxes and to pull caissons out of the mud. At night he slept in a cage, at the insistence of officers who feared their local hosts would otherwise object, but among the troops he was considered a member of the Division, a picture of a bear carrying a tank shell painted on the sides of all manner of vehicles. A wise senior officer overruled the colonels, brigadiers, and maybe even major generals when they attempted to invoke British Army regulations against animals in camp. Wojtek, in a small way, reminded them that, while they lived in Britain, and served under them, they were still distinct, and Polish.

The necessity of these nighttime inspections, like the marches up and down the beaches along the Scottish coast back in early '42, was questionable now, but as Ian learned during officer training classes, ensuring whatever was ordered was done correctly was critical. Keeping everyone sharp, not comfortable, would save lives and promote success when it came time to battle. As a new soldier, he'd attributed much of what he'd had to do to tradition or even maliciousness. Now, he understood that organizing people, units, vehicles, guns, supplies, goals, obstacles, intelligence, weather, psychology, and more into a force was, in many respects, similar to what the design and construction of a Suez Canal or a bridge across the Bosporus was. A massive enterprise is divided into parts and for each, a goal is defined, and the necessary resources and processes mobilized to meet that goal. Each manager or engineer or officer becomes responsible for planning and executing for their particular unit and goal, and if they do it correctly and well, a modern marvel to stand for decades, or victory in the battle and the war will result.

All was as expected at his first stops. No one was sleeping, or smoking, or in violation of any of the many rules, even if they were unhappy that they had this duty while their comrades ate and drank together. This was good training, and good men were doing their job. He stepped up his pace to finish with Wojtek's guards so he could go and warm up in the office before he did it all again at 0400.

Ian heard Wojtek snoring from yards away, he'd probably shared in some Christmas cheer. There was a shack next to the cage, where the two guards stayed, protected from wind and rain. They had a small wood stove as well, which made this assignment better than the furthest post or the western train line one. Ian wanted some of what that stove was producing and hurried to the shack. But it wasn't Wojetk who was snoring. It was one of the two sleeping men. It was Christophe.

They had barely spoken after what had happened on the ship. With the help of Major Wysoczanski, they'd wrapped the body in canvas and that night, while the Major kept watch, they brought it up to a deserted spot near the dark stern.

"Should we say something?" Christophe asked.

"What?" Ian did not understand what Christophe was thinking.

"I don't know. He was a priest, at one point." Christophe began a prayer in a low voice. Ian did not know if prayer was for Bloch's soul or Christophe's. Probably Bloch's since Christophe and the Major were acting as if all was as it should be. They'd caught him in time, so no harm, now let's do our duty and send his body to oblivion. Ian kept his confusion about the man, their time together, what he now knew about his previous life, and his death to himself.

Ian had felt ambivalent when, upon debarking from the *City of Nagpur* in Liverpool, he discovered that he and Christophe were assigned to the same Regiment, but as two out of ten thousand men in what was now a Division, they rarely saw one another. Christophe insisted on buying Ian a drink the first time he saw him with a second lieutenant's pips on his shoulders, and whenever they ran into each other in camp or town, they would stop, speak of home, remember Paul. Then, Christophe was posted to Ian's platoon as a tank driver. The temptation to see invisible forces behind such a long-shot circumstance was something Ian had to fight off. Now here he was sleeping on duty. No matter that he was guarding a bear rather than something of real military value, except Wojtek did have value for the spirt and cohesion of the Division. It all mattered, if not now, then when they went back to the continent to fight against seasoned Germans. Ian looked down at Christophe. He pictured him cooking in their apartment in Paris. He saw him proudly crowing about Paul's successes with the doorknobs. Through Christophe, they'd found a way out of France when the Nazis and their Vichy collaborators looked ready to swallow them up, and he had become indispensable in Casablanca.

The other man stirred, and a decision became necessary.

In the end, Christophe accepted getting demoted from corporal without anger or even surprise. He did not beg when Ian woke the two men and ordered them to put themselves on report. He appeared to understand that, as Ian told them that night, "It's for your own good. If you do this when we go over there, a Nazi could sneak up and kill you."

Christophe did not stare at Ian or avert his eyes at the hearing before the battalion executive officer, and he took the consequences of his actions like a good soldier, even saying, "Thank you sir, I promise this will never happen again."

Ian had the feeling that the next time they met, Christophe would act exactly as always, maybe even thank Ian for doing his job. He hated being an officer.

Henry — Ithaca, New York, 3 May 1974

Just before my first finals week was not the most convenient time for my dad to visit. I was fairly confident about the three exams, and the five-page history paper due before the end of the exam period. What I needed to focus on was the short story that would finalize my grade in my writing class. On the other hand, the visit was only a day and a half, plus I would get a good dinner out of it.

We rendezvoused at the main entrance to the campus, and I proceeded to show him around, explaining each landmark, or the purpose of each building, even when it had no relevance. I pointed to where the ice rinks stood in winter, and recounted the myths and stories associated with various sites. He seemed to enjoy the tour. He asked a few questions and made a couple of uncomfortable jokes about what the girls were wearing. He'd come alone because my mother could not take time off from her job as one of a thousand paper pushers at a big insurance company.

We sat on a bench on the patio outside the main library to take a break and enjoy the spring sunshine, talking about this and that.

"You have to choose this summer, no? What you will study from now on?" he casually asked me.

"Yes, it's called picking a major," I said.

"You still want to do that, be a writer?"

Nothing I'd studied so far had turned me away from that. If necessary, I figured I'd become a journalist to pay the bills before my own writing made me famous enough.

"We've never had a writer in the family," he said to no one in particular. "It's not something we do."

That's because this was a new continent, a new country, a very new time where whatever had kept previous generations from becoming writers no longer applied, I thought, but did not say.

"It's a good profession," he admitted. "Bellow, he makes a good living. That guy who wrote the book, they made the movie out of it, what's his name…?" I couldn't help him with that.

He and my mother must have rehearsed. After his opening gambit, he next asked how many hundreds or thousands of writers there might be for every famous one, adding a comment about how luck seemed to be an important factor. He asked me if I knew all the steps it took to become a writer. Was graduate school involved? Start with low-pay experiences, an office boy or intern? How many years before one could call oneself a writer?

Then he turned to the oft-told Uncle Max story. Uncle Max had been a successful lawyer in Vienna before the War. But when he came to New York, he was only qualified to open a candy store, where he spent the next twenty-five bitter and miserable years. "He was a famous lawyer and couldn't find a lawyer job! Think about how much harder it would have been if he'd been a writer!" Their solution was that I prepare for another job, like medicine, and write on weekends.

I defended myself. Many writers who weren't household names made a living. There were graduate journalism schools, and I didn't need to decide about them for a while. Writing was even more portable than law.

"As long as you speak the same language," he pointed out.

It wasn't just about practicality, I declared. I had the right to be happy.

He didn't challenge my right to be happy. His reply was worse.

"Maybe you aren't that good. Did you ever think that? I have read some of your things, and maybe you aren't that good. Just think about it."

Daniel – Onboard the *Na Vakhte*, the Caspian Sea and Baku, Azerbaijan, 19 May 1944

Daniel took up his position on the starboard side, a dozen meters from the bow, as the *Na Vakhte* backed from her berth and turned to port. He kept that watch until the boat slipped between Kosa Kasnovodskaya's sandy spit and Teozebad Island. Now, he had an hour to smoke a cigarette and even read if he avoided any mates or officers. He could choose between a copy of the Party weekly from Baku and a month-old *Izvetsia* from Moscow, left on a seat by a passenger the day before.

The papers reported good news. They always did, even when the Nazis stormed across thousands of kilometers to the edges of Moscow. Actualities did not matter. Even before the heroic victory at Stalingrad a year ago, only positive stories appeared in the local and national Soviet newspapers. The difference now was he trusted the reports of serial successes. A regular reader with some knowledge of geography could see the westward progress of the Red Army, that Leningrad was no longer under siege or that Crimea was back in Russian hands.

He stubbed out his cigarette and squirreled the newspapers away under coils of rope when he heard someone coming, but it was only Rasim.

"Hey, the second engineer wants us to look at something near Hold Twenty-seven." Rasim was a big man, with hands defined by thick, sausage-like fingers. His shoulders and his chest looked as if they'd been sculpted by years working on ships, even though he'd joined the crew of the *Na Vakhte* four months after Daniel. Young men were becoming rare, all gone to the army, and their jobs were now filled by women and older men like Rasim, even foreigners like Daniel. The ship's captain looked like he should have retired decades earlier. The second engineer was a woman, as was the radio operator.

Daniel and Rasim passed the kitchen on the way to their assignment, where they stopped and each had a glass of tea and some bread with honey. The second engineer looked annoyed when it took so long to meet her at Hold 27. She said nothing, merely pointing to the warren of pipes and the brown liquid that dripped steadily from one of them to form a fetid puddle.

"This section needs to be replaced. You know how?" she asked the two men. They nodded. "Then, get on with it. We have over three hundred passengers who will need to use the toilets again before we reach Baku."

She left them to their task. The hold was near the water line, and so it wasn't too hot. Without any air circulation, though, the smell ranked between strong and overwhelming, so both took off their shirts and tied them over their nose and mouths and they exchanged minimal words through their shirt-masks over the few hours. When they were done, Rasim went to find the nearest toilet to test flush it. Success.

Rasim smiled as he scrubbed his hands. Daniel assumed these successes gave someone like him great satisfaction.

"That was good," Rasim said. "Took long enough that we are now closer to Baku than Turkmenbashi."

"What?" Daniel asked.

"It's past four o'clock, so we are more than halfway across. Closer to Baku, my home."

Daniel shrugged. He rarely left the *Na Vakhte*. It saved money and confused the authorities. He could tell the Azerbaijani secret police he lived in the Turkmen Soviet Socialist Republic and vice versa. Only once, when the ship spent two months getting repairs, did he need to find a hole on land to crawl into.

"Hey," Rasim continued, as if he and Daniel were having a conversation, "we have sixteen hours shore leave. You should come to my home!" His face showed how pleased he was with this idea.

"No, thank you. That is kind of you, but no," Daniel said.

"Oh, come on! We have extra beds, real feather mattresses, not like what you sleep in," Rasim said, referring to the hammock Daniel strung up in his space. "You will sleep like you were back in your home!"

"That is unnecessary. Again, no thank you."

Rasim hesitated, and then went ahead with what he wanted to say, as was his nature.

"Forgive me for getting a little personal here, Daniel. We have worked together for quite some time now, and I consider us friends."

Daniel looked at Rasim, surprised that the message he wanted everyone to receive had failed with this man.

"Forgive me," Rasim continued, "but you are perhaps the saddest man I believe I have ever met. I mean, I know, we all have to keep things close, we don't know who will report something we say to the NKVD, at least that's what my wife worries about. 'One day,' she says, 'you will leave to work and you won't come home and it won't be another woman, it will be your damn mouth that has put you into jail.' But when you work close with someone for all this time, you notice things."

"You know all about me, Rasim. I am Polish, brought to Russia in 1939 and then released in '41. I am just trying to do my work and survive, like all of us," Daniel said.

"Yes, yes, we are. But you… Well, you look like someone who has lost something, or even everything, if you'll forgive me. A night with my family might do nothing, but it couldn't hurt."

Daniel reiterated his polite but firm decision and walked away to find another task with which to occupy the time, away from Rasim. Two hours out of Baku, while leaning over a rail to enjoy his ritual fourth cigarette of the trip, however, Rasim found him again. They both looked down to where the bow imposed its will on the water.

"How many trips have you made on this old bucket?" Rasim finally asked.

"I lost count after three hundred," Daniel answered.

"How many thousands of kilometers do you imagine that comes to?"

"I never calculated," Daniel said to the sea. He didn't want to know the total.

Rasim went on. "All these kilometers and you are still in the same place. That is why you are the saddest man. You travel so much, but not in the direction you wish to go. You are not restricted, like the Ukrainians, the Latvians, or me. You can leave, yet you stay on the *Na Vakhte*, eight trips a week, ending up where you started every time."

"Why do you care?" Daniel shot back.

"We are shipmates," Rasim said, as if that were enough.

"So what? Any of this can change in an instant. Someone somewhere signs a piece of paper and one of us is in Kolyma or marching into a battle."

Rasim's voice was just audible above the sound of the waves and the wind. "For the moment that isn't true, so we are shipmates. Tell me, unless you were an orphan, you have a home? A mother, a father? Brothers or sisters? Even a wife, maybe you were old enough?"

"No, nothing. It's all gone, all lost."

"All? I am sorry."

"My mother died before the war, when I was away at university," Daniel spoke to the waves, but Rasim heard.

"You went to university? I knew it! I told my wife that you were a smart one, like our Aliev. He was on his way to university before the war."

"Do you know where he is now?" Daniel asked.

"He died outside Stalingrad," Rasim responded.

"Oh. Now I am sorry, Rasim."

Silence again, then Daniel continued. "My father was shot by the Nazis. I don't know where my younger brother is. My home is gone, they told me that they stored munitions there and it blew up. My friends… I had friends in Warsaw, they were my second family. I also don't know where they are, likely dead. Everyone, it feels like, is dead. So many people I have known, every one that I can remember is dead."

"Everyone?"

"No. But I will never see them so that is the same thing. When I can't sleep at night, I don't count the number of crossings on this damn boat. I count the number of dead people, people I have lost. I am the anti-Noah. Instead of…" Daniel saw Rasim's face. "Do you know Noah?"

"A little. We were Muslim before the revolution, but also back then priests ran our school, where I went for a while. Noah was the one with the boat, the animals, right? I remember him, and I also remember Jesus, and Job."

"Yes," Daniel said. "Noah saved the animals when God swept away the people who'd disappointed him. Maybe God is doing this again, except he is amusing himself by using us to slaughter each other in ever more ingenious ways."

Rasim didn't know what to say to this, except reiterate his invitation.

"Come to dinner, Daniel, to sleep a little on land."

"I am not good company. And didn't you hear? I am Job, I am death."

"I don't believe that," Rasim said to Daniel and not the sea. "My father used to say, 'A plan is a bridge to a dream.' Now, you have no dream. You will forgive me, you appear to be a very smart man, you went to university. A plan will come to you if you allow it. And then you will find a bridge and through those two things, maybe a new dream. For now, come to dinner."

Rasim's house, a space only slightly larger than Nadhya's, was divided into several small rooms. The biggest, of course, was the kitchen, where his wife fussed over her pots, appearing both angry and pleased with an unexpected guest. Daniel sat in the best chair in the house and watched the large man play as gently as a mother bear with little Zenaida, his three-year-old granddaughter. She hung on his ankle as he bounced it over the fulcrum of his other knee, and Daniel admired how she laughed, a sound undiluted by thought or fear, containing only the joy of the moment.

There were five adults at the dinner table. Rasim's daughter-in-law, one of a million young widows, was Zenaida's mother. Framed by her headscarf, her face could have been the model for a Renaissance painting of Mary Magdalene gazing up at the crucifix. Another daughter-in-law named Sofia was not yet officially a widow, but they'd heard nothing about Rasim's younger son for months. No matter, they gathered to share food, cooked by someone who cared how it tasted, grateful that everyone who could be there was, including Daniel. The walls had holes, there were stains on the ceiling. Only little Zenaida wore clothes without patches. At the head of the table, Rasim sat back, his belly full. He went over to a cupboard and brought back a bottle of local brandy. He poured a finger each into two glasses, one of which he handed to Daniel.

"*Vashe zdorov'ye!*" he toasted and swallowed the liquor in one gulp.

Daniel took a swallow and failed to suppress the coughing spasm the harsh liquid provoked.

"It's good," he rasped.

Rasim laughed. "No, it's not. It's all we can get nowadays." And he poured them both another. "Here's to... Well, we toasted our health. Now, I drink to the safety of my son."

"I drink to that," Daniel said, and he did.

"Thank you, my friend."

The third toast was a silent one. Daniel could now swallow without suffering. Rasim proposed the fourth. "Here's to the *Na Vakhte*. That rusty floating... I don't know what. I hate every centimeter, every rivet. Do you know I get seasick? But it gives me what I need to keep those I love close and fed. And brings new friends. To the *Na Vakhte*!" They drank.

Rasim had one last toast, one he delivered to Daniel. "And here's to leaving that boat. You first."

Daniel – Occupied Bucharest, 30–31 January 1945

One visit to Rasim's family did not change Daniel right away. He did allow Rasim to sit with him more often in the ship's mess but they rarely spoke, although Daniel did remember to ask for news about the son every so often. Then, when little Zenaida fell ill in early summer, Daniel wanted daily updates. He attended the celebration of her recovery and slept at Rasim's for the second time. Next, Daniel stopped spending everything he earned and put aside a ruble or two to purchase some sweets or a little toy to bring to Zenaida whenever he accepted Rasim's standing invitation. By the fourth visit, he was also buying food to contribute to the household and the pleasure he felt at doing so felt vaguely familiar.

When he learned from the scavenged newspapers that the Red Army controlled Romania, Daniel was ready. He was no longer a wraith living in his deep hole, where the pinpoint of light above only reminded him how futile it was to think, let alone try, to climb up and out. It required only someone see him again as a unique individual for him to begin, very slowly, to see this in himself and to realize that the hole was a construct of his own mind. Action followed. He acquired warm clothes and enough money to buy a rail ticket from Baku to Tbilisi in Georgia.

There were no tears when he said bittersweet goodbyes to Rasim and his family. He accepted the food for his journey that Rasim's wife had prepared, but not Zenaida's offer of her favorite blue rabbit toy. Rasim wrapped his big arms around Daniel and slipped a piece of paper into his pocket. "It is someone I know in Poti, works on merchant ships. You never know, it could help."

Of Rasim's gifts, the greater was the one that rescued him from disappearing on the *Na Vakhte*, but without him connecting Daniel with the man who smuggled him across the Black Sea to Odessa, strictly based on Rasim's endorsement, he would not have arrived to Bucharest two months to the day from when he left Baku. One more leg, to Iasi and his family, and Daniel, son of Henryk, brother of Ian, architect, would be restored.

The irony was not lost on Daniel that finally he was in Romania, though five years late. This was where his sergeant wanted them to evacuate and where he planned to take his father on the back of that motorcycle. He and Ian had spent summers with their mother's family in Iasi, up north closer to the Polish border. Even though something had ruptured the affection, tolerance, or goodwill between his grandparents and his father after the death of his mother — maybe because she was buried close to her husband and her sons and not back where she was born and grew up — he was fairly certain that under the circumstances, he and his father would have been welcomed.

Today, he sat in a café at the foot of Udricani Street, sipping from a mug of hot water, the least expensive item on the menu. Daniel kept squinting at the map of Romania on the wall behind the cash register before the barman finally took it down and passed it over.

"Excuse me," he asked the barman. "Why are some of the towns underlined?"

The barman stared hard at Daniel. "Are you Jewish?" he finally asked.

That question again, the one that meant nothing to him and everything to others, the cause of so much of what had happened to him. The small, almost hidden, mezuzah on the doorpost reassured him that here he could give an honest answer.

"Those are where they had pogroms. Dorohoi. Galati. Bucharest. Iasi."

"Iasi?" Daniel said. "That's where I need to go, where my family is."

"I am sorry. They may be gone. Many were killed, in '41. Many were sent away and only a few came back. The fighting around and in Iasi last year took care of many more. Talk to that man over there, he arrived from the area a few weeks ago, maybe he knows something." The barman pointed to a figure sitting alone at a corner table.

"Excuse me, friend," Daniel said to the wizened, shrunken man. It was impossible to gauge his age. "The owner over there, he says that you are from Iasi. I am hoping to go there, to find my family, the Litwacks. Do you know them?"

The stranger turned to face Daniel to reveal that he had only one eye. The other was scar tissue. Daniel did not react. "Can I buy you something?" he offered.

The stranger accepted a large *tuica*. He did not speak until the drink came.

"I knew a few Litwack families. Can you be more specific?" he asked. Daniel listed all the names he could recall, starting with his grandfather, who, according to his mother, had been a very important and prominent member of the community. The stranger, however, did not know him, or any of the others.

"They all lived around each other," Daniel added, and he gave the address. The man fixed Daniel with his one eye.

"That was not a good place to be, in June of '41," he pronounced carefully, as if he needed to check his memory first. "That was where it started, the killings. Men, old people, women. Children, even. Hundreds. The streets filled with bodies and blood." He stopped, seeming to push himself past the scenes in his head. He drew a breath and went on. "They put many of us onto trains. Death trains. By the time we reached Hell, many were dead. I was lucky. By the end, I only lost this." He gestured to his empty socket. "I cannot tell you if any of your family are alive and still there. The odds are against it, but I just don't know for sure."

Daniel thanked him by buying another glass of *tuica* and went back to his room near the train station. He lay back on the thin mattress. He had often imagined the relief that would overcome him when he walked into his grandparent's home and felt their embraces. After a few weeks' recuperation, he would go in search of Ian, then maybe seek out Joseph and Sylvia, and begin to think about things beyond immediate survival once more. If the man in the café was right, though, the struggle to get to Iasi was likely to be for nothing. The man was not specific, not certain, … he realized that if any were alive and still in Iasi, it would be a miracle. Romania, he forced himself to conclude, was not the destination, it was only another way station.

Which way should he go? Beyond Iasi, there was Warsaw, which had just been liberated by the Soviets and appeared utterly destroyed in the newsreels. What about west, to follow Ian? The chances of finding his brother, one man amongst millions, who would have to have survived his own Hades, seemed even worse than the odds that one relative was alive in Iasi.

Daniel lay awake all night trying and failing to come to a logical decision. It took two more visits to the café on Udricani Street for him to conclude that, since all his destination choices were equally hopeless, the decision was random; another roll of the dice.

Daniel — Occupied Budapest, 29 April–9 May 1945

Daniel picked his way through hills of bricks, wood, wallpaper, pieces of furniture, and other remains from collapsed apartments. The air felt heavy, as if it took extra effort to move it in and out of his lungs. It wasn't incineration; the fires ignited during the siege and battle were all finally extinguished. Rather, it was pulverization. Explosives delivered by airplane, artillery shells and rockets, tank rounds, and grenades thrown by victorious Russians and retreating Germans appeared to have damaged or destroyed most of Budapest. A city with a long and distinguished history, a capital of empires, a mecca for the creative and ambitious of central Europe, rolled over by the summit of man's ingenuity to destroy. Anything still standing remained at risk of falling into more dust. Each of Daniel's hurried footsteps along the makeshift path raised little clouds of what had been cement or stone. In an hour, it would be another gray day. Rain would be welcomed, and not only to clean the air; the water mains were gone. The dead bodies still washing up against the pontoon bridge made the Danube undrinkable.

Under an awning leaning out from the intact façade of what may have once been a hotel, several women, children, and old men stood silhouetted around a small fire. This was the best time to be about, when the night patrols moved closer to their barracks as the day teams finished breakfast. At a point opposite the castle, right before where the Chain Bridge had previously stood, he turned his back to the river and weaved his way to a doorway lying several steps below street level, off an alley near Sas Utca. He'd wandered the shell-shocked city for several days after hopping off the boxcar that brought him from Bucharest, determined to survive no matter the cost, when he saw two teenagers disappear into what appeared to be a hole in the street, but which turned out to be this little hideaway. After another day watching the comings and goings, he cinched his coat, drew himself up into the posture of an NKVD man, and with his hand on the Nagant pistol in his pocket, walked in.

He spoke quickly, in Russian. "What is this place? Are you saboteurs?"

There were four boys and one girl in the room. The oldest might be fifteen, the youngest eight or nine. He glowered from one to the next, and when one of the boys moved to stand in front of the girl, he knew he'd found the leader.

"Quickly, tell me who you are. Do you have papers?" Daniel demanded of him. He repeated the question in the Hungarian he'd learned from his grandmother's maid.

They were orphans. This one was the brother of the girl he'd instinctively moved to protect.

"Stand there!" Daniel ordered, pointing to a corner near the lantern so he could watch them. They complied and then flinched when he went to bring something out of his pocket, but it was a small flashlight, which he used to inspect their space. One dirty mattress, a couple of blankets on the floor, the lantern, and a little pile of clothes held no interest. On the other hand, on a shelf behind a curtain, there was a small but neat stack of Red Army cigarettes, five packets of soldiers' rations and, most damningly, several identity cards, which he inspected closely. One sergeant and two Russian privates plus a card and paybook from a German *Unterfeldwebel*.

The leader stood in front trying to look brave. It was noble and pathetic, so much so that part of Daniel wanted to hug him. That would not do, of course. Kortnev, the Urka chief from the Gulag, had probably never hugged anyone in his life. Instead, Daniel walked over and slapped the boy across the cheek.

"You have a Nazi pass. You worked for them? You know the penalty for collaborators!"

It was the turn of the girl to protect her brother. "We are not collaborators, sir! We are children, we are orphans, we found these things on the street! We do this, we bring back things we think might be useful or valuable."

"Red Army soldiers throw their papers out by the side of the road, do they? And you happened to be lucky and find so many?"

They stared back at him, open-mouthed and wordless. He paced in front of them to make it appear as if he needed to decide their fate. He pulled a box from a corner and sat down, and from an inner pocket of his coat, he pulled out a sausage and a small pocketknife, with which he proceeded to cut the sausage into five equal pieces and handed one to each.

"I am not the police, or even Russian. What I am is your leader. You work for me now. I can use some extra hands, and you can do better with me than as a gang of children."

For the Soviet conquerors, there was easy access to food, potable water, safe, dry shelter and, when the urge came, a local woman or a girl. For the survivors, there was only the loss of so many fathers, husbands, brothers, as well as grandmothers, mothers, children, neighbors. Many mourned. Others worried over the fate of loved ones arrested or press-ganged by Soviet troops and commissars. Services from the new municipal leadership or the army appeared haphazardly and remained vastly inadequate. In this environment, it took only a few days for a grudging trust to develop between Daniel and his little group. For one thing, he didn't beat, shoot, or denounce them. He made them keep a kind of schedule, resembling in some way life with their parents: regular, if sometimes meager, meals, and lights out by sundown to save on lamp oil. Their diet improved by the end of the first week, when his schemes began to succeed. Daniel overheard Niklas, the oldest, finally admit to the others that this arrangement was worth continuing, for now.

"But we watch, and when things change, we leave," he concluded in a whisper.

This was life now in Budapest — at seven each morning, when the nightly curfew lifted, people emerged from their makeshift shelters to rush to the lines. The most important line was the one where each registered resident received their weekly ration coupons for bread, sugar, oil or butter, and either eggs or meat. Each item had its own distribution point, meaning its own line, and there were so few such points that each took a day. In other words, one day for the ration book, another for bread, and so on. No ration coupons, no food. Cash was de facto evidence of black marketeering, meaning summary trial and maybe execution. It was in this confusion of scarcity and desperation that Daniel operated. He traded the Russian IDs for local registration papers from men who needed to leave Budapest so, when added to the two documents that the girl, Dorka, produced — he didn't ask how — the six of them could claim to be ten different people. On coupon book day, they crept out early to be near the front of the line. The children first used the adult identifications they'd procured, claiming that they were standing in for their injured parent. They then ran to the end of another line to get their own coupons. Each child proudly brought their little triumphs back to lay on the table Daniel had found. There were now five chairs, and four mattresses, and blankets. A sheet provided privacy for those using the bucket.

Ration books and coupons had value in the unofficial economy, and that meant cash — and risk. Daniel always waited until Friday to sell their supply, two days before the new distribution.

"Patience," he taught his charges, "can be valuable."

For example, a bread coupon fetched up to forty percent more on Friday than on Monday. This meant that he often had to be away from their basement on Friday and Saturday, doing his business, but he made sure to be back before they all left for their assignments Sunday mornings.

**

It had rained the night before, and the air felt cleaner. His charges were all there, looking ready to go, and he had to hold back from tousling young Anton's hair. Kortnev would not approve.

"You all know what to do. Be swift," he said, and they were silently off. Daniel stood on the third step, his head barely above ground level, watching them go in four directions while he had a cigarette.

Not where he'd ever envisioned himself. Still, it was better than most of the circumstances in which he'd found himself the past few years. That he was using Kortnev as the yardstick against which to gauge his actions was not something he permitted himself to think about much. When he did, he told himself that it was temporary. He turned to walk back into their room, to freshen up before he went to his assigned line, when he felt more than heard a body jump down behind him, and a gun or finger or pipe jabbed him in his kidney.

"I have nothing, comrade," Daniel said first.

"That's a lie." The man spoke in Hungarian. "We know that you have your young friends doing a little racket."

"I don't know what you are talking about," Daniel said. He calculated as he spoke. A shot would draw serious attention from the Russians. His dead body would do the same, plus they were far from the river, so disposing of him among all the other floating bodies would not be feasible. Keep talking, he told himself. "What do you want?"

"You are a small annoyance, a pimple on our ass. Still, it itches, you know, and we are tempted to scratch it."

"What are you talking about?" Daniel was genuinely confused. He tried to face his assailant but was dissuaded by increased pressure from the object still pointed into his back.

"My boss, you may have heard of him, Farkas. You are his little pimple. We do not want you to grow, to get big, and then we have to pop you, you know what I mean? Don't get any bigger, get smaller, stop undercutting us for coupons."

He'd heard about Farkas, rumored to be a master at adapting his enterprises to the times; corruption and extortion under the Horthy regency, black marketeering under the Nazis, and now with the Soviets in charge, doing a little bit of everything.

"I don't know anyone by that name, and I keep telling you, I don't understand what you are saying," Daniel said.

"Just get in there, close the door, and think about it for two minutes if you don't want to get shot in the face."

Daniel waited twice as long while he considered what to do. It was too late to intercept each of his children at their different lines, so he cautiously left and got into his ration book queue. It was late before he got back, and by then, he had decided to say nothing about the threat. It was impossible to know how serious it might be plus, not only did he not have an alternate way to survive, he believed that Niklas, Dorka, Slava, Lukacs, and little Anton didn't either.

They laid low over the next few days, as usual. Niklas had a small side business in contraband cigarettes, which Daniel tolerated as it kept him supplied, and the boy put his profits into the communal kitty. When they couldn't stay cooped up in the basement anymore, he let them out for an hour with instructions to do nothing that might attract attention — for example no other schemes or thefts. He limited his own brief excursions to the early morning and the hour before curfew. Friday, though, he had to make his rounds to convert the coupons to cash. When nothing unusual happened, he decided that if they stayed within their routine, Farkas would leave them be.

By Tuesday, the warming spring encouraged him to go out in the daytime. A few of the major streets now had cars, the rare bus, and enough pedestrians for Daniel to feel relatively anonymous. He glanced behind once or twice and then forgot about it. He enjoyed being amongst people moving with non-lethal direction and purpose. There was blue sky visible now, and a hint of lilac, or maybe one of the women he passed was wearing perfume. When the crowds thickened as he neared the State Opera House, Daniel hung back, especially when he saw the two tanks and the Russian soldiers at its front. Except they were smiling. Russian soldiers never smiled.

Young women climbed onto the tanks to hand flowers to the men in the turrets. And there was dancing, men politely grabbing anyone, male or female, young or old, to kiss on both cheeks. He knew it before he heard any of the words: Germany had surrendered. The war was over. The killing was done. He avoided all but a couple of beery, sweaty, happy bear hugs, but he smiled back at everyone who smiled at him, which was practically everyone. He felt himself carried along by the happy throng until he saw Varosliget, the city park, and escaped to find a space where he could stop and absorb the news.

All the buildings in the park were damaged and there were rumors that a lion from the zoo now inhabited the nearby metro tunnels. He made for the one small section of green grass, like a sudden introduction of color into a black and white movie, which reminded him of Lazienki Park in Warsaw, where almost every summer Sunday afternoon, in another life, he met with his friends. He spread out his jacket and lay back to feel the warmth of the sun and listen to the rustling from the trees that still stood and managed to leaf in defiance of the trauma they'd witnessed. His weight pressed the grass down, and as Newton taught, the earth pushed back to buoy him up.

The war was over. He repeated this several times, in Russian, Hungarian, and in Polish, and it still felt foreign. He certainly felt relief, and happiness that the specter of perpetual war was gone. But the end of the war meant exactly what for him? The question had never come up before. It had never been relevant. He stared straight up and made a silly attempt to determine North from that angle. What was left in Poland? His father was gone, as was Ian. Warsaw and the life which had been interrupted, as if interrupted could even begin to describe it? Would Warsaw have cafés and architects' offices and work again? And would the Stasceks return, and be in charge?

He decided that he wouldn't waste too much time with this speculation for now, simply file this new information and see where it led him. He sat up, stretched, and rose to walk back to the basement. Searing pain in his belly came simultaneously with the sound of the gunshot. He screamed, his hands going to where the pain centered, and they quickly became saturated with his own warm blood. At the edge of the field he saw a man he didn't recognize pocket a still smoking revolver, then walk quickly past the trees.

Daniel lay on his back again. The sun, he knew, provided light and heat and energy and it shone every day without any deviation so that we always took it for granted, never gave it a thought. There was a sun in his belly, too, becoming slightly more tolerable over the minutes. The grass smelled like... it was a strange, non-grass smell, he noticed. He opened his eyes again. There were people around, glancing towards him, confused because the war was over and yet someone had been shot. They could take their time. All that had fueled his will, in the army, in the prison, in the camps, the forest, the tunnel, Nadhya, the roads, the trains, the boats, the cold permanently seated in his bones, all of it he could sense again, running out. Run out, run out. There was no reason to do any more. From his early teens. he'd fought to define and then live a life with purpose and now there was no purpose. Except to lie here for a few more minutes.

His life only mattered to one person, and if he didn't care, then it mattered to no one.

Ian — Wilhelmshaven, Germany, 9–13 May 1945

Shouting, cheering, sharing looted bottles of anything alcoholic, dancing with anyone within arms-length — the officers allowed it all to go on for hours, except for the fools who fired into the air — in celebration of the end of the war in Europe, the only one that mattered to the Poles. It was the occasion for a party unlike any other, by men who only hours earlier faced, at some level of consciousness, the possibility that they might die. NCOs hugged their captains and English nurses from the field hospital danced to exhaustion with privates. A few men slipped off by themselves to quietly cry and were quickly pulled back into the jubilee.

Ian stayed near the men he knew best, those in his three-tank platoon. Their brazen promise to each other to survive had come true. He moved aside for a minute for a cigarette and to attempt to grasp this wholly unfamiliar reality. The war which had consumed six of his twenty-five years, virtually all his adult life, was over. It had come to occupy all the spaces in his mind, leaving little room or time for anything else. He regretted how infrequently he worried about those he could not see. His father, Daniel, Alicia. Instead, he'd learned a new language and the rules of a new society, the army, as well as new skills. He had applied them at Verrieres Ridge and the Falaise hell-storm, and for the months after that: driving, halting, fighting, resupplying, and doing it all again and again.

Christophe liked to echo their brigade commander: "Don't think, do!" Ian, though, needed to think; about the overall mission as well as the welfare of the men for whom he was responsible. At each briefing, he factored terrain, weather, objectives, fuel, fatigue, light, cover, in whatever proportion he needed to balance safety with the mission imperatives, on how to instruct his men, timing, and other variables. When it was over and they were safe and in resupply — his unit never seemed to be in reserve — he thought about repair, rest, recovery, time, and supplies. At rare moments he recognized how this resembled how one approached engineering problems and wondered what might have happened had there been no war, but he let these moments be brief.

Once, on an August night at what the map called Hill 262 and the locals called Mont Ormel, it almost failed. The Germans threw everything at the Poles, desperate to create an escape valve for the thousands in danger of being surrounded. Wave upon wave of counterattack, incessant accurate artillery barrages, no clear front lines, complete confusion. Then came a lull. He was organizing the information needed with which to formulate his plans when they heard a 75 mm shell from a Panzer Panther glance off the top of their turret.

"Reverse, right turn," he yelled, as he rotated the turret left to locate what was shooting at them. At first, he found nothing. Then he saw a muzzle flash, and he heard the shell pass to their left. He yelled the range and direction to the gunner, who fired but missed. Lesczak the loader slammed in a new round in two seconds, and this one found the Panther. The rest of the night and the next day was as furious, and they survived, because they didn't think. Only did.

Celebrations kept reigniting throughout the night and those who had duties at first light bore the consequences without complaint. They were now an army of occupation. Ian's tanks, supported by an infantry company, drew the oil storage facility at Heppenser Groden assignment. They would take control from the Kriegsmarine and move whatever German troops were there off to prisoner of war sites.

"Prepare for resistance, but rules are to fire only if at risk of being fired upon, and only enough to dissuade further resistance." That was the order.

When Ian rolled up to the gate, a korvettenkapitan waited with his holster open and empty. He handed over his pistol and hopped on to the front of the Sherman tank to direct them to where his men sat on their parade ground in postures that signified resignation tinged with concern. It resembled a scene from one of the films Ian watched as a boy on Saturdays at the movie palace — *White Fang*, or maybe *Klondike Annie* — where the dogs sat waiting to be hitched to the sleds, except those dogs looked eager to go. The defeated Germans stood to shuffle off to their fate.

This became their days, liberating different areas of the city. The Royal Navy, now steaming toward their position, would take care of the ships anchored in the port. The army had responsibility for the shore. Their staging area was inland, at the sports complex, home of the *SC Frisia im 1903* football club. Between them and the shore were the naval base, the docks, the U-boat pens, the oil tanks, and the dry docks, all demonstrating how mercilessly Wilhelmshaven had been bombed with the resultant obliteration of almost all the buildings at the port, including many blocks of shops, libraries, factories, schools, and homes. The steeple on the Catholic church dedicated to someone called St. Willehad was gone so no bells rang to remind whoever remained faithful when it was time for Sunday services. Ian watched Poles join a few German civilians walking toward the church. The power of indoctrination in these people must be overpowering if it permitted someone to sit next to the enemy just because they shared a faith in something supernatural.

He turned away to walk south. On his left, two destroyers and several escort ships lay off the mangled docks. On his right were debris patterns where only an archeologist might discern that there had been buildings whose function could only be guessed at by the detritus, the modern equivalent of pottery shards. The first standing one within view was two hundred meters inland, some sort of barracks, though it was unclear for which service.

Might that have been where Lachance lived in 1918, before he left for Kiel? Ian had worked hard to forget the man and everything that happened from the moment they met at Zemmour's café to the black night they'd slipped his body into the Atlantic, and for the most part, he had been successful. Today, though, on these grounds, the demand for attention was too strong.

Lachance never explained why he joined the march on Kiel. Were he and the other marchers as afraid of dying as he had been since... well, the last six years? Or was it because they felt wronged? Lachance claimed they had marched to free their fellow sailors, and that is how it was portrayed in the history books. They were angry and so they were brave, a white-hot flame lit in the hearts of young men by pure motives, impervious to manipulation by evil leaders. But in truth, maybe they were like all soldiers: tired, maybe hungry, finally fed up. He rejected that, at least for the man he had lived with for all those months. Lachance would have ruminated about it for days, and when he finally acted it would have been from his own moral imperative. As noble and pure as he tried to be, though, it was not enough to protect him from his humanness, that mixture of thoughts, habits, desires, fears, principles, traditions, education, instincts, myths, hopes, facts, and misperceptions. Lachance strove so hard to control it all, first by adopting the mind and discipline of the church, and when that failed, with reading, philosophizing, contemplation, study, and isolation. Ian had the impression that, to the end, Lachance remained surprised that he could not escape his demons or his past, which may have been the lesson he was trying to pass to Ian. Whatever Ian's analytical mind achieved, no matter how practical it appeared at the time, was incomplete. This careful way of living and of thinking, would not work for normal aspects of life, but he knew no other way. Hell, he didn't even know what those other ways of living were. He was twenty-five years old, and he knew no more about himself than what he knew when he left Warsaw so very long ago, except that he could never be as certain about anything as he'd been then.

Daniel — Vienna, Austria, February 1947

The line moved slowly. That was not good. Daniel removed his hat to wipe the sweat from the inner band — showing any perspiration in this cold weather would certainly alert the guards — shuffled forward a step or two, and worried if his papers were good enough. They were from a well-recommended craftsman of the unofficial Viennese world in which he lived and worked. Demand for such materials continued to be high even now, almost two years after the end of the war. Since the four powers needed to agree on every rule and regulation, the veneer of civilization imposed by order was developing slowly in divided Vienna, to the delight of those businessmen and women working in the seams and shadows. Rates for goods and services, paid in cash or in coal, cigarettes, other contraband, or even in human beings, followed the market, so middlemen were available to broker a deal for whatever one might want, including a new identity.

Access to the platform for the Rome train required passengers pass through a single gate in the tall iron fence, where everyone's documents were inspected and stamped by men in four different uniforms.

"*Papiers!*" The first soldier was French. He took what Daniel offered, inspected them, stamped one, and passed them on to the American, who did the same. Halfway through. Daniel smiled at the Brit, who was too young to successfully grow a real mustache, which elicited no response but his papers were approved. One last step and he could enter the West.

"You are from our zone?" The Russian junior lieutenant was as young as the Englishman.

"*Da,*" Daniel answered. "I have permission to go to Wiener Neustadt to collect some leather goods for a contract. You see where it says this." The train to Rome stopped at Wiener Neustadt.

The Russian looked closely at one of the forgeries. He set it aside to examine Daniel's identity card and business license. Sweat threatened to visibly stain his hat.

"*Nyet. Nein.* Get out of the line."

Daniel's breath left him. What did this mean? He followed the junior lieutenant as he walked his papers along the fence to another table where four more senior officers sat. He watched them inspect the documents, eye him, confer. A French major delivered the news.

"You are not authorized for this train. There are local trains for Wiener Neustadt leaving from Ganserndorf, a station in your residential zone. You must go that way."

He should object, take umbrage at this outrage, at least demand reimbursement for the train ticket he could no longer use, but that would accomplish nothing, so he accepted the worthless papers back, minus the train ticket, and returned to the Soviet zone, to the apartment he'd hoped never to see again.

When he woke up in a hospital bed in Budapest, he realized he was alive, but he never learned how he came to be so. When they released him two weeks later, he went directly to the basement and was not surprised to find two strange families occupying it, his money, the goods, and the children gone. Ironically, it was Farkas who came to his rescue. Daniel, wandering aimlessly on the Pest side of the river, happened upon the storefront from which Farkas ran his little empire, and recognizing one of the goons loitering outside, made a snap decision to go in. Farkas either admired the courage or decided that someone with so little regard for their own welfare might be useful, and Daniel was back in business, this time paying Farkas the tax he demanded from each deal. They both thrived. It felt different though, less like a fully lived experience and more like he was a character in a book about a strange locale, like Tahiti or California. He thought of himself as simultaneously the character and the reader, but there was no author or hero in this book. Weeks later he recognized that he was in an even more unfamiliar state: no longer cold or hungry. He inhabited a life in which he reaped the rewards of working angles and schemes at which he was clearly adept. There had been moments when he felt warm, or full, but not consistently from his own efforts. It was novel and good.

Like a cancer that initially gives intermittent, vague, and non-specific signals of its presence, but continues to grow until it cannot be denied, eventually he could not ignore the vague unease underlying his satisfaction or pretend that everything was fine. The catalyst was when municipal services improved, specifically, law enforcement. Risks were now higher. One breach of the increasingly rigorous legal standards would expose him to more significant and more likely consequences. Worse, his only relationships were transactional and there were times when he realized he felt lonely. His body now healed, he had material security but spiritual emptiness. He worked harder, then drank harder but could not prevent something arising from a very distant memory, something he used to call a future. Lying on his cot at night, staring into the blackness, he began considering what he could do, what he should do. Asking these questions was a tonic and also filled him with fright, usually simultaneously. Only when he finally permitted himself to remember the young man who'd been consumed by dreams of changing how man lived, did he stop waking up in a cold sweat every night.

Eight years on, could he resurrect that passion or had the small flicker he felt when he spoke of it to Nadhya died when he left her? Was it still in Warsaw? If the others — Joseph, Sylvia, and the people at that party — were there, there might be a chance but all, he assumed, were dead or scattered far away. That left Ian's West, and though the contours of his future life there were indistinct, or even invisible, by resigned default, that was where he needed to go.

He thanked Farkas and Budapest for his nascent resurrection and came to Vienna because it was reportedly the easiest place from which to get from the Russian zone to the West. He tried to find legitimate work when he first arrived, however the Viennese did not welcome foreigners. With victors and occupiers, they had no choice and maybe it was penance for their sins, but work for refugees like him? *Nein!* The only job he found was removing rubble, together with other desperate displaced persons, or locals too damaged to do anything else, and his fiscal situation quickly deteriorated. He knew of only one alternative. Through Farkas, he brokered his first deal involving American stockings, French cigarettes, and tins of sardines from Turkey. The skills he'd learned in the Gulag, on his journey across Russia, and in Budapest, proved effective in Vienna; opportunism, care, suspicion, bluster, intimidation, lying, expediency. Within three months, he was living well again.

Forgers are, by and large, not brave men. They stay behind, under the covers, and let others take chances with their false papers, so Daniel had no trouble scaring the shit out of his forger, a Moldovan named Donici.

"I don't know why they didn't work, Herr Novak." This was how Daniel was known in Vienna. "Perhaps it was bad luck, perhaps you can try again, and they will work."

Daniel leaned in, his face a few centimeters away from Donici's. He spoke quietly, which he knew to be more menacing. "And maybe they won't, and I will be arrested and on a train to Siberia. Before they load me up, though, I am sure they will have questions, and they will keep asking them until I give them answers. What do you think those questions will be?"

There was no need for Donici to answer. Daniel let a long pause increase the older man's stress.

"Donici," he said, his voice now a little more conversational. "Who is the best forger in Vienna?"

"I am!"

"Let me put this another way. If I wanted to get on a train to Rome, with you as my travel companion, with your life dependent on not giving the soldiers any reason to stop us, who would you get your papers from?"

"I am not going to the West," Donici said.

"I will let you get off just before we leave Austria, Herr Donici."

Finally, the forger said, in his meekest voice, "I would use Herr Richter."

It took a week for Daniel to arrange an introduction to Richter, who worked above a women's hat shop behind St. Stephen's Cathedral, and then a month to accumulate the funds needed to pay the man, four times more than Donici's rates. But when Daniel settled into the second-class car on the 8:47 a.m. train to Rome, after having no trouble whatsoever at the gate, he felt relieved to be broke once more.

Florence, 7 September 1947

Dear Ian,

I believe it's been three years since I last wrote to you, and though there is not even an infinitesimal amount of evidence that permits me to believe you are still there, some-where, I have no one else I can tell these thoughts to. You were the first, listening to my dreams and plans in our bedroom, with such patience and without judgment. Later, there was Joseph, with whom I shared many ideas and hopes. But since 1939, there has only been one brief interlude, one other person, with whom I felt even a little safe. War and displacement cause many terrible things, one of which, I have come to learn, is isolation. Until I find someone, if I ever do, a letter allows me to imagine that I am with you in that bedroom back in Father's house.

I've been in Florence for about two months, and it should be a dream answered, like Paris would be for you. Did you ever get to visit Paris, before the war or after? I hope so. Florence is Brunelleschi and the Duomo, Arnolfo di Cambio and the Palazzo Vecchio, Santa Croce, the Palazzo Medici Riccardi... and I should be like a little boy given free and complete access to Kazimierz's candy store. Remember that place? I won-der if it survived. Did Nazis buy sweets to send home to their little murderous offspring, or just take them?

Sorry. That sounds bitter. I try not to be. There is no purpose to feeling that way; it doesn't change my circumstances. This is not where I imagined myself when we last stayed together in Warsaw and if you would have predicted that I would be studying architecture in goddamn Florence, I would have called you delusional, among many other names. Yes, I am back in school, in pursuit of a Master's degree. I left everything in Warsaw, including my diploma, and university records aren't available, so I need a new piece of paper if I want to go back and be an architect. Truth be told, I know that theorizing about how to craft space for a noble sociological or even metaphysical purpose doesn't make sense after what the world and I have been through, but it's all I know to do (aside from some skills I picked up in my travels, most of which are not socially acceptable). You probably would cringe if I said "Functional Humanism" after I talked your ear off over the short time we spent together. So long ago, in time and in the trajectory of my life. It is not a part of the curriculum and I have no patience for it now. What Florence has permitted me to rediscover is that I can still draw. My hand still connects to my eye through my mind. That is enough.

I worry that your studies were interrupted at an earlier stage. Have you gone back to school? I hope so.

This is getting depressing, and it is not why I wanted to write. Rather, it was to say that, while I am not and cannot be the same man with whom you stayed in Warsaw eight years ago, I am someone who, deep down, loves you and admires you, and misses you. If we could meet again, I promise I would show you that I can be a better brother.

Not sure if and when I will write again. If this miraculously gets to you, know that I send you all my love and hopes.

Daniel

Daniel — Florence, Italy, 17 November 1947

Daniel sat on the topmost step in front of the loggia which formed one side of the piazza, the best vantage point from which to see the complete face of the Palazzo Rucellai. With his pocketknife, he sharpened his soft graphite pencil, and went to work on his twentieth or twenty-fifth sketch of the Palazzo. Several of the previous ones were technically good — the professor even said so — but they were not good enough for Professor Michelucci. What was the old man not finding in them? What did he want?

Today was his third one on the steps, and he had to wait until the morning rain stopped. The streets now were full of people. Students like him, and also housewives and workers, American soldiers on leave, a smattering of tourists walking slowly as they swiveled their heads from their Baedekers to the real thing. They all distracted him, adding to his frustration. He tried blocking them out to concentrate on what Alberti, the architect of the Palazzo, had created.

Two more aborted attempts before he gave up. He bypassed the nearby cafés and went, instead, to the one near his rooms, across the Arno in the cheaper part of town.

"A beer," he ordered, and then had another. He opened his pad to see why all his sketches did not satisfy him. Why this effort to recapture his career looked increasingly like a mistake. The basics were still there, the lines and proportions correct and in proper relation, the shading evocative, equal to what he could do when he was twenty-five. At that age, though, he was consumed with architecture. Drink, food, song, and sex merely played minor supportive roles in his obsession with creation. His sketches had reflected the energy and purity of that drive. Now, at thirty-three, he was riven with a multitude of images and memories, all consequences of decisions and the results of chance. He snapped the sketchbook shut, paid his bill, and returned to his rooms until the sun rose the next morning.

Fortified with a latte and a roll, he arrived early to his spot in front of the loggia, determined to try again, because he was not ready to contemplate what an emptiness his future would be if he failed. He put a copy of yesterday's *La Nazione* between the cold stone and his rear end. The sun placed a wide diagonal stripe across the front of the Palazzo. Daniel noted a mother and her little girl, no more than four years old, sitting on one of the stone benches built across the lowest level. They had selected the one upon which the sun shone. He took up his pencil. With a few lines, he outlined the building on his page. Two perfect horizontal strokes, straight, without need for straightedge or measure, divided the space into the three stories. Now he filled in the details: the arches above the windows, the bold corniche of the roofline, the entablatures he knew that Professor Michelucci valued. Daniel had reviewed all his notes and underlined many passages from Alberti's famous treatise on architecture. He knew that there was something he was supposed to see and put into his sketch. He knew it wasn't in this one. He ripped the page off the pad and restarted.

Maybe if he worked quicker, with more intuition and less thought. He left his hand free to draw whatever it wanted. This time, after the outline and the horizontals, he started at the bottom and worked up. The child's legs dangled, too short to reach the ground. Mother and daughter wore matching wool coats, of a blue he recognized, like the sky on a very cold winter morning but he only had a black pencil. He finished the mother and daughter, then went on to the architectural elements. He was still drawing when the mother looked right then tugged the child to stand and they left their sunspot and disappeared from view. Daniel looked from the front of the Palazzo to his sketch, and he knew he'd found what he'd previously missed. All the elements, the strong foundation signaled by the cross-hatching rustication at the base, the impressive height of the first level, the lightness of the second and third floors where the family lived, the smooth pilasters conveying fortitude, the bold horizontalism, all the references to classical Rome. It was a great building and his previous sketches showed this. But Alberti was, first and foremost, a humanist. For him, form and ornamentation and the like were all in the service of people. Certainly, for the family who would live in the building. But he did not forget that people walked past, whether merchants or bankers, artisans or servants, some perhaps needing a place to rest, and so he gave them the benches. Benches that continued to serve the people centuries later. The commission came from a rich family, and it also had to serve the needs of that mother and daughter.

He recognized that he'd taken a step towards recovering an important part of himself, a hint that he still had a future in architecture. He kept it in perspective, because it wasn't Warsaw and it was no longer 1939, and manifestos did not pass exams or lead to real jobs.

Michelucci gave him only a passing grade for the work, which surprised no one, because he hadn't given a high mark in thirty years, but when he returned the sketch back to Daniel, there was a blue check mark above the mother and daughter.

Ian — Kelso, Scotland and London, England, November 1947–March 1949

Mr. Goudie had passed away in '46. "Old age what did him in, but he lived to see those Jerries properly lamped, he did," his wife told Ian, after she'd hugged him, cried, dried her tears, and prepared his tea.

Otherwise, nothing had changed. His room was as he'd left it more than three and a half years ago. Mrs. Goudie was maybe a little frailer but fussing over him restored her pep. The other widows on the block admired his loyalty or were maybe a touch jealous. Mrs. Lockart mentioned to her daughter, whom she worried might be moving a little past her prime, how considerate the Polish captain appeared to be.

"Aw, ma," came the response.

The daughter did notice that he seemed to always be sitting by himself when she and her girlfriends saw him at the cinema. He might be a little gawky perhaps, though not half bad if you looked closer. Being brought up proper, she waited for him to take the initiative, and when he never did, and a more attractive Polish corporal stepped forward, she forgot about Captain Ciszek.

Ian reacquainted himself with Ingrid, Lana, Rita, Gene, and all their screen sisters because there was little else to do — nothing to guard, no battles to prepare for now, and like all the men, he was grateful for the boredom. Checking inventories, listening to the engines when they fired the tanks up for five minutes each morning, and filling out reports meant ample time for attending the cinema. The soldiers made sure to arrive in time for the newsreels. A cheer greeted any voiceover or caption that alluded to something Polish, because, as hard as they looked, nothing appeared familiar. The photos and movies of Gdynia, Krakow, or Warsaw or of the Polish countryside were indistinguishable from those of Rotterdam, Dresden, Belgrade, or any European country, all showing lines of still shell-shocked survivors, some in carts pulled by cows or by women, walking towards cities and towns that only existed in their memories.

The contrast between these images and the pictures and stories distributed by representatives of the Warsaw government couldn't be starker. Rebuilding was almost complete, they affirmed. Crops were at record levels. Everyone smiled and looked welcoming. They proclaimed that opportunities to thrive in a new Poland were almost limitless. Whom to believe, the recruiters and agents of the government or the rumors that some returning from the West were being arrested as traitors or spies? The question could not be ignored. The men of the Free Polish Army were being forced to choose: go back after eight years to their family and home, or stay in Britain.

Ian worried about going back. Despite reassurances from the Communists, he wondered if the quotas and prohibitions that drove him to Nancy, and the epithets and caricatures his father chose to ignore, were gone. They might no longer be publicly acceptable, but could long held prejudices just disappear? He did note that in the vast mixing bowl that was Europe in war, people knocked together learned to confront and overcome their ignorance and prejudices when necessary, so it was possible, but would it continue in peacetime?.

His calculation ended up being rather simple because there was only one reason to return, and nothing he knew supported it, regarding his father or Daniel. Letters to them or to more distant family all returned unopened. Among the millions of names gathered by the Red Cross from displaced persons across Europe, there were no relatives. Each day without news became another brick in his certainty that they were dead. At night, though, as he lay on his narrow bed in Mrs. Goudie's back room, he took down that brick by asking how the lack of information could be considered definitive, and he remained suspended in his purgatory.

The Scottish weather was not following form. It was sunny, and no gale blew off the cold seas. Ian sat outside his office smoking a cigarette, admiring a migrating flock of Brant geese resting and refueling in the nearby field before going southward, when Christophe brought a chair from inside to sit next to him.

"I got a letter back from my father," Christophe said.

"That's nice," said Ian. "What's new?"

"The last time I wrote to him, I asked him about your family,"

"You did? Well, that was kind of you, you didn't have to do that," Ian said. He tried to keep stomach acid from refluxing into his mouth.

"Yes, I did," Christophe said.

Ian awaited the news.

"It's not good."

Ian was surprised at how far he fell in on himself. He managed to nod to Christophe to continue.

"That first winter, the Germans, they made all Jews move into one neighborhood, including those from the little towns in the countryside, you know, like the Rozenzveigs, Danny's family. They burnt the big synagogue, and all the others. It was bad, for everybody in the town, food shortages, no coal, no work, everyone was suffering. There wasn't much information coming from the Jewish quarter, he said, but he heard that your father organized a school there. Anyway, October 1942, my father says that over three days they marched every Jew to the train station and took everyone away. He says he saw your father, and he was a sight, standing straight, marching like he was still in the Polish Army. The thing is, in five years, no one has come back, Ian. I asked him to check at your home, and he says that there is another family there now and they yelled at him when he asked about your father. They said that they always lived there. My dad knows that is a lie, but he went by himself so... I am sorry, Ian."

Ian sat, his cigarette burning to ash.

"But no one knows anything for sure. You said it yourself, they are always adding names at the Red Cross, from Russia, from Bessarabia. You come back with me, so we will be there when they return," Christophe said.

Ian felt relief that his decision was now so easy. "Thank you. And thank your father. But they all left, and none have returned. Not in five years, not in the two years since the war ended. I am sorry, Christophe, there is nothing for me to go back to. What would I do, show up to our home and kick that family out?"

"We can go to the police. You could stay with us while you sorted it out."

Ian stood up and stretched. He turned to look directly down at Christophe. "You have a good soul, Christophe. You know that I was angry with you about what happened on the *City of Nagpur*."

"There was no choice. He betrayed us, and we almost got killed. It was war," said Christophe. "And he was also a thief."

"I was confused," Ian said. "Claude or Hermann or whatever his name was, he was… he'd been my friend. And I still believe that he didn't want to kill us. Himself, maybe, someday, but not us. He was forced into it."

Christophe answered directly. "You have said it yourself, Ian. We all have choices. Maybe it was his time, and I was the instrument."

Christophe was going back to Poland, and this was the last, and the first, chance to address what connected them like brothers.

"We have been together for so many years, and I have never met anyone who sees things so clearly as you do," said Ian.

"I have heard the comments. The others, they often think I am simple, that I can't understand what they are saying," Christophe said, without bitterness.

Would that they had more time. "You're shy, you get tongue-tied when you are around other people. But you do think about things, as much as many of the others and more than some, and what you do is refine them down to their essentials. You are Polish, the war is over, it's time to return to Poland. My family is not there yet, so I need to return to wait for them. Lachance betrayed us, put our lives in danger, he needed to die. Sometimes I wish I thought like you do. You always look like you sleep well. I wake up, my head full of conditionals and alternatives, calculations, contingencies. I try to quantify the unknowable. It feels like a curse, except it's who I am, like you are who you are."

"You watch me sleep?" Christophe asked. "That's creepy."

"Not really. I mean a few times when I woke and couldn't fall back asleep, I looked over to see if you were also having trouble, and you always were sound asleep. But it was during those nights that I finally figured it out, that you had to do what you did."

"You forgave me?" Christophe asked.

"There was nothing to forgive," Ian declared.

"But you were angry, for a long time."

"Yes, with Lachance for sure, and certainly with Hitler. And with myself. I am still angry, Christophe. I need to start over, and I don't know if it's too late."

"No, it's not. And if you come back with me, we can do it together, from where we started!" said Christophe.

"Except that my beginning isn't there anymore," Ian said. "When do they think you will be shipped back?"

"Seventeen or eighteen days. From Glasgow," Christophe answered.

Ian paused again, then asked. "Your father didn't say anything about Daniel, did he?"

"No, he didn't mention him," Christophe answered. "Do you know what you will do?"

Ian looked to where another dozen or so geese had arrived. Cycles of days, months or seasons were obvious. Civilization, or war, moved on a much vaster scale, their arc was unknowable, which made it feel linear. On a train taking a curve, one could see the last car passing the place where you had already been, but if it was going straight, there was only future.

"No," Ian answered.

Three weeks later, Christophe and half the camp left to their families and the new Poland. For the rest, clerks set up in a dozen tents to process all the forms necessary for demobilization and in another few weeks, Ian was in civilian clothes again. They even found him a job, office work in a London company quartered in a reconstructed block near Battersea Power Station, right off the Thames.

At the end of his first week, Ian left the office to catch the late train from Victoria Station and arrived to Paris early the next morning. The city was far less damaged than London. It still felt familiar, and this gave him hope. But the new concierge at their old apartment building on the rue Chevreau indignantly denied knowing her predecessor, Madame Durand, denied that any woman had ever lived in the apartment under the roof and denied knowing anyone named Alicia. There was nothing at the 20th police prefecture because records from 1940 had been moved out the year before. The Ministry where she'd worked was closed on Saturday. His last hope, the Communist Party headquarters at 44 rue le Peletier, evaporated when he learned that to protect itself during the Occupation, the party had destroyed its membership rolls. He returned to London unsure about how he felt.

With his second pay packet, he began setting a little aside towards a fund he planned to use for something, maybe a restart of his engineering studies. He didn't go to the pub or the track. His only indulgences were a weekly visit to the cinema and attending the monthly dance at the Polish Officer's Club in South Kensington. His manager permitted him to leave a half hour early on those Fridays, so he had time to stop in at the Tracing Service office of the Red Cross, to check in and post another query to Daniel.

On his fourteenth visit, Daniel's letter from New York was waiting for him.

Ian and Daniel — Queens, New York City, 12–27 June 1953

"You've thought this through carefully?" Daniel asked, gently.

"Yes, of course," Ian responded.

"Excuse me, does anyone else want some?" Clara, Daniel's wife, reached across him for some more potato salad because she'd grown up with three brothers and one sister, and preemption was a necessary dining skill. It still surprised her how well these two brothers got along.

"Yes, please," Ruth said. "It's delicious."

Ruth had only had one sibling, yet she shared Clara's gift of smothering emotional eruptions, and Clara had taken an instant liking to her when Ian brought Ruth to meet them. The two had become as close as sisters over the months they'd all lived in the same apartment.

Ruth spoke up for her husband. "We went over this many times. As Ian said, it will take at least four more years until he has his degree, and opportunities like this may not happen again."

"It would be shorter if he went full time," Daniel pointed out.

"There wouldn't be enough money to live, especially now with the baby coming," Ian said.

Daniel swallowed any offer of aid. It was reflexive, and while Ian would see the fraternal benevolence behind it, he would refuse help from his older brother. The mention of the baby, though, put a smile on Daniel's face.

Clara deftly pivoted the conversation to Ruth's condition, how she was feeling, the preparations, whether the girls at her office knew. The women got up to clear the table. As happened every Saturday, the husbands stood to offer their help and when that was declined as usual, they exited onto the tiny balcony to sit on the two bridge chairs, an ashtray perched on the TV tray table between them. It pained Daniel to be out there. The balcony was so narrow that his knees pushed up against the railing when he sat. The stupidity of this design constantly offended him.

Theirs was one of three identical buildings defining a square of dust that the super insistently called the lawn. Four floors of brown brick interrupted by windows as insufficient as the balconies, three of hundreds of similar structures warehousing families in Queens and beyond. Cheap, soulless, thoughtless. At least the interior was bigger than their first place. Soon after Ian and Ruth moved out on their own, he'd reclaimed the second bedroom as a small office, with a drafting table and towers of books waiting for him to install real shelves, but while he appreciated having his space, he also felt that having Ian there for not quite two years could not compensate for the time they'd lost. He was so fortunate that Clara welcomed first Ian and then Ruth into their apartment for as long as the brothers needed.

"You think that the managers at this new firm won't find out that you don't actually have a degree?" Daniel asked his brother, picking up the topic from the dinner table.

"No. I am fortunate, they have hired many from overseas in the last few years, and they know things like diplomas were lost. The one who interviewed me is a Jew from Prague and when I told him that I fled with nothing but the clothes I was wearing, he said the same thing happened to him," Ian said. He'd heard about the job, which paid significantly more, through the refugee grapevine, except it required a bachelor's degree in engineering. He was confident that he had the ability to perform what they required. His analysis led him to conclude that the risks, while not zero, were low enough to be tolerable.

"Will you tell them after you graduate?"

"No, I think that would put them in a difficult situation. I'll change jobs." Ian took a few seconds to organize what he wanted to say. "Ruth and I went over this for weeks. Our expenses are going to take a big jump soon, while the income goes down when Ruth has to stop working. Con Ed doesn't let women with babies work in their offices. Or even pregnant, so once the managers figure it out, that will be over. We looked at all the options. I could take a second job, which would leave no time for classes. I am already a senior draftsman. There's no percentage in staying where I am; the next step at my firm also requires a degree. When I heard about this position, I had that ridiculous feeling that it came to my attention for a reason, you know. Not that I believe that."

"Me neither, but I know what you mean," Daniel said.

"We all lied during the war. Hell, my name was Claude Pronovost for weeks. That means that, despite what I will teach our child, to lie is not absolutely prohibited. We know it is circumstantial," Ian spoke out to the early evening light.

"We are honest with each other, I hope." Daniel wanted the reassurance.

"Yes," Ian answered. "More than anywhere else." Every time he explained his plan, to Ruth, to Daniel, to himself, it made sense, and it still left him disturbed.

Ian and Ruth had met through her cousin, who was married to one of his office mates. He fell quickly for this vivacious petite brunette, a fellow refugee, in her case from Croatia, and when his brother and sister-in-law approved of her too, that sealed it. After she moved in, however, the geometry of the household became rectangular, known to be less stable than a triangle. One evening after dinner, Ruth decided to address the tension.

"We all have our stories of how we came to be here, and I am certain that there are parts that are painful, but I think it would be good if we told them to each other just once and then we never have to do it again." She told Ian, when they were alone, that she thought maybe knowing some of each other's secrets would cement the trust between them.

Ruth went first that evening. She described her first husband, an athlete who before the war competed in the Maccabiah Games, the Jewish Olympics, in Palestine. Their war did not arrive until 1941, and it was their Ustashe neighbors who paraded her grandfather, the chief rabbi of Zagreb, through the center of the city before shooting him and leaving his body in the street. Ruth and her husband left that night to the mountains, where they'd previously holidayed, to join Tito's partisans in the forests. Her husband became a soldier, Ruth a courier. Slavko — that was her husband's name — was killed near Lake Modrac in January 1944, she reported, the pain still apparent on her face.

"There were some narrow escapes, but overall I stayed safe," she said, skipping any details. When it was over, she returned to Zagreb but found no one, not parents, not her brother, nor uncles, aunts, or any of two dozen cousins. The sole living relative, one of her father's brothers had emigrated to the U.S. before the war, and he sponsored her application to join him in New York, which was granted three years later.

Ian felt pride for his wife's courage, both then and now. He put his arm around her shoulder to give a squeeze as she appeared drained by the effort of revisiting these memories, reinforcing his impression that she had set the bar for honesty. He already knew how much she'd loved Slavko.

The next night, after clearing the dishes, Clara volunteered to speak. The war came to her family in Vienna early, in March 1938. As life for Jews became increasingly unbearable, her father used his connections in the city to buy forgeries that re-identified his family as Catholic.

"I became Maria Hofer, went to mass twice a week, and recited the rosary," Clara told them.

They moved to Graz, where fewer knew them. She and her older sister worked in a factory alongside her parents while the boys went to school. Her father never stopped looking for ways to get out of Austria. Once they drove to the Swiss border, where one of the guards was supposed to let them through in exchange for a large bribe, but he didn't appear, and they had to turn back. Finally, in early 1944, her father arranged for the sisters to cross into Italy. They stayed in a displaced persons camp for two months and, as the Allies fought their way up the Italian peninsula and order disappeared, they walked out one day and traveled to Rome. It was still under German occupation.

"I was still Maria Hofer," Clara said. "I went every day to sit in St. Peter's Square because the Gestapo couldn't go there."

After the liberation of Rome, Clara got a job as the manageress of a British officer's club and, compared to the majority of Romans, had a comfortable and sometimes even fun time. But she and her sister heard nothing about their family in Austria until official word came that they had all been betrayed and sent to Mauthausen concentration camp, where they had been killed.

Clara went on. "But then things changed. My sister met another refugee, Baruch, and maybe a week later, while we were walking near the Villa Borghese, a handsome young architect came into my life."

This was pure Clara. She would never permit darkness to exist, if she had any control, always looking hard for a counterweight.

The brothers had to wait until the next weekend for their turns. With his new job, Ian was too preoccupied to think, or worry about how much he would say, until Saturday morning when he realized it might be that night. As searing as their wives' stories were, neither had spoken of any horrible choices they had to make. Ian wanted to honor his wife, and Clara, but did not know how much he could reveal.

That evening, Daniel joked that, as the elder, he should go first, and Ian did not object. Daniel began with the bombing of Warsaw, how it disrupted everything, how he bought the motorcycle and left with every intention to gather up their father and get him to Romania.

"I kept heading east, even though it was the wrong direction. I kept getting further and further, but every time I tried to turn south, to go around, it was blocked. When I joined an army unit, I only wanted to use them to get over the river and then I would somehow find a way to Father."

On the word father, Daniel's voice stopped. He lifted his shoulder once, twice, as if he was having trouble catching his breath. His racking sobs, when they came, seemed to be from an untouched place deep within him.

"I'm sorry," he finally was able to say directly to Ian. "I'm sorry. It was my responsibility. The oldest son. I needed to go and save him. I waited. Too long. No reason. I failed." Fourteen years of pain was being released. "I'm so sorry, Ian. I am so sorry."

Ian rose up to embrace Daniel, to comfort him, to try and absorb some of his pain. "It's alright," he kept saying. "There was nothing you could have done. It's alright." It was strange, the younger comforting the older but they weren't back in the bedroom they'd shared. Clara brought out tiny glasses that she filled with a liqueur, and they all sipped quietly. The other three objected but Daniel wanted to finish, and he described the battle by the bridge, the sergeant who gave him the papers from the dead soldier, the cattle car across Russia, the two camps, and the long journey back to Italy, in barely more than an hour.

A week later, it was finally Ian's turn. He started with why he went to Nancy, followed by the months in Paris, the escape to Casablanca, the *City of Nagpur*, his army service, and the last years in Britain. He didn't plan what to omit yet when it came time to describe the truck hijacking, Alicia, and how Lachance died, he said nothing.

At the end, his relief was shared by the others. Despite whatever each might not have said, it felt as if when each spoke, they were shedding their clothes to show each other their scars, some obvious — puckered skin, pink or brown, sunken or raised — some deep and visible only by their effects, but all marking them. As Ruth had known, each realized that here were three equals who would support them without hesitation.

It was still warm on the balcony as the evening darkness deepened. Ian looked towards Daniel, knowing that there would be no judgment.

"I am going to be very careful. They will initially have someone checking my work, because I told them it had been a few years since I'd practiced real engineering, so I can ask for help without raising suspicion," he said.

"You don't need to convince me," Daniel said. "If not for the war, you would be an engineer, with a diploma and all that. You will still get there."

"Four years though. And it's harder now, to sit and listen to someone instruct you on secondhand wisdom. Dammit. I want it to be over."

"We all do," Daniel said. "But it can't ever completely disappear. What happened was too severe, it went on for too long, and I think it was at the wrong time of our lives."

Clara called out that dessert was on the table and that it was time for Twenty Questions on the radio.

***

"Is Ian okay?" Clara asked her husband as they readied for bed. Daniel reassured her that he would be fine.

"What about you?" he asked her.

"What do you mean?" She said as she looked at him.

"The baby." A year after they'd arrived to New York, he rushed Clara to the hospital because of bleeding, and she required a hysterectomy. The doctors never explained why. Daniel remained convinced that it had something to do with the war, perhaps something that Clara could not permit herself to share.

"No, that's fine," she laughed, as if it was too silly a thought. "I am happy for her. Truly."

Whenever she said that, Daniel believed her, and then he wondered if being so selfless was possible, especially if it went against biological imperatives.

"This child will have four parents," Ruth proclaimed after she'd announced that she was expecting.

They named the boy after Ian and Daniel's father.

"The next one will be named for someone in my family," Ruth laughed, but there never was another one.

Daniel and Ian – Queens, New York City, 15 April 1957

"Aunt Clara!" Little Henry gave her a quick squeeze before running past to find Uncle Daniel. He loved coming over. He had his own corner of the living room, filled with books and toys. He sometimes spent the night in a little bed Daniel had placed in the extra bedroom after removing his drafting table, ostensibly so that Ruth and Ian could have a night off from parenting but, in truth, to give Daniel and Clara time to share the child, to contribute to what was being created and nurtured, someone who, to their amazement and gratitude, appeared untouched by anything that had happened to his family.

"How do you have time to bake?" exclaimed Clara when Ian handed over Ruth's hazelnut apricot torte, which Daniel loved.

"We missed last Saturday so I thought we should do something a little special. Henry wanted to know whose birthday it was!" Ruth laughed.

Clara looked through several drawers for candles after dinner, when Henry began to cry that not having any would ruin the birthday cake. She managed to locate a box of menorah candles and stuck two into the torte. Henry proudly blew them out. The brothers played a game with him, and Clara gave him a bath and read him a story.

"Pancakes for breakfast?" she asked him.

"Yes, please!" he answered.

She sat in the dark room as he fell asleep, absorbing something invisible emanating from the child's presence, to store for when she needed to pull it back out when he wasn't there. She went out to help Ruth finish the dishes. The brothers were on the balcony, in their coats. Daniel still smoked.

"It's good to see how well your job is working out," Daniel started off.

"Thank you, yes. They said I will become a project manager in the next six months, with three junior engineers under me," Ian said. He still liked the smell of cigarettes. He watched a squirrel begin its tightrope walk along a clothesline from their building to the next.

"Will that make changing jobs difficult?" Daniel asked.

"What do you mean?"

Daniel reminded him of the need to move to a different company when he finally could honestly claim to be an engineering graduate.

"I'm sorry, I never told you. I stopped school this fall." Ian said.

"What? Why?" Daniel asked.

"Many reasons. They think I am doing good work at my firm. Three promotions in four years. Henry is needing more attention and I don't want Ruth to have to do it all while I am at work or school or the library doing homework. Plus, frankly, I don't want to miss anything."

"That's understandable," Daniel agreed. "You're so close though." Rein it in, he admonished himself. Ian did not want, or deserve, unsolicited advice or implied criticism.

"Another year. But I can't anymore. I was the oldest person in my class, by almost a decade. They were all polite, but I could see them wondering what I was doing there. You see that question in their faces and you start to ask it of yourself. Ultimately, though, it is difficult to care about some old man's judgment of my work. You wonder, as you watch the professor stand at the front of room and talk on and on, what they did during the war, whether they risked, or suffered, or lost anyone.," Ian explained. He summed it up. "It's too late, Daniel. My time to be a student passed."

"Mmm," Daniel said. One confession deserved another. "Did you know that I went to Boston last weekend?"

"For work?" Ian asked.

"No," Daniel took out another cigarette. He rarely had two on the balcony, especially when it was this cold. "You remember Joseph? You met in Warsaw."

"Of course!"

"I went to visit him. Him and Sylvia," Daniel said.

"What? How? When did you find each other?" A connection to someone from before the war was rare and prized.

"In the office, in a copy of the Architectural Record magazine, about three months ago, there he was, looking at me from a photo. I recognized him right away. He's on the faculty at Harvard and working with a famous Spanish architect named Sert."

"Wow!" Ian exclaimed.

"I know. His articles and his book gained him enough of a reputation it seems, although I am embarrassed to admit I never came across them. They weren't relevant to general commercial practice, I suppose."

Daniel was now a principal at a small firm in the new field of shopping center design. "It's a very good book, though. I can lend it to you."

"Is it Functional Humanism?" Ian asked. Daniel was touched that he remembered.

"No," Daniel answered. "Well, not directly. I can see aspects of it within his overall thesis, but I may be the only one who can." There were actually several significant sections that he thought came from some of their draft manifesto.

Daniel went on. "I went to see them last weekend. In Cambridge, actually. They have two sons, smart kids, and a charming house. It was both a little surreal, and deeply touching to reconnect, you know." Ian nodded.

"Here's the thing. He wants me to join him. He asked me to stay through Monday, and go to Sert, to tell him to put me on the faculty. At Harvard!" Daniel chuckled.

"Wow! That's fantastic." Ian said, excited for his brother. "I hear Boston is a wonderful city! It's a few hours by train, we can visit easily."

"I turned it down," Daniel interrupted him.

"You did? Why?"

"It was so clear, his book, how he thinks now. He still has that singular belief in yourself and the ability of your mind and your ideas to influence the world. I remember how fervently we felt it back in Warsaw. But he spent the years since in Sweden, then France and now here in the US. I didn't... Part of me feels sullied, too dirty to deal in theory or with such ambitions anymore. I can't completely explain it but I do understand that those overarching precepts we were formulating, and that have carried over in his work, they're prescriptions. '*Do this according to what I say, and you will be happier.*' I can't do that. And if I'm honest, when I look back at the me who thought that way, I think '*What a fool!*'"

"They were good, important ideas. Maybe ahead of their time!" Ian protested. "Joseph's success with them proves that."

"Maybe. I don't know anymore. Sometimes I believe that those ambitious dreams of the young, they can spark changes, important changes because the young don't know any better. But I am not who I was before, and I can't be again. We have to leave that to people like Joseph., who stay young. The lucky bastard." Daniel flicked his cigarette butt over the railing.

Ian spoke. "Every so often I remember how some things tasted stronger, how the color of someone's eyes was more memorable, how what I felt, somehow it felt deeper." He looked through the glass at their two wives sitting and talking like sisters. "So many other memories, though."

The brothers went inside. It was time for Twenty Questions and maybe a game of gin rummy.

Henry — Great Neck, New York, 1993–2010

My uncle was eight years older than my father, and so he died first. Turned out he'd had a chronic kind of leukemia and, of course, he told no one. One night, as he was returning from a trip to the bathroom, he fell and hit his head. He made it back to bed before passing out as his cranium filled with blood. The doctor explained it to us before leaving the room, where my aunt, my parents, and I stood around his hospital bed watching the ventilator breathe, waiting for someone to speak, hoping it would be him. The struggle to understand that he was likely dying and that if not, it would be with significant brain damage went on within each of us.

The doctor came back in and asked, "What would you like to do?"

"I don't know," my aunt whispered. My father said nothing.

My uncle never woke up. He officially died the next morning, without anyone needing to decide anything except funeral arrangements.

As if planned, eight years later my father returned home one evening from dinner out with my mother and, on his way to the closet to hang up his jacket, fell down dead from a heart attack.

Neither had a lingering death, one where they received a terminal diagnosis and had time to get their affairs in order and help their wives prepare and not suddenly become devasted. To crack open the lockbox of their stories and share them. If their need to protect me was so ingrained that it could not be overcome, maybe they could have told it all to my children, and they, in turn, could tell me after the old men died. No. They stuck with the plan.

Thirty years after leaving it aside, I began writing fiction again. It was the only way I could finally complete the two stories that I needed to know.

 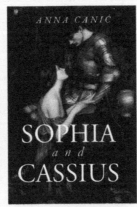 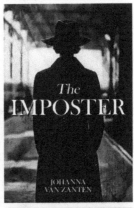
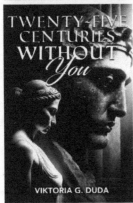